Just
NEIGHBORS

CHARITY FERRELL

Just
NEIGHBORS

CHAPTER ONE

Chloe

EVERY DAY, without fail, my hot neighbor tells me good morning.

And, every morning, I tell him to fuck off.

Today will be no different.

"Good morning, Chloe!"

The abrupt sound of his voice cuts through the morning air and slices away my good mood. His deep voice brims with authority and masculinity, and I clench my jaw in irritation. His voice and I share a love-hate relationship. It makes my panties wet, but I wish it belonged to someone who wasn't an asshole.

I rush down the stairs, my coffee mug clutched in my hand, and speed-walk toward my car. I pause on my way for what I give in to every morning, and my pride flips me off the second I cast a glance in his direction.

I can't restrain myself. His voice demands attention, as if he were a king, and shamelessly, I need to worship the view of him. He's standing in his daily spot on his porch—shirtless, no doubt another device to make me miserable. It's fall, and the weather is peaking in the low sixties. No sane person hangs out on display this time of year. I'm curious if he'll carry on his half-naked greeting when winter hits.

Fingers crossed his balls freeze off, and he learns his lesson.

Gray sweatpants hang low on his waist, the drawstring loosely tied, putting his six-pack on display. My pride then rolls in its grave when my thighs clench together under my pencil skirt as my gaze falls to the deep V disappearing beneath the waistband. His chestnut-colored hair is a tousled mess, as if someone were pulling it all night—which wouldn't be a shocker to the world. There's been a regular cycle of women coming and going from his home.

He's Blue Beech's favorite bachelor. It's unfortunate the people who worship him don't know what a terrible person he is. This crazy-attractive man has done nothing but ruin my life and reputation.

My cheeks blush when he confirms he caught me checking him out with a mischievous smile.

"Fuck off!" I yell when I pass him.

He ignores my response and whistles loudly as if I'd catcalled him back. "Looking professional today, babe. I prefer today's skirt to yesterday's. It's tighter. Shorter. Sexier."

Arrogant prick.

I grip the door handle and stop before getting in. It's a dangerous game to play with him, but I can't stop myself. "I don't care what you prefer, jerk. I don't dress to please you."

Mental note: buy fifty of the skirts worn yesterday and burn this one.

I slide into my car while ignoring his laughter, slam the door shut, and situate my bag and coffee. I hold my hand up and flip the bird when I cruise past him. He only laughs.

Kyle Lane, the man I've despised since sophomore year of high school, moved into the house next door three months, six days, and twenty hours ago. The jerk wore out his welcome within five seconds.

Correction: he was never welcome in my neighborhood.

If I had known the world's biggest jackass was shacking up

next door, I'd have burned it to the ground. Being around him is the equivalent of menstrual cramps.

His irritating morning game began our first day as neighbors. He scared the shit out of me the first few times, and I made a fool of myself—tripping, spilling my coffee on my white blouse, spraining my ankle once.

Initially, I ignored him, assuming it'd last a few days, but here we are—three months into me possibly being on my way to prison for neighbor homicide.

Kyle does it for his sick entertainment.

The man gets off on making me miserable.

I brake at a Stop sign and scrub my hands over my face while taking a deep breath. If there's any day I don't want to deal with his bullshit, it's today. I've been dreading this day, stabbed it on my desk calendar with a red pen as if it'd declared when I'd die.

But there's no avoiding it.

———

MY OFFICE IS on the second floor of the building.

I pass crowds of people and separate offices on my way there. To dodge the curious stares often filled with pity, I take the stairs in favor of the elevator. Cardio isn't my favorite morning routine, so my ass had better thank me for it later.

"Nuh-uh, nope. You turn around before I drag you outside and shove you in the trunk of my car, and we take a paid vacation until tomorrow," Melanie, my assistant, declares when I shuffle into the office, resembling a frazzled mess.

I drop my keys in my bag. "I'm not running from my problems."

"Maybe you should. Running from your problems is better than committing murder."

I groan. "Oh my God, I'm not running away or killing anyone today."

She raises a brow. "Though, tomorrow, it's a possibility?"

I signal to her computer with my coffee while passing her desk on the way to my office. "Work on a new résumé. I'm firing you."

She flips her shiny blonde hair over her shoulder. "Don't dial my number when the new one is lame and won't help you bury a body." A smile dances on her lips when I glance at her.

"I appreciate your loyalty, Melanie. You've earned yourself another week of employment."

"And I appreciate yours for not firing me after the six hundredth threat." She swivels her chair and looks at me. "Are you taking calls today?"

I shrug—an attempt to fake indifference. "Yes. I doubt anyone will call."

"More reason for us to haul ass out of here."

I sigh. "I'll be in my office if you need me."

But please don't.

I have a bag of mini Snickers, plenty of coffee, and a flask if worse comes to worst to survive this day.

She salutes me. "Sounds good, boss. I'll be on Pornhub, so please don't need me."

I can't stop myself from cracking a smile while shaking my head. "One of these days, I'm going to fire you."

"And that will be the worst day of your life."

"Yeah, yeah, yeah," I mutter before disappearing into the solitude of my office.

I shut the door, collapse in the uncomfortable chair behind my desk, and vacantly stare at the stack of papers in need of editing. This office is what I've wanted for years, what I've worked my ass off for. I'm the editor in chief of *The Blue Beech Register*. The number of scandalous stories in our small town is that of *Sesame Street*, but it's given me a job, experience on my résumé, and the opportunity to move up in the field.

————

"WHAT THE FUCK, CHLOE?"

I hear the very familiar and very pissed off voice in the reception area outside my office, and my back stiffens in my chair. His tone is the opposite of what it was this morning when he was hanging out, half-naked, on his porch.

I toss the pen in my hand on my desk, preparing myself for the incoming shitshow when my office door flies open.

I need that flask, stat.

I straighten myself, squaring up my shoulders, and scowl at the man taking residence in the doorway. "Excuse you. Who do you think you are, barging into my office?"

Melanie is definitely getting fired.

The next task on my to-do list is hiring a secretary who hates my neighbor and won't mind taking a criminal charge for kicking him in the nuts.

The walls vibrate when Kyle slams the door shut as if he owned the place, and he stalks the few steps until he's directly in front of my desk. He spreads his feet and crosses his arms across his broad chest. "Your neighbor. Your proclaimed enemy. The man whose dick you've wanted to ride since sophomore year."

Oh, this motherfucker.

"True. True." I sneer at him in repulsion. "And *you wish.*"

He stares me down, and his tone turns serious-slash-pissed again. "Word is, you're poking around about Lauren Barnes's assault, so you can publish about it in your pitiful paper. What the fuck?"

I've been dreading this conversation. I knew he'd come roaring in here, prepared for war, and he wouldn't understand my reasoning for writing the details of what happened to his best friend's fiancée.

"It's a story worth reading," I reluctantly answer.

Kyle's hands move from his chest to his pockets, and he shuts up long enough for me to appreciate the sight of him in his police uniform. I'm positive they're tailored to fit every inch of his tall, muscular stature. His hair is now brushed, and a light scruff scattered along his cheeks complements his stupidly handsome face. A small cleft rests in the center of his chin, and he has cheekbones any Real Housewife would beg their plastic surgeon for. The early morning, shirtless view of Kyle is nice, but, *damn*, so is this. I hate my attraction to him.

My eye-fucking assault breaks when he starts bitching again.

"It's a desperate attempt to publish something *scandalous*." He says the last word dramatically. "It's bullshit. Stick to your boring stories about food drives and petty crimes and keep your mouth shut about anyone close to me."

I wince at his insult but compose myself. "It's not a *desperate* attempt. The man was running drugs in this town, harassing women, and assaulted your best friend's fiancée and his father. They're giving him a slap on the wrist because his family is loaded, and that's bullshit. I'm a journalist, Kyle. Reporting these stories is my job."

"Find another story." His strong jaw clenches. "You publish it, and I swear to God, I will ruin your life in every way possible."

"Are you threatening me?" I swallow hard.

He leans forward and plants his hands on my desk, the smell of teakwood and citrus taking over my space. "Consider it more than a threat. What happened between us in the past will seem like a fairy tale compared to what I'll do. I will arrest every person you love. Every day, your mother and sister will get a visit from an officer. Do not fuck with me on this."

I straighten my palms and flatten my hands on my desk, mirroring his stance. "Acting like a dick isn't helping your case in getting what you want."

He scoffs and shifts closer. His cool, minty breath brushes the side of my face. "I'm not one to beg, but I am one to make a point. Don't act like you don't know that I can destroy a person in one night, *Fieldgain*."

I flinch. It's known I despise my last name. I've never liked it because of the people I share it with, but my hatred for it increased after it was turned into a taunt—thanks to him.

Our lips are inches apart with neither of us dropping eye contact. This will result in one of three ways: one of us killing the other, us fucking each other, or me kicking him out of my office before either of the first two happens.

I pull away with the hope he'll do the same and sit back in my chair. "Leave my office, or I'll write a story about you."

He remains in his stance and releases a hard laugh. "Oh, sweet Chloe, you're smart enough to know you can't touch me. Don't act clueless to that fact and make sure you remember it. I will always have more power than you do in this town. Period."

That's not a lie.

But I hate him for pointing it out.

Kyle is Blue Beech's golden boy and man-slut, and he's basically royalty here.

He pulls away from my desk and takes a step back with tightness in his eyes. He knows this story will kill Lauren and Gage. "Don't fucking run it, Chloe. Unless you want hell to pay."

"The story goes out in two days," I argue. "I need a front-page story."

"Print one about fucking puppies for all I care." He turns to leave but halts to throw me a cold smile. "And have a *good day.* It's a special one, isn't it?" He snaps his fingers and points one at me. "Shouldn't you be in a wedding dress?" He snaps again and places his fist to his lips, letting out an amused laugh. "Oh shit, wrong girl."

"Fuck you," I bite out while gripping the arms of my chair.

"Word is, we've already done that." He winks.

Oh, this motherfucker.

"I hate you!" I pick up the first thing I can—a stapler— and fling it his way.

Okay, not at him.

I can't exactly assault a police officer.

It hits the wall, leaving a mark, and falls to the floor.

"Whoa, I should arrest you." He grabs the handcuffs from his belt and holds them in the air. "You ever worn a pair of these?"

I flip him off.

"Is that an offer?" He swings the cuffs back and forth like a pendulum. "We can put these to enjoyable use."

I point to the door. "Get out."

"By the way, work on your aim." He smiles, taps my door with his knuckles, and leaves the room without shutting the door.

I take a few minutes to make sure he's gone before jumping up from my seat and charging into the reception area. "You're fired, Melanie. Quit watching porn and watch who comes into my office instead."

Melanie peeks up from her desk, faking innocence. "I wasn't watching porn. I was waiting to hear a live show while you two screwed in there. Figured it'd be much more entertaining."

I shoot her an annoyed glare. "Shut it."

"The sexual tension bled through these walls and practically gave me an orgasm."

"You can't have *sexual tension* with a man you hate."

"That's where you're wrong, boss lady. Hate sex is the best sex."

I retreat to my office and grab the flask.

Screw it.

I'M CHLOE FIELDGAIN, and I am a walking, talking cliché.

I caught my boyfriend cheating—and I stupidly forgave him.

He proposed—and I stupidly said yes.

I caught him cheating again—and I stopped being an idiot and dumped his ass.

And what do I earn for my train wreck of a five-year relationship? Hearing the gag-worthy story of him proposing in Town Square to the woman he cheated with, and the second embarrassment of knowing that they're tying the knot today—four months after we broke off our engagement.

Today is the wedding, and no amount of alcohol will help me forget.

That doesn't stop me from trying, and where better than in a public place? That's why I'm stupidly getting my drink on at the Down Home Pub—the only bar in Blue Beech.

I took a sip from my flask after Kyle's departure earlier today and then put it back in case anything work-related dropped onto my desk. When five o'clock hit, I headed straight to the pub, and I'm now sitting at the bar in the corner where the brokenhearted linger.

A slight buzz is hitting me as I trace the names scratched into the wood of the bar with my finger. All day, I've forced myself to remember the worst of Kent—the cheating, him being not so great in bed, and his shitty sense of humor. My intoxicated mind needs to be reminded that dropping him was the best thing to happen to me.

Who wants to live the rest of their life with shitty sex and a cheating bastard of a boyfriend?

Not this girl.

"Well, well, well, if it's not-my-favorite reporter. You here, stalking around, waiting for someone to create a scene, so you can write an article about it tomorrow?"

That motherfucking voice.

I knock back the rest of my drink, needing the liquid courage, and tilt my gaze forward to find Kyle sitting a few stools down from mine. Unlike me, he's changed out of his work clothes and into something more comfortable. A red buffalo plaid flannel covers his shoulders, and a backward ball cap hides his hair.

"If it's not-my-favorite asshole," I reply before swirling my tongue in my mouth to capture any lingering excess alcohol. To deal with him, I need to be as drunk as possible.

"Oh, *favorite*? I like that." He winks, stands up, and comes my way even though I'm not sending an *I want company* vibe. "Maybe I'll work my way up to your favorite fuck."

I roll my eyes. "I take it back. Just asshole, delete the prefix."

His scent and proximity drag me into a high stronger than anything behind the bar will.

"What do you want, Kyle?"

He smirks—a sign he came over to fuck with me. "Didn't expect you to show your face in public tonight."

"Fuck off."

"You're plastered," he states.

I shoot him a glare. "And you're an asshole. A smart one, with your very intelligent revelation, but still a definite asshole."

He rests his elbow on the bar and leans into it while facing me. "Are *asshole* and *fuck* your favorite words in the dictionary?"

"Only when it comes to you."

He places his palm over his chest. "Aw, I'm flattered I have a special place in your brain."

"Fuck off."

"And there you go, thinking about me again."

"What do you want?" I repeat. "You want to rub my shitty life in my face?" I pause. "Wait, why are you here? Isn't everyone and their damn dressed-up dog attending the stupid wedding of the cheaters?"

His eyes meet mine with humor. "Shouldn't you be there, objecting?"

"I hate you," I grumble.

"Good." He sets his beer down and situates himself into the seat next to mine as if my insult were an invite.

"*Now*, what are you doing?" *Why am I constantly asking him this?*

"I'm giving you the pleasure of my company to help clear your head," he says as if it were as obvious as my Social Security number.

I hold my empty glass up. "I've already found the solution. Go annoy another poor soul." I'm not surprised when he makes himself comfortable.

"You know what would do an *even better* job?" he asks.

I hold my cup up. "Shattering this glass and then slicing your genitals off with a broken piece?"

"Damn, you're brutal." His attention swings from me to the bartender, Maliki. He yells out an order of fries and water.

Maliki nods in response and then calls out the order to the kitchen. Maliki owns the Down Home Pub and insisted all drinks were on him tonight when I plopped down earlier.

Kyle stays quiet while sipping his beer, and I play with my glass, uncertain if I should order another vodka I can barely stomach.

What's his play here?

He doesn't speak again until Maliki slides the fries and water down the bar, and they land in front of me. I glance over at Kyle in question, and he snags a fry before holding one out to me.

"Eat up, drunkie," he demands. "And drink the water if you don't want a hangover tomorrow and risk oversleeping. It'd be an unpleasant start to my day if I couldn't annoy your ass while enjoying my coffee."

I narrow my eyes at him but bite off the end of a fry. He's right, but I won't admit that to him. When I finish the fry, he pours ketchup on the side of the basket and slides it closer to me. My stomach growls. I had no appetite earlier and worked through lunch and dinner.

He snags a few fries, and we eat in silence until his arrogant voice breaks through.

"Aw, we're sharing a meal, Fieldgain," he teases. "Consider this our first date. Do I get laid?"

I wince at his comment. It sickens me more than the alcohol and breakup heartbreak combined. He had to bring up our history, knowing today is already hell for me.

I throw down the fry in my hand, sick and tired of his games. "Did you forget that happened years ago?"

The playfulness on his face falls into regret. "Chloe."

I brush my hands together, removing the salt on my fingertips, and push the basket of fries toward him. "Save it. I don't want to think about it tonight. I have enough disturbing memories to drink away. I don't need another on my list."

He leans back and snags another fry. "Fine by me. I'd prefer not to talk about it either unless you give me the chance to explain myself."

"Hard pass."

He grabs the water and hands it to me. "How about we make a toast?"

I take it from him with a frown. At least he's changing the subject.

"No."

He grabs my wrist, pulls my hand up, and clinks my water against his beer. "What if we toast to douchebags?"

"To you then."

He shrugs. "I was thinking more of your ex, but I'll take your verbal abuse because I'm a nice guy." He sets his glass down to settle his elbow on the bar again and puts his attention on me. "Why are you upset though? Word is, you cheated on Kent before he fucked around with Lacy."

"Cheated?" I scoff. I'm tired of Kent using it as an excuse

for his unfaithfulness. "I hardly believe it's cheating when it's with yourself."

His head cocks to the side as he blinks in confusion. "I'm sorry, what?"

I want to stop talking, but the alcohol forces me to defend myself. "I *cheated* on Kent with myself."

His lips curve into a wicked smile. "Explain, please."

Oh shit, Chloe. Abort confession. A-fucking-bort confession.

The confession pouring from my mouth seconds later informs me that I'm no longer sober enough to make responsible decisions. "He caught me, uh ... pleasuring myself ... you know ... doing his job." The words come out in slow stutters.

His mouth drops open at the same time he knocks over his drink with his elbow. I've never seen him so flustered before. I smile, knowing I caught him off guard.

He stares at me with interest. "Are you telling me, he got pissed at you for playing with your pussy?" He grins. "Damn, I thought I was possessive."

"Don't say it like that," I grumble, wishing I could cut and run from this conversation. Unfortunately, I'm certain I can't even get off my stool without falling on my face.

He grabs a napkin and cleans up his mess. "So, he's labeling you a cheater for getting yourself off?"

I avert eye contact. "Yes."

Half his body slides off his seat when he moves in closer. "Can you please provide details of what happened, so I can determine if he's correct?"

I press him into his own space. "I gave you the details."

"You didn't give me shit for details. Was it with your hand? A sex toy?" He tilts his head back and groans. "Fuck, this makes my night."

I hold my hand up as a flush of embarrassment hits my cheeks. "Oh my God, I'm not doing this with you."

He runs his tongue over his lips. "Come on," he begs.

"Give my imagination something pleasurable to think about when I'm home with my hand around my dick."

Oh my God.

I shut my eyes and pull at the collar of my top, suddenly burning up.

Is he saying he'll jack off to whatever I confess?

"I'm not giving you any *details*. I don't want to conduct a casual conversation with you, let alone one about my sex life." I shove his shoulder. "And don't talk about having your hand on your dick around me."

He eyeballs the bar. "Why? It's not out of the ordinary to play with your pussy. Ask anyone in here."

"Quit calling it playing with my pussy!" I hiss. "And I'd rather not poll that right now ... or ever."

He chuckles. "You masturbate. Good for you. I do it on the regular *right next door*. I've made it clear how much I love those skirts of yours."

I'll smack myself for this tomorrow. "We were, uh ... you know ..."

Thankfully, he catches my drift in seconds. "Fucking?"

"Yes, *fucking.* It was in the morning, before work. He got off. I didn't. When he left, I grabbed the vibrator he knew nothing about from my bedside drawer."

He grins, eating this up. "Wait, so this happened frequently?" He appears baffled, disgusted, and entertained, all at the same time.

"Quit interrupting, or I'll stop," I warn.

He holds his hands up. "My bad, my bad. Do continue the Chloe Masturbation Saga."

"So, I started to, uh ... take matters into my own hands."

"You played with your pussy," he corrects.

I push him again and shyly glance away. "Yes. I didn't hear the front door open. I was almost there, and next thing I knew, he came barging into the bedroom. He'd forgotten his wallet."

"And, also, to give you an orgasm."

"He got pissed, accused me of emasculating him, and called it cheating, arguing he should be the one giving me orgasms. He'd already been sleeping with Lacy, but he uses that as an excuse to make me the bad guy. Kent knows I won't defend myself and tell people he caught me masturbating, not cheating."

I cover my mouth with my hand and want to curl away in embarrassment when I realize what I confessed and *who* I confessed it to. Kyle is the last person I should've told. I wait for the snide comments from him, but they never come.

He licks his lips and stares at me in fascination. "If you were mine, I would've sat down and enjoyed the show. That's *after* I had given you the best orgasm of your life. Then, you'd go to work, missing my cock and rubbing your thighs together, anticipating me doing it again. During your lunch break, I'd visit you in your office, spread you out on top of your desk, and eat your pussy. Later, when we were in bed, I'd fuck you all over again."

Jesus. This man and his words.

Those words in that voice.

Heat shoots up my spine while I fumble for a response. My heart races as I imagine him doing all those things.

Maybe a one-night stand will help rid me of my thoughts of Kent the Cheater.

No. Nope.

This is Kyle Lane.

I clear my throat when our eyes meet, hoping it will kill my dirty imagination. "So ..." I stutter out. "That's how I cheated."

"It's not cheating, but at least it helped you dodge a bullet with that one. Dude is an asshole. He was the backup to the backup quarterback in high school. The fuck were you thinking, being with him?"

I narrow my eyes at him. "He was the only guy who'd talk to me, thanks to you."

Guilt creeps up his face again. "Returning to the subject at hand ... *your hand* on ... or in your pussy."

I cover my entire face with my hands this time.

He removes them one by one.

"Can we not talk about this ... or act like we never *did* talk about it?"

"There is no chance in hell I'll forget this conversation." He winks. "I'm starting to like you more, dear neighbor."

———

I'M drunk off my ass with the man I hate sitting at my side.

Last time we hung out, it crushed me.

Kyle chuckles, drags my drink away from me, and sets it out of my reach. "Cut-off time for Chloe."

I scowl at him and gesture to the bar. "Look at that, ladies and gents. The life of the party has graduated to the party pooper. Is the music too loud for you? Should I ask Maliki to turn it down a notch, so you can get your full eight hours of sleep?"

"I love wasted, smart-ass Chloe." He smirks.

I'm clueless as to how long we've been sitting here with each other. Kyle's company has outshone every thought of Kent. Being around him is entertaining and much better than drinking myself into a stupor alone. I'm an emotional drunk. The first time I got wasted, I blubbered about losing a pet goldfish before puking and passing out.

Hanging out with Kyle—if that's what you can call it—has been interesting. We argued when I attempted to order a drink stronger than the vodka in front of me. Five minutes later, I realized I had no choice. When I yelled my order to Maliki, Kyle shook his head, and Maliki turned around like a traitorous little shit.

Somehow, Kyle volunteered for Chloe babysitting duty—not surprising. He's always enjoyed being in charge and bossing people around. Sober me does not like him being in charge and bossy. But drunk me—good ole stupid, drunk me—loves his authority.

Somehow, the liquor numbs my hate for him. His attractiveness is the culprit of my sliding closer to him as the night grows later. My attention closes in on his hair as I think of how amazing it'd be to mess it up, run my hands through it, while he touched me in places he shouldn't. The flannel hugging his muscular arms looked hot when he sat down, but my mouth watered when he unbuttoned it later and revealed a black V-neck tee. He hung the flannel on the back of his stool and stretched his arms out on the bar.

I knew vodka went straight to the head, but I didn't know it messed with your head like this.

Maybe I should drink away those thoughts.

Excellent idea.

I need to up my alcohol intake.

I reach for the half-full glass of vodka soda he confiscated, but he grabs my hand. His finger massages the space between my thumb and finger before sliding the drink farther away from me.

"Nice try," he says.

"But it's half-full!" I argue as if he took my favorite toy. "Isn't that a drinking foul?"

"True, but you're *way* over being tipsy." His response drips with authority, and I shiver.

"*Duh.* It was my game plan tonight."

He cocks his head toward the door. "Come on, my drunk Nancy Drew. I'll drive you home."

I cross my arms. "No."

"Yes."

"I can find my way home."

He snorts. "It's not like it's out of my way or anything."

"I'm not getting in the car with my archnemesis."

"Archnemesis?" he scoffs. "What are we, a fucking high school drama?"

"Piss off."

"Come on, I'm a nice guy. I ordered you fries. Mean people don't order other people fries. They keep them to themselves." He elbows me. "So, admit it. I'm a nice fucking dude."

I reach for my water, which he allows, and play with the straw, staring at it instead of him. "Maybe now … but not then."

His eyes narrow my way. "I was a stupid teenager, Chloe. Get over it."

"*Get over it?* You don't understand the consequences I had to deal with because of your *stupid teenager* actions."

He throws cash onto the bar and rises from his stool. "Stand up before I call your ex-fiancé and ask if he'll ditch his wedding to pick you and your vibrator-loving pussy up." He pauses and grabs his flannel, throwing it on over his tee. Then, he leans in. "On second thought, I won't even need to call him. The groom's party walked in. Now, you can either leave with me and not face your ex and his new wife or you can keep your ass in this corner and watch their happiness. It's up to you."

I glance up to see Kent's best man walking to the bar with a bridesmaid at his side.

This is where they chose to reception it up?

I grab my purse. "Fine, but how am I getting my car in the morning?"

"I rode with my sister. She helps Maliki close sometimes. I'll drive your car." He holds out his hand. "Keys, neighbor dearest."

I roll my eyes but grab them from my bag and shove them in his hand. "Can we go out another way, so they don't see me?"

He nods toward the back exit and grabs my water. "Sure can."

I allow him to take my hand, and he guides me down a dimly lit hallway. My head spins, and I use the wall and him to level myself. The chilly night hits me when we make it outside, and my car headlights blink when he hits the unlock button on my key.

Opening the passenger door, he assists me into the seat and then moves to the driver's side.

He hands me the water and helps me with my seat belt. "Drink this," he orders.

I gulp it down, realizing how thirsty I am.

He rests his hand on the top of my seat while reversing out of the parking spot. "See, I'm a nice guy, babe."

"Fries and rides don't make everything better," I mutter. "They don't erase my hate for you, so, no, you're still not a nice guy."

"I'll prove it to you then."

I narrow my eyes at him. "What does that mean?"

"You shall see, dear neighbor."

CHAPTER TWO

Kyle

FIVE DAYS out of the week, my mornings consist of showering, pouring myself a cup of coffee, and then walking outside to fuck with Chloe before she leaves for work.

I consider it our cute little routine.

She most likely thinks of it as a prologue to the day she murders my ass.

I tap my fingers against the steering wheel of Chloe's Honda and peek over at her slouched in the passenger seat. She's desperate if she's publicly drinking and allowing me to drive her home.

I ditched the guys as soon as I caught sight of her sitting in the back of the bar, resembling an old heartbreak country song. Gage gave me a glare and then a sly smirk when I instructed him to bury my body next to my grandmother's in case she killed me, and my sister sent me five smile emojis after I sent her a text saying I didn't need a ride home. They've been up my ass about getting a girlfriend, like it will establish world peace.

"Quit staring at me like that," she snarls.

"Like what?" I ask.

"Like you pity me."

"I don't pity you." I stop to correct myself. "Scratch that. I do pity you."

"Someone grew up and put their honest undies on."

I soften my tone and explain myself. "I don't pity you for the reason you think. I pity you for having a boyfriend who failed to get you off."

My response is met with silence.

"Was it every time?"

Groaning, she shifts her neck from side to side as if it's sore. "I'm not discussing this with you. I should've never told you in the first place."

"Jesus, Chloe, I won't tell anyone you own a vibrator. It's not uncommon, but if you're ashamed of your sexuality—"

"I'm not ashamed of my sexuality," she snaps with a sneer.

"Appears that way to me. You pleasure yourself. Who the fuck cares? I'm more concerned that you consider it weird that you masturbate but not weird that your boyfriend didn't give two shits if you were satisfied."

"Contrary to your belief, not every relationship is about sex."

"True, but Kent not giving a shit about satisfying you wasn't a healthy relationship. It was a selfish one."

"I don't like being around you," she huffs out.

"Tough shit. We're neighbors. Get used to it."

She shifts in her seat to face me. "Speaking of that, why would you buy the house next door? What's your play here?"

"Don't flatter yourself by thinking I'm secretly in love with you," I say with a laugh. "It's a nice home in a decent neighborhood with great landscaping."

Lies. The landscaping sucks ass.

"Oh, look, we're here," I say while pulling into her driveway. "No more time for your paranoia of me moving in to ruin your life."

"Until you tell me why, it's what I'm assuming."

I park the car. "Keep assuming wrong then."

She starts to talk, no doubt to continue this ridiculous argument, but her hand closes over her mouth. "Oh shit," she groans.

Fuck!

Those are never good words to hear from a drunk person with, most likely, a low alcohol tolerance.

I turn off the car. "Oh shit, what?"

The door flies open, and her head disappears from my view.

Motherfucker.

She's a damn puker.

I unbuckle my seat belt and walk to her side. Sure enough, there's vomit. It's not just outside but also on the side of her mouth and on her top.

I drag my flannel off, step to the side of the puke, and wipe her mouth with it. "Swear to God, you'd better not fucking flip me off tomorrow morning."

After I'm finished using my favorite shirt as a puke rag, I assist her out of the car. She doesn't argue, doesn't fight me, but I can see the humiliation on her face. I'm the last person she wants help from. My arm is on her shoulder, the other at the dip of her back, and her side is resting against mine. She points to the door key on the ring, and I unlock the door before walking in. A lamp in the room's corner provides light for me to walk through without running into furniture.

"I'm usually not up for drunk babysitting," I say when she points toward what I'm guessing is her bedroom. "Not even for my little sister, who can hold her liquor better than you. Jesus, you damn lightweight."

She argues with a groan and a tip of her middle finger, and I can't stop myself from laughing.

This is my first time stepping into her house. It's nice—

plenty of feminine shit everywhere. We pass a child's room, and she points to an open doorway. I flip on the light and take in her bedroom. It's not what I expected from her—not uptight. It's bright purple with gold accents scattered throughout.

"Come on, let's get you in bed," I say, jerking my head toward it.

My statement is more of a guess.

Does she want to go to bed?

Shower?

Sleep by the toilet?

I take the bed as her decision when she allows me to lead her there and grab her waist to steady her. The way I deposit her on the bed is far from graceful, and I hear a thud when her head hits the headboard.

Whoops.

I'm not trying to be Mr. Romantic over here anyway.

She rubs her head while chewing on her lower lip. "I'm going to bed alone."

I hold my hands up and grimace. "The frilly-ass bed is all yours. Taking advantage of puking, drunk chicks isn't a hobby of mine. I wouldn't kiss you right now if you begged me. French-fry vomit is not a turn-on."

She makes herself comfortable, still wearing her clothes and shoes, and I wonder if it's how she'll sleep. I'd offer her help, but I'm not risking her losing her shit on me. She stretches out on the bed and pulls the blanket until it smacks her chin. Her blonde hair is half-smashed against the headboard and half-down in tangles, and she stares at me with mascara smudged around her baby-blue eyes.

Even when she's a drunken mess, there's no mistake that Chloe is fucking gorgeous in every sense with her light skin, freckles scattered along her nose and cheeks, and plump lips that tasted like candy the first and only time we kissed. I wonder if they still taste the same.

"I thought any woman willing to sleep with you was a turn-on," she replies, proud of her comeback.

"As usual, your thoughts are inaccurate, Nancy Drew." I do a sweeping gesture to the hallway. "By the way, are you hiding children in here?"

She could be dating someone with kids. But he'd have to be against staying over or going out in public with her because I've never seen anyone.

She shakes her head and then hiccups. "I help my sister with my niece and nephew."

I draw in a breath. "Ah, I've seen her drop them off a few times."

"You need to quit stalking me."

"You need to quit thinking I find you important enough to stalk."

That shuts her up real quick.

I walk backward while staring at her. "Anything else you need?"

"Nope. I'm good."

"You sure? Water? Advil? Your vibrator?"

She grabs a pillow and hurls it at me. "Get out!"

I turn around but glance over my shoulder at her before taking off. My voice softens. "And, Chloe, thank you for not running the story."

I asked a woman who works at the printing company, and she confirmed Lauren's name was nowhere in the paper.

Her eyes narrow in my path. "You're not welcome. I'm risking a potential promotion—all because you threatened to blackmail me."

She's right.

It didn't feel good, threatening her, but I protect the people I care about.

I turn on my heel, her keys still in my hand, and leave the room. I lock her front door behind me, the key ring swinging around my finger on my short walk home.

I started my day telling Chloe good morning.

I'm ending my day telling her good night.

Tomorrow, she'll tell me to fuck off.

It's the circle of us—enemies since my balls dropped.

MY PHONE VIBRATES with a text as soon as I stroll through my front door.

Gage: You home?

I drop both our keys into my designated key bowl before replying.

Me: Just walked in. What's up?

Gage: You home alone?

Me: Why? Does Lauren want to come over and give me company?

My phone vibrates in my hand seconds later, and I answer it after two rings.

"Say something like that again, and I'll come over and beat your ass," Gage warns as soon as I pick up.

I chuckle. "You're not doing a satisfactory job as a fiancé if you're calling me this late and not snuggled up with her … or whatever you lame, monogamous people do these days."

"I don't share my bedroom talk."

Gage is my best friend, but Lauren is a delicate subject for him. He loves her more than anyone—has since we were kids.

I fake offense. "Not even your best friend?"

"Especially not with my best friend, who referred to her as Satan for years."

"Some would find the name flattering. Now, to what do I owe the pleasure of a call so urgent that it couldn't wait until tomorrow?"

Gage is my partner, and I'll see him bright and early in the morning, so we rarely do nightcap conversations.

"Call me curious, but I was wondering if you were sleeping over at your neighbor's."

I stroll into the kitchen, snag a bottle of water, and head to my bedroom. "Mrs. Kettle? We went to school with her son. Gross, man."

He laughs. "Hey, maybe it's time for you to change your type. Nothing else has worked out for you."

I'm not looking for anything serious and unsure if I'll ever be. "I'm not at Chloe's. Drunk chicks who can hardly walk don't make my dick hard."

He releases a long breath before responding. "Jesus, Kyle. I wasn't referring to you fucking her. I want to know where her head is regarding publishing the story."

I toss my puke-decorated flannel into the hamper and undress. "You're asking if I questioned her while she vomited?"

"No. I'm asking if you questioned her when you visited her office *or* when you spent your night canoodling with her in the pub's corner. Please make sure the story isn't run."

"I know for sure she's not running it in this week's paper. How did you know I was in her office today?"

"Her assistant, Melanie."

"Is Lauren aware you're chatting it up with Chloe's assistant, Melanie?"

"I'm not *chatting it up* with anyone. Melanie is fooling around with Joey and told him. Joey relayed the message to me."

Damn Joey.

No more women advice from me for him.

"So, you used Joey's big mouth to your advantage?" I ask.

"Obviously." He sighs. "Give me the fucking details on what's running through her head."

"I was hoping for a bedtime story first."

"Once upon a time, a dude needed to give his friend details. He didn't. Got his fucking head ripped off. The end."

"I love a happy ever after." I grab a towel and turn on the shower. "I think I made myself clear, but I'll talk to her again, okay?"

"Thank you." He sighs again. "Tell her she owes you a favor for your drunk babysitting."

I grin. "Don't worry; I intend on letting her know."

CHAPTER THREE

Chloe

YESTERDAY MORNING, I thought my ex tying the knot would be the lowest thing to happen to me. I was so wrong. Somehow, my mission to escape thoughts of Kent derailed me straight into the company of a man I'd been avoiding for years.

I drank with him, allowed him to drive me home, and gave him the keys to my house to escort me inside.

He was in my bedroom, for Christ's sake.

I'm appalled at myself for admitting how I received most of my orgasms in my last relationship.

Today's to-do list: research realtors and vacate my ass out of here ASAP.

While I shower, my head pounds with a reminder of every sip I took last night, praying Kyle doesn't deliver his morning greeting. Maybe he'll see me as a weird, self-pleasuring freak he no longer wants to live next to.

Maybe he'll move.

Fingers crossed.

Doubt it.

He pressed me for every detail about the morning Kent had walked in on me. I don't know if it was the drinks I'd consumed or Kyle seeming sincere for once in his life that drove me to spill the embarrassing story.

I get dressed and opt for flats rather than heels. It's easier to run in them. Operation Avoid Kyle is now in full force, and my first mission is to sprint to my car as soon as I open my door. I find my bag on the couch and shuffle through it in search of my keys.

Nothing.

Maybe he left them in my car.

I suck in a calming breath and open my front door.

"Good morning!" His voice is louder than usual, closer than usual, more annoying than usual.

I shriek, my coffee falling from my hand and splattering onto my porch, and my heart stops in my chest.

Kyle is standing on *my* front porch, smiling in front of me.

My mouth drops open. "You've got to be kidding me," I mutter under my breath. I guess I didn't scare him away last night. "This is getting out of hand," I add when he bends down to pick up my coffee mug. "And stalker-like."

He sets the cup and lid on the porch railing, and there's mischief in his smile.

Oh shit.

"What? You spilling your coffee? It is clumsy, you know."

"No. You showing up at my door."

"I was in your bedroom last night."

"That doesn't sound less stalker-like."

His smile turns playful. "Shut it, Fieldgain. I didn't come over to admit I peeped through your windows and sniffed your panties. I came for reimbursement."

I blink. "I'm sorry, reimbursement?"

He nods. "Yes. It's time to pay your debt."

"Excuse me? I don't owe you shit unless it's a swift kick in the nuts for being on my property, *uninvited.*"

He appears entertained while leaning back on his heels. "I

was invited last night. The invite is valid for a full twenty-four hours."

I roll my eyes. "Seriously?"

"Yes. You told me to stop by whenever I wanted, remember?"

I park my hands on my hips. "Those words left my mouth alongside the vomit?"

"You. Owe. Me. Now, I have a few options on payment."

I scoff, "I owe you for being a decent human being?"

He points to me and snaps his fingers. "Correct."

I clench my teeth and tap my foot. "I can't believe I'm entertaining this, but what are my *options*?"

He holds a finger up. "One: we have morning sex."

I snort. "Not happening."

He holds up a second finger. "Two: we have sex after work this evening."

"Next."

He adds another finger to the mix. "Three: you take me to breakfast." When I don't answer, he gestures to my empty cup. "Unless you plan on slurping it from the ground, you need a fresh cup."

While taking my sweet time to determine my next move with him, I get chills when I realize he's not bare-chested today.

What a shame.

Instead, he's giving me the gorgeous view of him in his blue uniform again—another one fitting him perfectly.

Definitely not a shame.

Whichever sight he delivers never fails to turn me on. My nipples tighten, and I wonder what it'd be like to strip his uniform off and for him to use his handcuffs on me.

I nearly fall over in embarrassment, and my eyes meet his at the sound of him clearing his throat.

A cocky smirk plays at his lips. "Chloe, while I appreciate

you checking me out, unless you plan on doing something about it, let's not make my dick hard, okay?"

It takes me a moment to pull myself together, and I gesture to the door. "If breakfast is what you want, come on in. There are Cheerios and Pop-Tarts in my pantry. Have at it."

Here I go again, being stupid.

Who invites their enemy into their home *again*?

People in horror movies who wind up murdered —that's who.

"As much as I'd love to come in and have you serve me breakfast—" he begins.

"Serve?" I interrupt with a snort. "I'd throw it to you and walk out the door."

My answer further amuses him. "Shirley's Diner. I can drive us, or you can meet me there in five."

I feign annoyance.

He grins.

"Fine," I deadpan. "Thirty minutes. One pancake."

"Forty minutes. *Two* pancakes."

"Jesus. Just fucking follow me." I yell his name to stop him, and he turns to leave.

"Decide on a better offer, one involving us in your bed?" he asks with a raised brow.

"You wish. Where are my keys?"

"I might know the answer to your question."

"Are you kidding me?" I screech. "You jacked my keys?"

"Technically, you gave them to me, but I kept them to lock your door on my way out. You should thank me for eliminating the risk of you being executed in your sleep."

I push my open palm his way. "Hand them over."

He pats the pocket by his groin, and I notice the outline of keys underneath the fabric. "I'd prefer if you grabbed them. The pockets are tiny, so smaller hands would do better to rescue them."

I take a deep breath. "The longer you play your games, the shorter time we spend at breakfast. Choose your battles, Lane."

My mouth waters at the idea of going forward and startling him by grabbing my keys. I'd love to watch his reaction if I did reach in, graze his cock, and then pull them out slowly and torturously.

I don't though because not only am I a chickenshit, but he also drags them out and dumps them in my hand seconds later.

"I hope you bring your appetite." He shifts around and strides to his new Jeep.

I further check him out and shrug with no shame before walking to my car.

———

SHIRLEY'S DINER is packed with people stuffing their stomachs with every breakfast food imaginable. The diner has been a staple here for longer than I've been alive. Blue Beech, Iowa, is a small town where everybody knows everybody. Most residents reside in town, in comfortable neighborhoods void of dilapidated homes, or are lucky to own acres of land.

Me? I was raised on the outskirts, given the name West Side Trash decades ago. There's no cute '50s-themed diner within walking distance of the west side. It's at least a mile walk anywhere—the school, Town Square, any stores.

I pledged I'd move from the west side trailer park I had grown up in when I made enough money. I did. Unfortunately, my sister and mother refuse to do the same. They both live in the same run-down double-wide with my niece and nephew. Don't get me wrong. I don't judge people from there, but it's where most of the crime takes place.

Shirley gives Kyle a grin when we walk in and seats us, muttering something about giving us his favorite booth.

Of course he has a favorite.

Unlike other patrons who aren't the biggest fans of my family, she greets me with a friendly smile while we sit down, and she takes our orders.

No matter what other people think about my family, Shirley has never let outside influence change her opinion of me. In high school, I'd come to the diner to do homework, and Shirley always brought me free milkshakes.

I order a coffee, scrambled eggs, and toast. If I'm stuck with him, I might as well eat.

"What's your favorite breakfast food?" Kyle asks from across the booth when our food is dropped off.

"I don't have one," I answer with honesty.

He dramatically gasps at my answer. "What? Who doesn't have a favorite breakfast food? Pancakes or waffles with delicious maple syrup." He tips his head back and groans. "Mmm … chicken and waffles."

Goose bumps run up my arms. His food-loving groan turns me on.

I am ridiculous.

When he glimpses at me, I shrug, acting like I wasn't imagining him making the same groan while inside me. "I grew up on generic cereal and toast, so I wouldn't consider any of those as my favorite."

Even now that I can afford decent breakfast foods, it's never been my thing—most likely because of skipping meals in college in favor of studying.

His eyebrows scrunch together. "I'm sorry, but what does that have to do with not having a favorite breakfast food?"

I straighten my napkin in my lap. "I'm not a breakfast person. Sue me."

He points his fork in my direction, syrup dripping from the ends. "One day, I'll make you breakfast in bed. You'll eat my pancakes while naked and love every bite. Watch and see."

I snort. "You've lost your mind."

This conversation needs to take a different turn, pronto. It's making me imagine things I shouldn't. Eating his pancakes while naked *does* sound like a fun time.

He drops his fork and focuses all his attention on me. "All right then. Chloe Fieldgain is not a breakfast person; got it. Let's move on to the next question. What is your favorite food then?"

I chew on my lower lip. "I don't have a favorite food."

I'm not a foodie. I live on a diet of salads and quick meals. It's not entertaining, cooking for one.

He gapes at me. "Everyone has a favorite food, Chloe. If you picked one thing to eat for the rest of your life, what would it be?"

I hate the question. It's a typical first-date question that no one has ever asked me.

Shit.

This is most definitely not a date.

I drum my fingers against the table while thinking. "Uh … grilled chicken, I guess."

"Grilled chicken?" he slowly repeats in a disapproving tone, making me feel judged. "Grilled chicken is the one thing you'd pick to eat for the rest of your life?"

I shrug. "Why not? It's healthy and easy to make."

I had my fair share of cooking for four when I was younger. It's a chore now.

He gives me a confident smile. "Jesus, as your neighbor, I'm officially taking it upon myself to change your favorite meal into something less boring."

I glare at him in reluctance. "All right then, favorite meal judge, what's yours?"

It doesn't take him but a second to answer. "Pussy." The word falls from his lips with pride and no shame, as if he'd said it was chocolate cake.

The one word causes me to spit out my coffee.

He smirks at my reaction. "It's organic."

I cover my face with my napkin and shake my head before cleaning up the mess. "There are so many things disturbing about your answer … about your *favorite food*."

"*Disturbing?*" He raises his brow as a teasing smile plays over his lips. Yes, the man loves fucking with me. "What is so *disturbing* about it?"

I start to answer, but he cuts me off and continues talking. "I'm not surprised that someone whose boyfriend never sufficiently ate her pussy would find my answer disturbing. I'm sorry your orgasm-abandoned personality finds it disturbing, but a quick tip for when you find another boyfriend: you'd better pray it's his favorite meal." He grabs his coffee and leans back in the booth. "I'd suggest making it a first-date question."

I can't stop from smiling even though he just talked shit about me and insulted my personality. *Orgasm-abandoned? Who says that? Hell, what does it even mean?*

"You're seriously depraved." I grab my coffee and rest my elbows on the table as the cup dangles from my fingers. I take a slow drink and continue. "Maybe it's why I've hated you all these years."

He sets his mug down and leans across the table, lowering his voice so that only I hear. "You didn't hate me that night."

I push against his forehead with my palm, and he relaxes in the booth, not one bit alarmed I forehead-slapped him.

"You need to quit with that bullshit before I throw my coffee in your face."

He drapes his arm along the booth. "In high school … I did a shitty thing."

"No shit, Sherlock."

As painfully as I want to deny it, regret is on his face.

"I've felt like a douchebag since then."

"You should."

My gaze lowers to my eggs before reaching Kyle's eyes again. We're inches apart, and it takes us seconds for our gazes to connect. I can't resist pouring all my emotions out, needing him to witness the hurt he caused me, and we create the connection I wanted with him so many years ago.

"You could've fixed it, you know," I say, soft-spoken.

He doesn't look away. "It wasn't that simple."

"It was that simple."

He gulps, his Adam's apple bobbing. "I'm sorry."

A child screaming in the background breaks our connection, and I shut my eyes, shake my head, and withdraw, my back against the booth again.

"Whatever," I finally mutter, opening my eyes. "It doesn't matter anymore."

"Obviously, it does since you bring it up every time we talk." His face remains serious, and he pinches the bridge of his nose. "I'm fucking sorry, Chloe. I don't know how many more times you want me to say it. Tell me what I need to do to make it up to you. Go ahead. As long as it's not cutting off my balls or some shit, I'm willing."

There's nothing he can do to change it now. The damage is done. Although this is the first time he's offered to make up for what he did instead of giving me a simple apology.

"I don't like this Kyle," I grumble. I need the smart-ass Kyle who's easier to hate to return—not the guy who takes care of me when I'm drunk and then insists on having breakfast together.

He raises a brow while studying me. "What Kyle?"

"The nice, no-ulterior-motive Kyle."

He takes a bite of his neglected breakfast and swallows it down. "How do you know I don't have an ulterior motive?"

"Do you?"

He shrugs. "Possibly."

I glare at him. "Of course you do. You want to make sure I don't run the story about Lauren." I shake my head and roll my eyes. *Go figure.* "We've been neighbors for months, and you've never invited me to breakfast. Will you threaten and harass me about her story until the day I die?"

"Technically, you telling me to fuck off daily never gave me the notion you'd enjoy a meal with me, but last night confirmed you don't hate me as much as you lead on." He smirks. "And we both know you're smart enough not to run the story since I made myself clear on the repercussions."

I narrow my eyes his way. "What makes you so sure I won't?"

He shrugs and settles back so casually that you'd think we were discussing the weather. "You're smart. Always have been."

"Except when I hang out with you."

"No, that's smart. Who doesn't want to hang out with me? You seemed to enjoy it last night. I'm cool as shit."

"Negative. Men who are *cool as shit* don't do what you did, and they most definitely don't threaten women not to publish stories in what you so kindly referred to as a *pitiful* newspaper. So, what gives?"

"I was a fucking kid, Chloe, for the millionth goddamn time. Kids do stupid shit."

"You're right. Kids toilet-paper houses or sneak out. They don't cross lines like you did."

He pushes his plate forward and stares at me with intent and annoyance. "My only *ulterior motive* is convincing you to get to know me and realize I'm not the villain you paint me out to be. I want us to share some meals and *maybe* share some orgasms. You know, I've wanted to finish what we started in high school."

I pour more sugar into my coffee even though it's unnecessary. His words piss me off. "Your behavior didn't show that."

"True, but I'll make it up to you. Don't waste orgasms by giving them to a vibrator."

I take a drink and cringe at the sweetness. "How do you know I don't have a boyfriend?"

"I was the one who took you home and tucked you in last night, and you're having breakfast with me. If you do, he's another shit boyfriend you should dump."

"And what?" I raise a brow. "Sleep with you?"

"If it's what you need, I don't mind taking on the job." He holds his hand up but drops it as soon as his phone buzzes with a text. "It's Gage. He'll be here in five to pick me up."

"In the squad car?" I question.

He nods.

"Does he always drive?"

I've seen them come and go, and Kyle always seems to be riding passenger. I'm not sure why I've paid attention. It could be because Kyle enjoys being in charge, which means, being in the driver's seat, so it makes me wonder why he doesn't ever drive.

He nods again.

"Do you feel emasculated?" *Ugh, I sound like Kent. Ew.*

"For not driving? Fuck no. Gage has gone through some rough shit. If driving helps him, he can have the keys anytime he wants."

"Things like what?" I've heard the rumors but never known what was true and what wasn't. I considered writing a piece on it but decided against it after no one would say a word to me.

"I would never put my best friend's business out there. Loyalty is a big deal to me."

"But you had no problem putting my business out there," I fire back. "You had no problem with people talking about *me*."

"You weren't and aren't my best friend." He says it matter-of-factly, no bullshit, like his loyalty only falls on those he deems worthy.

"Glad to know. I'll be sure to never tell you my personal business."

He cocks his head to the side and smirks. "Earn my loyalty, and you can."

I ignore his comment and take another drink of the Candy Land–tasting coffee. Our teenage waitress, who should probably be on her way to high school, hands him the bill without even glancing at me.

He pulls it away when I go to grab it.

"I've got this," I say in a demanding tone. I try to snatch it from his hand but with no success. "You said *I* owed you breakfast."

"Did I?" He fakes confusion and scratches his head. "I thought I said I'd take you to breakfast."

I push my hand out further. "Give me the damn bill."

"How about ... no?" He pulls out his wallet and drags out a fifty without bothering to glance at the bill. "Keep the change," he says, handing it to the waitress.

She gives him a girlie smile I would've given every Backstreet Boy in my day. "Thank you so much, Kyle."

He smiles in return—not in a disturbing, *I like to creep on younger girls* way, but more of a genuine one. "You're welcome."

What gives?

Why would he tip a pre-algebra student so much money?

The waitress skips away in excitement, and I scoff.

He flinches. "What?"

"Look at you, Mr. Dreamy Eyes Keep the Change."

"Mad I'm not making dreamy eyes at you?" He inches forward. "I'm not hitting on her. Her father walked out on the family a few weeks ago. Her mother works here as well, and they're barely making ends meet. If an extra tip helps them out, then I'll give her an extra tip."

I hate that this turns me on. "That's, uh ... very nice of you."

"Again, I've tried to tell you that I'm a nice guy. Let me know when you're done lying to yourself."

I roll my eyes. "Okay, okay, you're *such a nice guy*, Kyle. There's no other man nicer than you. When people tell tales about this century, you'll be the man they call the *nicest*. You will be put in history books as Mr. Nice Guy."

He grins. "Quit giving me the sarcastic attitude, Chloe. It makes me want you more."

My stomach flutters, and my gaze on him softens.

God, why do I have to hate this man?

Why can't he stay Voldemort evil?

I push my coffee up the table and set my napkin next to it. "I need to get to work. We've shared a meal. Now, we're even."

He shakes his head and clicks his tongue against the roof of his mouth. "Wrong. We're nowhere near even."

"The hell?" I do a sweeping gesture of me in the booth. "This was my payback."

"No. Breakfast was for me driving you home. You still owe me for dealing with your puking ass. Three shared meals in return for my kindness."

"Are you kidding me?" I yelp. "You never mentioned there were numerous debts owed."

He bites into his lower lip in humor. "I must've forgotten that part."

I throw my arms up and then drop them to my sides. "I don't have time to play games with you. I have a job to get to."

"Second order of business: as previously discussed, no digging up information on people I care about. Promise me."

So, this is why I'm getting nice Kyle.

Duh. He's not doing this for no reason.

"You know damn well I can't promise that."

"Actually, it's quite simple for you."

"*Fine*, I won't publish any stories."

He nods, accepting my answer as if he were my authority. "Third order of business: have dinner with me tonight."

"Not happening."

He crosses his arms behind his neck. "I'll visit you at work for lunch then. We'll enjoy a romantic picnic in your office. I'll find a basket and a red tablecloth to set the mood."

My gaze darts around the diner. Briefly, I forgot we weren't alone. "Fine, dinner at *your* house."

"Cool. See you at six."

"Whatever. I have work to do."

He tilts his head toward the window when Gage pulls up. "Me, too. See you tonight." He winks. "Wear one of those cute skirts I like."

"Wear that muzzle I like."

He grins. "I love when you get kinky on me."

CHAPTER FOUR

Chloe

Age Thirteen

DEAR DIARY,

I hate my bedroom.

My friend Holly's is prettier.

It's pink, and she has a real bed, not a mattress on the floor like mine.

She lives in the same trailer court. Her parents are poor, too, but at least they give her something pretty.

Meanwhile, my bedroom walls are a dingy yellow from cigarette smoke.

I throw my diary down and lower my head, glaring at the worn, stained comforter.

Ugh. Just writing about it makes me hate my life more.

I pick up the book next to me and open it.

Time to take myself to a happier place where I have a father, a mother who doesn't suck, and an older sister who isn't mean fifty times a day for no reason.

"Hey, Chloe. What are you reading there?"

I peek up from my book to find my sister's boyfriend, Sam, standing in the cramped doorway. I smile before holding up the book, so he can read the cover.

"*The Lion, The Witch, and The Wardrobe*, huh?" he asks. "Your sister said you enjoyed reading."

"I love to read." I wait for him to make fun of me like Claudia, my sister, does.

She's been dating Sam for a few months now. I only saw him a few times before, but lately, he's been coming around more. My mother hated him at first, calling him filthy names and then sinking so low as to demand he pay her to see my sister. She needed the money to buy drugs and alcohol.

He pays her now—most likely because my sister is younger, and I'd guess he's around my mother's age. Now, she doesn't mind as much.

Neither do I.

Sam is handsome. He reminds me of a character from some of the romance novels I shouldn't check out of the library. He's tall with dark hair and broad shoulders and maturer than my sister. It's not unusual for her to date older men, but she's never brought someone home like Sam. He doesn't lick his lips or ogle me, making me uncomfortable because my mom won't buy me a training bra, and my nipples poke through my shirts.

He leans against the doorframe. "Girls who like to read are those with a bright future ahead of them. Their imaginations can take them anywhere."

I crawl to the edge of the mattress and settle myself Indian-style. "My sister doesn't like to read."

He chuckles. "Yes, I am well aware."

"Why do you like her then?"

Claudia is gorgeous, and even at eighteen, she could pass for someone old enough to get into bars. Mama lets her go with her sometimes, too. Claudia is also mean and selfish, and she isn't the big sister girls dream of.

"Your sister excels in other areas," he replies.

"Like sex?"

My response surprises him.

He raises a brow and points to my book. "Keep reading. Excel at that."

He walks away before I can reply.

The next day, he returns with a box of books—brand-new books!

"These are for you," he says. "Keep reading, Chloe."

"Thank you!" I squeal, hastily searching through the box. I grab a copy of a Sarah Dessen book and hug it to my chest. "Thank you so much!" The book hits the floor with a thud when I jump up to give him a hug.

When he leaves, I grab my diary and write about how nice Sam is.

CHAPTER FIVE

Chloe

MY STOMACH FILLS with dread when I see the name flashing across my phone screen. My finger wavers over the Ignore button for a few seconds but eventually moves to answer it.

I clench the phone in my hand. "Hello?"

"What is wrong with you?" Claudia shrieks on the other line. "Marsha said she saw you having breakfast with Kyle Lane this morning."

My sister is best known for her overdramatic behavior.

Scratch that.

She's best known as being a scam artist.

An alcoholic.

An opportunist.

Overdramatic runs in fourth.

"Good morning to you, too," I grumble, rubbing my forehead.

I can't share pancakes with someone without it being talked about. *Good thing I run the headlines in this town.*

"Did you fall and smack your head? I know you're still mourning the loss of your snooze-fest relationship with Kent, but Kyle Lane is bad news."

"Noted."

She's irritated, but her not continuing her rant confirms this isn't a courtesy call. She wants something from me.

"Go ahead and say it," I finally mutter.

"I need you to watch the kids tonight."

"I can't. I have plans."

I'm not a fan of helping and enabling her, but normally, I have no problem with babysitting my niece and nephew, Gloria and Trey. I wish she'd act like a mom and take responsibility for them instead of putting it all on me.

"With who?" she snaps, the attitude resurfacing. "*Kyle?*"

Even though she can't see me, I tip my chin up. "My plans are none of your business."

We've never had a relationship where we share beauty secrets or boy advice. We only share conversations when it concerns the kids or she needs money.

"Do those *plans* involve Kyle?"

I release a long sigh. "It's a work thing, not that it's any of your concern. I'm available after seven."

"Cool. I'll drop them off then."

The line goes dead.

Claudia is as grateful to me for watching her kids as those obnoxious twits on *My Super Sweet 16* for their extravagant birthday parties.

Helping her is expected of me—has been for years. Like my mother, whose demise will be her strict diet of vodka and endless opiates, she's entitled. If someone has something of value, she demands a slice. Free rides are hitting the jackpot, and Claudia views me as her money train to support her partying.

I drop my phone in my bag before getting out of my car and heading to my office. My head throbs with every step I take up the stairs. It's not even lunchtime, and I've already dealt with Kyle and Claudia.

"Homegirl, you are in *trouble*," Melanie sings as soon as I walk in, her feet kicked up on the desk.

Her loud voice makes my head hurt, but it's nothing compared to the shrill of Claudia's.

I shrug off my jacket and settle it on my arm. "I can be late for once."

She snorts and drops her feet, smoothing out her skirt. "I don't give two shits about your punctuality. What I'm referring to is, you looking like you were up all night, drinking or sexing it up—or possibly both."

"You have no idea," I grumble while heading toward my office.

"The rumors are true then?"

I stop mid-step. "What rumors?"

She sits on the edge of her chair in excitement. "Word is, you left Down Home with Kyle last night and then had breakfast with him this morning."

Seriously?

Joke's on me. The woman who writes other people's stories is now the face of the town gossip.

"Word is, people need to mind their damn business," I grumble.

This is not what my hangover needs at the moment.

"He took me home and left last night. This morning, I spilled my coffee when he came over to give me my keys, and he offered to buy me another. Just two neighbors sharing a meal. No biggie."

She glowers, confirming I'm full of bullshit, before her face turns somewhat serious. "You know I'm all for you getting laid, but make him a booty call only. That's it. You get an orgasm and get the hell out of there, girlfriend. His family is no joke about protecting their image and not letting outsiders in."

She's right. Like Kyle, his family is royalty here. His dad is the mayor, his grandfather a judge, and his mother the biggest philanthropist in the town. Blue Beech isn't full of people with money, except the Lane family. They've owned this town for decades.

"Trust me," I say. "There's nothing going on between us."

———

I DON'T WEAR one of those skirts he likes.

I wear yoga pants and an old tee.

"I'm actually doing this," I say to myself while pulling my hair into a sloppy ponytail.

Sure, I've shared drinks and meals with Kyle, but dinner at his home is intimate. There will be no crowd around and no puking involved. Kyle obviously wants to have sex, and I'd be a liar if I said I didn't want the same.

Last time we had dinner, it ruined me. No one was supposed to find out, but they did.

When they did, Kyle came out unscathed.

Everyone loved him, his family, and their wealth.

Guys wanted to be his best friend. Girls wanted to be his girlfriend or current screw. Even I was guilty of the last two, which was what pulled me into the mess of him. He was nice when no one else even glimpsed in my direction.

Turned out, he wasn't the nice guy he'd played off to be, and I'm scared he's playing the same deprived game.

I walk through Kyle's front door without bothering to knock. He doesn't respect my privacy. Therefore, he doesn't deserve his. I check out the living room after the door shuts behind me. I expected the interior of Kyle's home to scream bachelor pad with neon signs and poker tables, but it's nowhere close. While there is a flat screen TV set up on the wall and a saddle-brown leather sofa, it's clean with dark pillows and a bookcase filled with books and pictures of him and his family.

I follow the noise of dishes clinking and the scent of food

into the kitchen to find Kyle standing at the island with a beer in his fist and dishes set out in front of him. I figured we'd have pizza or takeout, but it smells of comfort food—similar to how Kent's mother's would when she spent all day in the kitchen.

What the …

Surely, he didn't cook for us.

"We need to make this quick," I say.

He grins as if my outburst wasn't rude. "Mmm … I'm not normally into quick the first time, but I'll make an exception for you."

"Hilarious," I deadpan. "I'm babysitting in an hour."

"Not cool. You agreed to dinner." He's scolding me as if I were a child, like he's the one who has to babysit *me*.

I throw my hands up. "I'm here, aren't I?"

He sets his beer down and walks around the island, resting against the counter and pushing his hands into his pockets. He's in jeans, a tee fitting the vast expanse of his chest, and barefoot. "And? Our dinner will take longer than an hour."

I blow out a frustrated breath. "Wrong. Whatever you're cooking will take me ten minutes to eat." I smile. "I'm a fast eater."

He tsks under his breath. "You're lucky your escape plan is kid-sitting. Otherwise, I'd make you cancel."

Make me?

He's given himself the control tonight, and apparently, my spine has flattened because the urge to take that control back is nonexistent.

"How sweet of you," I mutter.

He shoves off the counter, takes the few steps separating us, and captures my chin in his hand.

I draw in a breath and surprisingly don't jerk away.

He uses one finger to tilt my chin up before cupping it, his finger sweeping along my skin, and his emerald-green eyes scream determination while he appraises me as if I were an expensive item he was debating on purchasing. "I'm sweet when necessary, dear neighbor, and as you're well aware, not sweet when necessary."

Is he flirting with me or threatening me?

I don't catch my breath until he drops my chin and turns away. I glance around the kitchen, debating on if I should leave.

"We should get started. You're not bailing before dessert," he says. He snatches his beer again and points at me with it. "What's your drink of choice?"

"Water, please."

Alcohol combined with Kyle is a bad idea unless my plan is to drop my panties or throw up on him—or possibly both.

"Water it is." He opens the fridge and draws out a bottle of water *and* a wine cooler before holding the cooler up. "In case you do want a drink, I snagged a few of these. When my sister was a teenager, she'd sneak and drink them. There's hardly any alcohol in them. Serving you anything stronger might result in you painting my walls with the wonderful dinner I've prepared for us."

His joke eases me, and I smile. "With the hangover I'm suffering from, I don't even want to think about consuming alcohol."

He settles the drinks down in front of me, and a pleasant smell covers the room when he opens the oven, drags out a pan, and places it on the island. I push forward on my toes to get a better view.

My attention flies to him. "You cooked this?" *There's no way.*

Chicken coated with spices, vegetables, and potatoes are in the pan. My stomach growls at the sight. I haven't had a home-cooked meal like this since last Christmas with Kent's parents.

"Negative," he answers. "My mother did. I'm heating it up. It has to count for something, right?"

I can't help but smirk. "Aw, how cute. His mommy made dinner for his forced non-date."

He drops the oven gloves on the counter and smiles at me. "Shove it, Fieldgain. My mother's cooking is the fucking best and is better than anything I can pull together. I prefer to impress you, not give you food poisoning."

I tilt my head his way. "Appreciate that."

I drag out a breath, watching Kyle move around the room to gather up everything. It's hot. He's not the chef tonight, but he's no stranger to the kitchen.

He prepares our plates, grabs the silverware, and directs me to the four-person table across the room.

He takes the chair next to me when everything is situated. "How was your day, honey?" His fingers circle around the neck of his beer, and he takes a drink while waiting for me to answer.

I narrow my eyes his way. "Don't make this all domestic."

He's not thrown off his game at my response. "All right then, how the fuck was your day, you goddamn pain in the ass?"

I shrug. "Now, that brings me back to my dinners as a child." At least, when my mother wasn't too drunk to sit with us.

"Same."

I raise a brow at the same time I snort. "Yeah, right. The Lanes are the picture-perfect family." I cough. "I mean, it's what everyone says. I wouldn't know."

He sets down his beer and leans back in the chair. "Looking in from the outside? Sure. Inside? No. My mother and father despise each other. They're experts at hiding it in public."

His parents not having a healthy relationship isn't surprising. His father is an asshole. Most people in this town, friend or foe, wouldn't dare mutter a bad word about the mayor. The people on the lower end of the totem pole, we speak about him. It might be in hushed whispers, but it's known that his father isn't a stand-up gentleman.

"Dig in," he says, breaking me away from my thoughts. "We only have an hour."

I take the first bite and moan.

It's delicious.

I'd so hire Kyle's mom as my chef if I ever won the lottery.

"This is amazing," I comment before taking another bite.

He sticks his chest out in mock over-the-top pride. "Ding! One point for Kyle."

"One point for Kyle's mom," I correct.

"Give a man credit now. You said your favorite meal was grilled chicken. I made sure that's what you got." He shrugs and moves in closer until our elbows are touching. His eyes meet mine. "Maybe I'll get my favorite meal tonight, too."

I nearly choke on my bite and use my water to help me swallow it down while he laughs in the background. "You enjoy catching me off guard, don't you?"

"I enjoy it more than you think. Hearing you tell me to fuck off is music to my ears."

I take another drink of my water. "Subject change, please." I glance at my watch. "You're running low on time, Officer Lane."

"Okay, Miss Fast Eater, let's see the proof."

I take a huge bite, and he laughs.

He's hardly touched his food. All he's doing is giving me the same deep stare he gave me earlier when I first walked in. His gaze is intense, but his words are playful. "Any hot plans this weekend? Going out, searching for a new boyfriend?"

I swallow down my bite. "Hey now, someone who's single can't talk shit about a fellow single person. At least I've been in a long-term relationship."

"How do you know I haven't had or am not in one now?"

That shuts my ass up for a moment.

He laughs. "Wow, I've never heard you go so quiet before. I'm patiently waiting for your smart-ass response." He takes a drink. "And for your information, I have had a serious relationship. Becky Binds, to be exact," he says proudly. "You going to run a story about that? I can give you plenty of details if need be."

I snort. "That does *not* qualify as a long-term relationship."

"Why, Ms. Relationship Expert 101?"

"It wasn't real. It was superficial and lasted, like, three months." I slam my mouth shut. *Oh shit.* Now, I seem like a total stalker. It's embarrassing, but I paid attention to Kyle and his relationships after our fallout happened.

"Is there a statute of limitations for relationships?" he asks.

I'm relieved at his lack of teasing about my knowledge of his bullshit relationship statuses in high school. I hated Becky's guts. They dated after our incident, and she made it her mission to make my life a living hell, even spreading rumors about me and creating the not-so-original, taunting chant that followed me down the high school hallways.

"High school relationships don't count," I state. "Are you currently the boyfriend of a poor girl who needs to find better taste?"

"*Poor girl?* Interesting, coming from a woman having dinner with me at my house, and even more interesting since said chick had drinks with me last night."

"The woman who was *forced* to come to dinner and can leave at any time," I correct with a cold glare.

"No one forced you to walk your sexy ass over here. You could've easily stood me up."

I hate that he's right. "*Fine,* I was hungry. Now, any crazy girlfriends I should worry about that will make it their mission to ruin my life if they find out I'm having dinner here?"

He lets out a breath. "Not dating anyone, so I'm all yours, babe."

I ignore the *all yours* comment. "I was right then."

"Not entirely. I recently ended a relationship."

I perk up in my seat. "Why?"

He shrugs. "It wasn't there."

"Do I know her?"

"No. Lauren set me up with a nurse from the hospital. It was fun for a while, but our schedules were chaotic and made it difficult to see each other. She wasn't next door and available whenever I needed her."

"I'm not sleeping with you, so if that's your game plan here, you're wasting your time. I'm sure it won't be hard for you to find another Becky Binds."

He strokes his chin and laughs. "My sweet Chloe, were you jealous of Becky Binds for having me?"

I fake a grimace. "Negative. How could I be jealous of someone who possibly had chlamydia and was a terrible person in high school? Again, I'm not sleeping with you." My repetition is to also convince myself.

"We don't have to sleep together. We can do other things and then go sleep in our own beds."

I suck in a breath. The thought of not sleeping but sleeping together turns me on more than it should. "You'd better quit before I leave."

He holds his hands up. "Okay, okay. Let's eat."

Our conversation takes a turn, and I'm surprised by how comfortable we are with each other. He tells me about the police station drama, and I complain about my office being a snooze-fest. As our plates clear, we take things to a more personal level, and I tell him about Gloria and Trey and how they're the reason I'm still in Blue Beech. I don't trust Claudia to care for them. Kyle has still made his fair share of smart-ass comments, but nothing to make me want to kick him in the balls for.

My phone beeps in my bag. There hasn't been one boring minute with us, so there was no need to check it.

"Check it," Kyle says, referring to it.

I grab it to find a text.

Claudia: Be there in 20.

"Your sister?" he asks.

I slip my phone into my bag. "Yep."

He wipes his mouth with a napkin. "How much time do we have?"

"Twenty minutes." I stop and hold up a finger. "Fifteen. She can't see me leaving your house."

"That pipes up a man's ego."

"She'll give me shit. She hates you."

He scrunches his face up. "She has no reason to hate me."

"She hates you by proxy. I hate you, so she hates you."

I set my phone down without bothering to text her back and grab my plate to clean up.

Kyle rises from his chair. "Don't worry about it."

I shake my head. "Nope. You cooked—*heated up*." I laugh. "It's only fair I clean."

I move faster than him, but he catches up seconds later and grabs the plate from my hand at the same time I'm about to set it on the counter.

He whips me around to face him and stands inches from me. "I'll let you clean next time."

"Whoa," I say, forcing myself to make my response sound like a joke, but inside, my heart is racing. "What makes you so sure there will be a next time?"

His hands go to each side of me, his palms resting on the surface of the counter, and his arms block me from moving around him. I inhale his masculine scent before peeking up at him in time to catch the way his eyes skim up and down my body.

"You promised me three dates, sweet Chloe," he whispers, tipping his head down and burying his face in the curve of my neck.

Goose bumps travel down my spine, and my traitorous

body aches for him to touch me, to kiss me, to do all the things he's made comments about doing.

I gulp, fighting to stand my ground. "Three meals," I correct.

He groans into my neck before dropping kisses along my sensitive skin. "Fine, three *meals*, but you're bailing early on this one. So, you owe me another half." He sucks on my skin next, as if he wants to mark me.

I release a heavy breath and throw my head back, stupidly giving him better access.

Jesus, why am I allowing myself to get caught up in him like this? Why am I so weak?

I clear my throat. "Why are you so adamant on hanging out with me, Kyle?"

"Why are you so adamant on not being around me, Chloe?" he whispers into my ear before nibbling my earlobe.

"You know why," I hiss, balancing myself against the counter. My knees are weak, and if I fall, it'll put me in line with Kyle's waist—with his crotch.

"Why?" he asks. "Is it because you hate me *or* because you can't control yourself when I'm around?" He skims his hands up my sides, causing me to let out a light whimper. "You're so used to being in control—in charge of your emotions, your life, every single thing. You've never handed control over to anyone else, have you?"

Desire rushes through me, and I blow out a nervous breath when he withdraws to lock eyes with me.

"Yes," I stutter out. "Once. I gave it to you."

He flinches but recovers. His fingers curl around my waist, and I gasp when his erection presses hard against my core.

"Do you remember how good it felt, losing control?" he asks.

I inspect the floor, but he grabs my chin again, forcing me to meet his eyes—the same as earlier.

"Be honest. I won't judge you. I'll never judge you."

His deep-set eyes impale mine. This is too personal, and I've never been this charged up before, not even with Kent— the man I planned to marry.

I finally gain the courage to say, "I'm not going there."

Before I can say or do anything, his lips capture mine.

And, just like that, I'm gone for him.

I exhale a sharp breath, and he wastes no time before sliding his tongue into my mouth. He tastes of beer and is skilled as we make out against the counter, his excitement rubbing against mine ever so slightly. I drop my head back when his lips return to my neck, sucking and licking.

"I wish I could take my time in pleasuring you," he whispers into my ear. "Unfortunately, we don't have that. You're about to receive the fastest orgasm you've ever had."

I open my mouth to object but moan instead. I could use an orgasm right now. It's been a while since I've had one not given via the vibrator Kent resented. There's no objecting to Kyle having his way with me, so I allow him to take control.

Seconds later, his fingers dip underneath the hem of my yoga pants, and he stretches them out far enough to dive straight into my panties.

"So wet for someone you hate," he says, running a finger through my drenched slit. "You might think you hate me, sweet Chloe, but your pussy seems to like me. Maybe next time, I'll bring my dick out to play."

I open my mouth to question the *next time* comment but whimper when he tugs my pants down.

"Spread your legs wider and let me get one leg out," he demands.

I do as I was told. Denying him isn't an option, but I'll regret this in the morning.

"How much easier would this have been if you'd worn the skirt like I said?"

"Quit bitching," I mutter. "We're running out of time."

And I desperately need an orgasm right now.

"Oh, how the tables have turned, my dear neighbor." He plunges a finger inside me before adding another seconds later, sliding them in and out of me. His fingers are thick and skilled, hitting me in all the right places.

I should unbuckle his pants and return the favor, but I'm too caught up in the moment. I rest my hands on his shoulders as he finger-fucks me hard.

"Does that feel good?" he whispers against my lips as he uses his thumb to circle my clit.

I nod.

"Wait until you find out how good my cock feels."

I stop myself from telling him it won't be happening, but hell, at the rate we're going, his cock will probably end up in every hole of my body.

"I need to taste you. *Fuck.*"

I moan.

"Fuck it."

My breathing hitches at the loss of his fingers, and he drops to his knees. He braces one hand against my thigh, and I shiver when he plants a kiss at my opening. There isn't a long wait until his tongue dips in and out of me, and I throw my head back. It's fast. We're both sweating, and I grip the edge of the counter when his fingers work me again. His tongue moves from my slit to my clit, from my clit to my slit, repeating the teasing action.

It doesn't take long to set me off, and I'm shaking with an orgasm. He grips the outside of my thighs and holds me up.

"Holy shit," I say, catching my breath.

I glance down to find him staring at me with a wide grin and a face filled with need. He kisses both of my thighs before standing up, his hands moving to my waist.

"Holy shit," I repeat. "I cannot believe we did that."

He kisses my forehead and I'm thankful when he pulls my pants up because, right now, my body is useless.

"It's hard not to believe it when your body is trembling,

and if I wasn't holding you up, you'd most likely fall to the floor."

"God, I hate you," I say with a shudder.

"I'll take that as a compliment since you just had an orgasm as a result of my tongue-fucking you." He nuzzles his head in my neck while I pull myself together. "Thank you for letting me play with your pussy tonight and for bringing dessert." He kisses my cheek. "Time for you to babysit."

I turn away in embarrassment when he draws back. "Thanks for, uh … dinner." I clear my throat. "I guess I'll see you tomorrow morning."

"See you then."

He doesn't kiss me again or make another move while I straighten myself out, grab my bag, and head to the door with so many thoughts spiraling through me.

"Oh, wait," he finally says as I'm about to walk out.

I turn around, and he hands me a plate full of brownies.

"Dessert. The kids will enjoy these."

My phone beeps.

Claudia: About to pull up.

Fuck!

"They will. Thank you." I rush out of the house and make it to my porch at the same time she arrives.

What in the flying fuck happened?

———

CLAUDIA IS two hours late to pick up the kids.

No surprise there.

She dropped them off without dinner in their bellies, so I took them to the diner. When we returned to my house, they devoured a brownie each, and then I went into full parent mode. With Gloria being four, she needs more attention than Trey. I gave her a bath and then read her a story before she crashed out in the bedroom. Trey has graduated to the guest room with a bigger bed and a smart TV.

"Is your homework finished?" I ask when I walk into the living room.

A glass of milk is in his hand, and a brownie sits on the table next to him.

He groans. "Yes, boss woman. I'm not dumb enough to bail on homework with you. Mom, yes. You, nope."

"Smart boy." I sit down on the couch across from him and cross my legs, a mug of tea in my hand.

Trey is fourteen and at the age where he'll pick up on the environment he's living in. He'll do one of two things—want a better life for himself or fall into the black hole. My sister had him young, so he grew up faster than most kids. Him being born also made me grow up faster. I fled that life as soon as I could, and I want him to be able to do the same.

"How's everything going at home?" I ask.

"Mom has a new boyfriend," he states with a straight face.

"I'm sure he's a real winner," I mutter before I can stop myself. Even though it's difficult, I try not to talk shit about Claudia in front of him.

He snorts. "Oh, yes, like all her others." He frowns. "Are you sure there's nothing you can do for us to live here?"

As much as Claudia loves to pawn her children off on me, she refuses to grant me custody. She uses them as a power trip and exploits my love and concern for them to her advantage. If it wasn't for the children, I'd have nothing to do with her.

"Trust me, buddy, I've tried," I answer with disappointment. It hurts my heart as much as it hurts theirs.

"I know," he says with a hint of a frown.

He picks a channel, a show of viral videos of people's failed stunts, and I grab my laptop to get some work done.

An hour later, Claudia pulls up. I make sure she's not high or drunk before letting the kids know she's here.

"You're late," I say when I step outside.

She brushes away her bleach-blonde hair from her face and takes another puff of her cigarette. "Shit happens, Chloe. Damn. This is your niece and nephew. Don't you love spending time with them?"

I fan the air in front of me to get rid of her cigarette smoke and draw back. "Don't patronize me. I spend more time with them than you do. Tonight, Gloria asked me why you never want to be around her like other mommies and their kids at her school. Get your shit together."

"Or what? You'll ask for custody like always?"

"I don't understand why you won't." I lower my voice. "You obviously have no interest in being a mother."

She sneers. "You're jealous." She tosses her cigarette on the ground and stomps on it with her heel. "You're childless, and your fiancé left you for another woman. Maybe you need to pay attention to your pathetic life before insulting mine."

"Fuck you, Claudia," is all I say before turning around.

I don't want my niece and nephew for my lack of children. I want to protect them from the life she's giving them.

I've adapted to her and my mother's insults, and mostly, I have become immune to them, but there are still times—*times like this*—that remind me of my misfortunes. She uses it to trigger me even though I've done nothing but help her.

People can be assholes. People can throw your misfortune in your face, even when it's unnecessary, even when you've done nothing to them. Some people aren't nice, and if there's anything I've learned from my chaotic childhood, it's that hurt people hurt other people. Misery loves company, and my family is always ready to hurl insults.

"I'm sorry. That was harsh," she calls out.

"It's nothing worse than what you've said before," I mutter while shaking my head.

I grab Gloria when she and Trey step outside and help her into her carseat while Claudia lights another cigarette and stands to the side. When she's finished, I stand on my porch and wave good-bye as they pull away. I take a deep breath and am about to go in when I hear it.

"Good night, Chloe!"

The words shoot through the night from Kyle's front porch. I glance over to find him standing beneath his bright porch light, shirtless, with a bottle of water in his hand. I shake my head, fight my smile, and flip him off before walking into my house.

At least he made me smile after the Claudia Horror Show.

CHAPTER SIX

Kyle

I'M WAITING for Chloe as soon as she steps out onto her porch. From now on, I will deliver my good mornings face-to-face.

"Good morning, my dearest neighbor," I greet, not startling her this time. "I enjoyed our dinner. Next time, maybe you can bring your vibrator as the guest of honor."

I can't stop thinking about last night.

Like yesterday, I'm dressed in my uniform. I promised Gage I'd come in early and help with extra paperwork, but I didn't want to miss seeing her.

"Fuck off," she replies, fighting a smile.

Another one of those black skirts I love hugs her hourglass curves and stops at her knees, and though it's not revealing, it's sexy. Her white button-down blouse is thin, and evidence of her hard nipples shows through.

"I was down for it last night and will be later this evening. Care to make a date for it?"

She hands me her coffee tumbler and tugs her jacket over her shoulders. "Last night was a mistake, and I'd appreciate us acting like it never happened."

"A mistake I'd love to make again." I inch closer. "I'll

relive it repeatedly. My brain will never forget the sound and sight of you coming for me."

Flustered, she snatches her coffee back. "I'm being serious."

"Let me remind you that, every time I've touched you, you've enjoyed it. Keep attempting to persuade yourself otherwise, but we both know you love my hands on you."

She blushes. "You're right. I enjoy you touching me. The problem is, I've never enjoyed the consequences."

We're side by side as we step off her porch and walk to her car.

"I see you still hate me for that."

"I will always hate you for that."

"Hate is an expensive grievance to carry in life. It shortens your life span, triggers depression, interrupts sleep—"

"I've hated you for years, so what harm is a little more?" she interrupts.

"Do you know what *does* lengthen your life span? Orgasms—"

She interrupts me again. "This is the part of the morning where I instruct you to fuck off."

"You already said it."

"Then, *fuck off* again."

"Wow, Chloe, way to make a man feel used," I say when we reach her car.

Instead of getting in, she rests against it, grips her coffee, and stares at me, not interested in ending our conversation.

"I seriously hate you more than the Grinch hates Christmas."

"You need to work on your insult game. That was the worst I've ever heard." I smile. "All joking aside, have dinner with me again tonight."

She smiles back, surprising me. "*Fine*, I'll do dinner with you tonight at *my* house, but keep your hands to yourself. Got it? This is because I don't make deals with people and not keep them."

I hold my hands up. "These bad boys will stay to themselves—unless you beg me for them. Deal?"

"Yeah," she draws out, "not happening."

I open the car door for her and help her in like the upstanding gentleman I most certainly am not, and she slides in.

I wiggle my fingers. "We'll see. Next time, you might ask for another body part of mine."

She swats at my hand holding the car door open. "You're seriously a child."

"You know that's not true." I wink and turn around at the sound of Gage pulling into my driveway. "I need to get to work now and make the world a better place. You can reward me for it later."

Fucking with Chloe Fieldgain is fun.

I wonder what fucking her will be like.

———

GAGE EXCHANGES A GLANCE with me when I'm inside the car. "I see your neighbor has yet to murder you. First, you're having breakfast with her, and now, you're walking her to her car in the morning. What's up with that?"

"Good morning to you, too," I answer, grabbing the coffee he brought for me from the cupholder. "Jealous I didn't have breakfast with you or walk you to your car?"

"Hardly. I'll let you keep those favors for girls you tormented in high school."

"I didn't torment her. We had a rivalry."

He snorts. "Some rivalry. You wanted to bang her. She wanted to kill you."

I shrug. "Something along those lines, yes."

"She forgive you?"

"I'm working on it."

"You're wasting your time. She's despised you for over a decade. *A fucking decade.*"

"How do you know she still hates me? Until recently, you were MIA from this place for years."

He grabs his coffee and takes a drink. "Hmm … I didn't notice, dipshit."

"Don't take it as an insult. I'm damn happy you're back. Focus on our current conversation."

"I was updated on all Blue Beech–related drama," he grumbles, not impressed.

Like me, Gage couldn't give two shits about gossip.

"The big-mouthed future baby mama? I told you she was trouble."

"Shut up before I throw you out of this car."

"Yeah, yeah, yeah, so you tell me daily," I joke. "Chloe has no reason to hate me now. We're mature adults."

He gawks at me. "Holy shit, you're banging her, aren't you?"

"If only," I mutter.

He narrows his eyes and studies me. "Correction: you haven't screwed her, *but* something happened between you two, considering she didn't have a gun to your balls seconds ago." He lowers his voice. "I hate to bring this up, but do you think … *dating* her will cause tension with your father?"

"I don't give a fuck what he thinks."

The mood turns somber. "You and your dad still not speaking?"

"When necessary … for my mom." Not that I have an issue with that. The less I talk to my dad, the better my day goes.

"Maybe your relationship will get better over time—you know, like your and Chloe's."

"My relationship with him gets worse with time, and unlike Chloe, I don't want to be around him."

"I understand, man. So, you're into her, huh? I knew you crushed on her in high school, even after she told you to get fucked, but I thought you had grown out of it. You're like a kid on the playground again. How many valentines are you putting in her basket this year?"

"Piss off."

"My best friend is infatuated with a chick who hates him."

———

I SMILE before answering the phone. "Hello, world's best mother."

"Hi, honey," she says on the other line. "Can you pick up a few things for me at the store before coming over tonight?"

I stop walking on my journey to my desk at the station. "Tonight?"

"Yes, for your sister's birthday dinner."

I frown and pull my phone away to check my Calendar app. "Her birthday isn't for another three days."

"She has plans with Devin, so we're doing it tonight."

Devin the Douchebag.

My younger sister lives for dating the wrong dudes. They're not even the bad boys, more along the lines of fuck boys who wear sweaters with cardigans over their shoulders— which is surprising. She's the wild child out of the bunch.

"I'll be there. Send me a list of what you want me to pick up. Seven?"

"Yes, seven. I'll see you then."

I need to tell Chloe about our change of plans. I open the database and find her phone number—perk of being in law enforcement.

If texting doesn't work, I can persuade her better in person; I wouldn't mind stopping by her office for a quick visit.

CHAPTER SEVEN

Chloe

I GRAB my phone from my desk when it beeps with a text.

Unknown: Hey, gorgeous.

I hit reply.

Me: Who is this?

I'm certain I know the answer to my question.

Unknown: Your favorite neighbor.

Me: Mrs. Davis?

Unknown: Let me elaborate. The neighbor who made you come last night.

Me: Mr. Davis?

The Davises are my eighty-year-old neighbors.

Unknown: Hmm … seems you need to be reminded of who your orgasms belong to. A do-over is in the works.

I sigh. I'd love for a *do-over*, but I'm not sure if sleeping with him would get in the way of my job. Not to mention, what it would do to my heart. I vowed to never let Kyle in my heart, and here I am, practically handing it over to him on a platter, ready for him to shatter it.

Me: What do you want, Kyle?

Kyle: This is a reminder of our dinner plans tonight.

Me: I don't need a reminder. I've been dreading it since this morning.

Kyle: Aw. I'm looking forward to it, too. I'll pick you up at 6:30.

Whoa. Whoa. Whoa.

Me: Pick me up? You're coming to my house, remember?

Kyle: Change of plans, sweetheart.

Me: I'm not going to your house or anywhere in public with you.

Kyle: What about my parents'?

Me: HELL TO THE NO!

I wait for his response but nothing.

Melanie groaning drags my attention from the phone to her as she staggers into my office with her hands filled with file folders.

"Hey, here are the documents you asked for," she says.

I stand to gather some from her hands and settle them down on my desk while she does the same with hers. "Thank you."

Her green eyes study me in interest. "Damn, you look hot this morning. You're sporting a special *glow*. Did you finally bang Kyle?" She winks and places one hand in a circular motion before putting her finger through it.

I came in early, so she lost her chance to interrogate me this morning.

"God, why do I like *and* employ you?"

"Because I'm awesome ... and my stalking skills are legit."

She leaves when my phone rings, and I pick it up, expecting it to be Kyle, but it's someone I'd rather not talk to more than him. I roll my eyes before accepting the call.

"Hey, I need you to babysit," Claudia says as soon as I answer. "I'll drop the kids off at five."

"I have plans."

"Seriously? I need you, Chloe. I need to work to make money to take care of my family like you've lectured me about."

I scoff. "Quit lying. Your boss sent me your schedule."

"That motherfucker," she hisses. "*Fine,* I have a date."

"So do I," I lie. I have to *hang out* with Kyle.

"With who?"

My tone turns sharp. "None of your business. Maybe you should spend time with your kids for a change."

"Oh, here she goes again, Ms. I'm Better Than You."

"Never said that."

"Fuck you! I won't ask for your help again."

The line goes dead.

Doubt it will happen.

———

"HELLO, DEAREST NEIGHBOR."

My heart races, and I jump up from my chair. I was so preoccupied with my work that I didn't hear my office door open.

"Melanie! You're fired!" I yell when I recover.

"Melanie is going out for lunch and has seen nothing," she yells from the reception area. "You kids have fun! I'll be back in *one hour,* so make it quick."

I cross my arms and settle down in my chair. "What are you doing here? We've been seeing each other more than necessary, and I'm not a fan."

Kyle smirks, shuts the door, and stands at the head of my desk. Earlier, his demeanor was carefree. Now, he looks determined with his eyes on me.

"You're not a fan of having lunch with someone?" he asks.

I gulp but hold myself together. Why does him looming

over me like this make me nervous? "I prefer to eat solo, like I did throughout high school."

He shrugs off my response. "Good thing we're not in high school anymore."

"I'm not hungry for your food or your games, Kyle. I have work to do."

"So selfish," he says, casually strolling around my desk. "What if *I'm* hungry?"

I tense up but keep my voice level. "Go feed yourself then. I'm not your mom who will bake chicken whenever you ask. Go find yourself a nice Martha Stewart to hang out with because it will not be me."

"Now, why would I want a woman who cooks when I can have that smart-ass mouth of yours? Keep throwing the attitude at me. It makes me want you more."

I gulp. "The feeling is not mutual."

I hold in a gasp when he grabs the chair and turns me to face him.

"What time do you want me to pick you up? Dinner is at seven, but we can spend time together beforehand if you'd like. Maybe a quickie in my backseat?"

"Never o'clock."

"Come on, Chloe. You *loved* my mother's food along with some other perks I won't specify in your workplace. Don't you want more of that?"

What's disturbing is, I *do* want more, and him standing in front of me with his crotch practically in my face isn't helping the matter.

"What is wrong with you?" I ask, irritated. "You want me to go to the house of the man who proposed moving city lines, so the neighborhood I grew up in wouldn't be in it? He called us scums of the sewer."

"My father won't be there. He doesn't show up to family functions."

"Still not happening."

Heat spreads through my chest when he drops to his knees and glances up at me with a grin. My skin flushes when he grabs the hem of my skirt, and a chill hits me when he yanks it up. He's keeping a slight distance between us—most likely in case I kick him in the face.

"What do you think you're doing?" I hiss. My stomach tightens, and instead of kicking him in the face, I want it between my legs.

I'm frozen in place when his hands splay across my bare thighs, leading my breathing to rise while I await his next move.

"I told you, I'm hungry," he mutters. He shoves my skirt until it's scrunched around my waist, and he settles himself closer. His mouth is so close to my core that I feel his breath against it. He groans. "And no panties. I love it when you leave my snack unwrapped."

I hold in a breath when he tilts his head forward to flick his tongue up my slit.

"Oh my God," I moan.

"Spread them wider," he demands before sucking on my clit.

He grips my waist to lift me enough to adjust my skirt, settling it underneath my ass and against my back, until I'm exposed for him.

"Good girl," he praises.

His attention sets on my core before he buries his face there. I throw my head back when he dips his tongue inside me.

"How do you like me tasting your pussy?"

I answer by rocking my hips forward to meet his tongue and can tell he approves of my response when he slides a finger inside me, causing me to lose a breath.

He caresses me a few times with that single finger before dragging it out and glancing up at me. "Tell me, sweet Chloe, if I reward you with my mouth, will you come with me tonight?"

"Reward me?" I raise a brow. "You came into my office. It seems like I'm doing *you* a favor, Officer."

He chuckles, his finger running along the seam of my opening but not pushing inside, teasing me. "Oh, trust me; you're definitely doing me a favor by letting me lick this pussy. *But* I'm not asking for anything sexual in return. Like last night, I'll deal with my blue balls. All I'm asking for is your company tonight."

"My company, so you won't end up with blue balls again?"

"Blue balls and I will become great friends the more I hang out with you." His head lowers again to suck on my slit while his finger continues to torture me. "Say you'll come with me tonight, Chloe." His mouth moves to my thigh, raining it with light kisses while refusing me what I want.

"It's not a good idea," I stutter. I reach down and wrap my fingers around his neck, sinking my fingernails into his skin, attempting to push his face closer.

Instead of giving in, he retreats more.

Well, that sure backfired on me.

"But you think me giving you an orgasm is a good idea?"

"Obviously." I snort. "Why else would I allow your face in my lap?"

"Then, say you'll come with me, and I'll give you an orgasm."

I dig my nails harder into his skin. "Not fair. You can't extort me to go to dinner with you by orgasm."

"I can convince you to do anything I want with my fingers." He pushes his finger inside me again. "With my tongue." He licks the inside of my thigh. "And with my cock when the time comes. I can do whatever I want, Chloe. It's the first thing you need to accept in our relationship."

"We don't have a relationship." *I cannot believe we're having this conversation with his head between my legs. What is really going on?*

"I'm about to eat your pussy. Do you not have a relationship with other people who stick their tongue in your pussy?"

"Please," I whisper. *No! What am I doing? I do not beg Kyle for anything.*

"You want me to finish what I started? Then, say you'll come to dinner at my parents' tonight."

"Fine."

I grip his neck, and this time, he allows me to pull him in closer.

I might hate the man, but I love his mouth between my legs. His mouth goes straight to my opening, his tongue diving in and out, before he slips two fingers ... then three into me. He rotates them to the side when he knows I'm about to come. The pad of his thumb goes straight to my clit, massaging it. He's everywhere, touching me in all the right places. Seconds later, I cover my mouth when I come apart.

He waits until I stop shaking before placing a single kiss to my clit while I collapse in my chair. He stands, and I fight to control my breathing. He wipes his mouth with the back of his hand. When my arms are no longer shaking, I hastily pull down my skirt in embarrassment, like he didn't just have his face buried between my thighs.

He watches me pull myself together as if I were his favorite show. I catch my breath as he licks his lips.

"Thank you for lunch. I enjoyed it."

My gaze drops down his body, and I notice the bulge between his legs. This time, I lick my lips as my mouth salivates for him.

He drops a kiss onto my forehead, his crotch nearly shoved in my face. "See you tonight." The erection in my view leaves when he turns away.

I grab his hand to stop him. "Wait."

He stares at me with interest.

"Don't you want me to ..." I nod to his waist.

"Return the favor?" he clarifies.

"Yeah … I mean, I know you said blue balls and you would become friends, but …" I lower my gaze while the words stutter from my lips, as if I were twelve and had never seen a cock before.

He shrugs casually, as if he were asked the question daily. "I won't stop you, but it's not why I came. I had a craving for your pussy. If you have a craving for some dick-sucking, mine is all yours."

My gaze slightly moves up, and I bite into the edge of my lip when I notice his handcuffs. If we ever have sex, I want us to use them. I shut my eyes and imagine the things he'd do with me.

I rest my eyes on Kyle's lap as if it were *my* favorite meal.

I stand up, surprised I can support my weight after the mind-blowing orgasm he gave me, and his eyes widen in interest as I take the small step to him. They turn hungry when I sink down to my knees, and they harden while he watches me unbuckle his duty belt.

His hand folds over mine, stopping me, and I peek up at him as he drags the belt off—along with his gun—and carefully sets it on the corner of my desk. This gives me better access to unzip his pants, and I easily tug them down along with his briefs until they hit his knees. My mouth falls open when his cock comes level with my face.

The asshole has a perfect cock, too.

Go figure.

He's huge and engorged, the tip of it red and glistening with pre-cum.

I settle my knees on his boots to give me better height and wrap my fingers around his dick. It jerks under my palm. When I glance up, his wild eyes meet mine.

"This never happened. Do you hear me?"

His cock twitches.

He holds his hands up. "Chloe never had her hand

wrapped around my cock; got it. Can we also act like your lips around my cock didn't happen either?"

Instead of answering him, I take him fully in my mouth, causing him to gasp. I nearly choke when the tip of him hits the back of my throat. I try to stop myself from gagging, and before it happens, his cock slowly moves out until the tip is at my lips.

"Shit, Chloe," Kyle croaks out. "You don't have to swallow my cock. Make yourself comfortable. Relax your jaw. Do it the way you want to."

It's like he read my mind. I shut my eyes and do as he said, slowly sliding my mouth up and down his length. With every stroke, I grow more comfortable. His hand dives into my hair, but he lets me keep my pace. I pray to God Melanie or anyone else doesn't walk in. The door is closed, but not everyone is polite enough to knock.

I know he's close by his breathing and the shaking of his legs.

"Fuck, Chloe," he hisses. "Let me fuck you. *Please*, let me fuck you." His pleading turns me on more.

I shake my head, and his cock slips from my lips. "No." I return to the task at hand.

I *want* to have sex with him. But I can't.

"Your mouth is amazing." He winces when I take him deeper. "We've already crossed a line. What's one more?" He groans. "We can say it never happened."

That awful idea turns into a good one at the sound of his moaning.

I keep sucking him without answering and smile in satisfaction when he releases in my mouth.

I'm forming a relationship with Kyle, but it's only sexual.

We have a relationship based on oral sex.

We're oral sex buddies.

And I intend to keep it that way.

What harm can a few shared orgasms do?

"ARE you sure me coming is a good idea?" I ask from the passenger seat of Kyle's truck. "Your father despises me."

He glances over at me and raises a brow. "My father doesn't know you. How could he hate you?"

I run my hand up and down the seat belt. "Correction: he hates everyone *like me.*"

"No, he doesn't."

"He refers to us as scum of the city. Dirtbags. Cockroaches. Along with some other choice words."

He winces at his father's comments. "He won't be there. My mom said he's attending a work event."

I deviate the conversation to one I've been wondering about after hearing the gossip around town. "Was he mad when you didn't go into the line of work he wanted you to?"

Everyone knows Kyle had been groomed to go into law and politics like his father. He went as far as attending law school before dropping out his first year.

"How did you go from future attorney to a police officer?"

"Because it's what I wanted to do, and I won't allow anyone else to declare my future. Was he happy about it? No. But I am, and that's all that matters."

"Your father seems like an asshole who always gets his way."

He chuckles. "You must know my father."

Everyone has their opinion of Michael Lane. Some glowing. Some distasteful.

In my opinion, Michael Lane is trash.

But most of Blue Beech practically worships their beloved mayor.

"I've heard rumors. How mad was he when you dropped out of law school?"

"We barely speak," he answers, rubbing the back of his neck.

My face falls. "I'm sorry."

He's not upset—annoyed if anything. "Don't be. Hearing less of my dad's voice is a goddamn blessing."

I chuckle to lighten the mood. "I take it, you aren't a daddy's boy?"

"Never have been. Never will be."

I can't stop the grin playing at my lips. "So, you're a mama's boy?"

His voice turns humorless, surprising me. "I love my mother more than anything. If it classifies me as a *mama's boy*, so be it. She doesn't pay my bills, but I will damn sure always protect her."

All right then.

Let's add protective and sweet to Kyle's Pros.

We pull into the nicest neighborhood in Blue Beech, and he rounds a corner before parking in a circular drive of the largest home on the block.

"This is it."

I eyeball my surroundings before glimpsing his way. "Why don't you live in this neighborhood?"

He raises a brow in confusion.

"You can obviously afford to live in a nicer neighborhood than mine."

"You do realize I'm a police officer, right? We're not raking in the money."

"Yes," I draw out. "But your family is loaded."

"Doesn't mean I am, nor do I want their money."

I snap my mouth shut and unbuckle my seat belt, feeling awkward over my question. Of course Kyle, as a grown man, doesn't allow his family to support him.

"And to feed your curiosity, I moved there because it was the house my grandmother grew up in. She talked about it all the time and how she missed living in a simple neighborhood. Someone bought it and renovated it. I put in an offer when it went back on the market. Trust me; it wasn't because you lived next door even though it is a plus." He winks before opening his door and getting out.

Circling around the truck, he opens my door next before offering his hand.

"Are you doing this to make sure I don't get out and make a run for it?" I ask.

He chuckles. "No. I'm doing it because I'm romantic as fuck."

I grab his hand with reluctance.

"I promise it won't be dreadful. I enjoy your company, and deny it all you want, but you also enjoy mine. We'll eat dinner, sing 'Happy Birthday' to my sister, and then bail. If you're uncomfortable, we'll leave."

I release an overly exaggerated breath and hop out of the truck.

———

KYLE'S INTRODUCES me to his family. His mother, Nancy. His younger brother, Rex. The birthday girl and younger sister, Sierra. And the youngest girl, Cassidy. Sierra's boyfriend is here, appearing nothing like I'd imagine her with by looking at her. Sierra is sporting a black leather jacket and bright red lips, and she's wearing heels. Her boyfriend is in a sweater and a pair of Sperry slip-ons.

Sometimes, opposites do attract.

No Michael Lane in sight. Good. My appetite won't be ruined.

We're seated at the table, about to dig in, when the front door slams.

Uh-oh. Front doors slamming are never a good sign.

The room goes silent.

No one takes a bite or drink.

"Sorry I'm late."

I stiffen at the sound of his voice.

Shit.

I hold my breath, awaiting his entrance. He stands in the entry, arms broad with an expensive suit and a face full of smugness. For a small-town mayor, he thinks he's hotter shit than he is. He hardly has any pull, but word is, he's trying to move up the totem pole and make it to Governor of Iowa. Then, Senate. Then, however higher he can manipulate his way up.

He walks around the table, giving his wife a kiss on the cheek before doing the same to Sierra and Cassidy. He gives Sierra's boyfriend a head nod but pays no attention to Rex or Kyle before taking the empty chair at the head of the table.

"I thought you couldn't make it?" Kyle asks with a slight hiss in his tone.

Michael gives a crooked politician's smile. "Didn't think I could, but there was a break in my schedule, so I figured, *Why not?*"

I'm not sure if he's noticed my presence.

Rex snorts. "Yeah, why not show up to your daughter's birthday dinner?"

"Rex," Michael warns.

I like Rex and his little smart mouth.

"Don't get mad at me for stating the obvious," Rex argues.

"Some of us work for a living to provide for a son who wants to take a year to defer from college to jerk around," Michael bites out with a glare toward Rex.

"Or maybe your son decided he won't be a puppet and follow in his father's footsteps. I'm not attending the college or majoring in what you want. Just like Kyle, I don't want to be Michael Lane's protégé. You've shown me firsthand your *business*, and politics are something I never want to be a part of."

This sure is fun.

Very entertaining.

I'm at the best dinner show, and I didn't pay for a ticket.

"Everyone, shut up," Kyle finally snaps. "This is Sierra's birthday dinner, not a pissing match. If we want to do that shit, we'll do it later. So, eat your fucking dinner and shut your fucking mouths unless it's to wish her a happy birthday."

Well, damn.

"Thank you," Sierra says.

Kyle glances over at Nancy. "Sorry, Mom."

I don't pay attention to Nancy. My eyes stay on Michael. I watch the way his upper lip snarls at Kyle. He clearly likes to be the one in charge. He's about to most likely lay into him until his eyes flicker my way. I receive a dirtier look than anyone at this table so far.

"I see we have company," Michael says, jerking his chin toward me.

"Yes, sorry for the lack of introduction while you came in, talking shit," Kyle says.

I've never seen him like this—so condescending and defiant. It's a major turn-on, given he's being a total dick to an asshole I don't like.

Kyle tips his head my way. "Chloe, Mayor Lane." Then, he tips his head toward his father. "Mayor Lane, Chloe."

Michael rubs his chin. "Welcome to my home." He says it with such distaste that more than one person at the table flinches.

"Dad," Kyle warns, "you're not even supposed to be here. If you plan to insult people, leave."

His glare confirms I'm not welcome here.

———

"HOW LONG HAVE you been dating my brother?" Sierra asks when I walk out of the bathroom and into the hallway.

I don't see Kyle anywhere in sight.

Dinner was awkward, to say the least. Nancy forced conversation, asking what everyone had been up to. Sierra recently graduated from college. So did her boyfriend. Cassidy's college choice was met with approval from Michael. Rex got skipped, considering he'd already told Michael to get fucked. The same with Kyle. When Nancy came to me, Michael interrupted the conversation and began discussing a charity function.

I nearly fall on my face at her question. "Negative thirty minutes."

She blinks. "Huh?"

"We're not dating."

"So ... just friends?" she asks.

I shrug. "Just neighbors."

She leans against the wall, and I don't know if she was passing by when I walked out of the bathroom or if she was waiting for me.

"I think you two would make a cute couple."

I shake my head. "No. It's a bad idea."

"Hmm ... doesn't seem that way, but if you saying that makes you feel better ..." she says before smoothing a hand down her blonde hair. "Thanks for coming to my birthday dinner."

With that, her boyfriend appears, and she leaves with him.

I walk down the hall and out the front door, in need of fresh air. I inhale deep breaths while standing on the front porch.

"How dare you step foot into my home," Michael says, coming to my side.

He was waiting for the perfect time to pounce.

"I'm unsure of why you're so angry about it," I reply, trying to keep my voice as firm as I can. *You don't scare me.*

He rests his elbows on the railing next to me. From the outside, we resemble two friends sharing a friendly conversation, and I hate how close he is.

"You don't belong here. My son hanging out with you will tarnish my family's image."

"Your son is a big boy who can make his own decisions. Maybe you should look in the mirror and realize what a deceptive liar you are."

He lets out an arrogant laugh. "That's where you're wrong, Chloe. I'm not a deceptive man. I'm a man who wants the best for the town he's in charge of, and if I have to get rid of the people who pollute it, it's what I'll do."

"I wouldn't brag about that."

"Oh, really?"

I stare straight ahead. "You're a *fighter* who will do anything to get what he wants even if it means stepping on the less fortunate. As our mayor, maybe you should fight for them instead."

"Life isn't fair. Accept it. It's a lesson you should've learned early, but I'm sure your single, drug-addicted mother didn't instill it." He cracks a smile.

I push off the railing. "Don't talk about my mother. Don't talk about my family. Matter of fact, don't come near me again."

"Chloe. No one cares about your dysfunctional family. You're the one who stepped into my home, unwelcome. I'm well aware that you see my son as an opportunity. I guess the apple doesn't fall far from the tree, seeing as you're trying to fuck your way into getting my son's money."

"You don't know what you're talking about."

"You of all people should know how powerful I am. Remember Sam?"

I wince at the name. "Go fuck yourself, Mayor Lane."

He laughs while I walk away.

CHAPTER EIGHT

Kyle

THERE'S a knock on my office door.

My father walks in.

Great. He's most likely not here to ask for my Christmas wish list.

"What's up?" This conversation needs to be as short as possible.

He shuts the door behind him and takes a seat. "I don't think it's a good idea for you to be hanging out with Chloe Fieldgain."

Ah, there it is. This isn't a social hello, unsurprisingly. I expected a call, but it seems he felt the need to show his face instead.

The tension between my dad and Chloe was strong, and I can't blame her. Even with my mom's discouragement, he judges those less fortunate in our town.

Last night, I could tell we were both exhausted, so I didn't ask Chloe to hang out, and we went into our own homes.

"Who I hang out with is none of your business," I reply.

He laughs. "Tell me it's only sex and you're using condoms."

"It's not only sex, and we're not using condoms. I'm

hoping to give you fifteen grandchildren with her." *Take that, asshole.*

"Son, if you're having an issue getting women to sleep with you, I can find someone to help get your rocks off."

I hold my hand up and cringe. *Fucking gross.* "Calm down. I'm not sleeping with Chloe."

"Good. You might be smarter than I thought."

I scoff. "Smart because I'm not sleeping with someone?"

"Smart, like your father, who knows where he sticks his dick is important."

"That's where you're wrong. I never want to be a man like you."

"A man like me?" he asks, insulted.

"Yes. A shitty husband. A shitty dad. A man so hungry for power that he can't realize his plate is already full."

He pulls at the collar of his suit. "I'm beginning to think my daughters carry more balls than my sons. Rex wants to be ... fuck, I don't know what, and you want to screw a woman who grew up in the trailer park."

"*Again,* I'm not fucking Chloe. We're friends and neighbors."

He smiles. "Be safe with her. The last thing you need is a baby with the woman. Fuck her all you want, but be careful."

"Leave her alone," I instruct. "Don't you dare give her the same warning, or there will be problems."

He huffs. "Since when do you think you have authority over me?"

"Since I decided I'm not afraid of you and not a puppet under your bullshit. I thought I'd already proved that to you. It's been fun." I tip my head toward the door. "You know the way out."

"Selfish bastard."

"I wish I were a bastard."

———

"AND THERE'S our favorite third wheel," Lauren sings.

"Piss off," I grumble when I slide into the backseat of Gage's truck. "If you two weren't forcing me to come, I wouldn't be a third wheel. My mom, who is the queen of throwing parties, never had a gender reveal party. Next, you two will be drinking hipster beer and eating avocado toast."

"Avocado toast is amazing, for your information," Lauren replies with a laugh. "Stop being a hater."

I run my hands through my hair. "Can't you post the baby's sex on Facebook like normal people do? Why are you throwing a big party?"

I'm curious as to whether I'm having a godson or goddaughter, but they want to find out the sex with balloons filled with confetti. Chloe wouldn't be into this shit. I pause.

Why am I thinking about her and what she'd do if she were pregnant?

"Lauren wanted a party. We're having a party, so shut your mouth, or you won't be the godfather," Gage replies.

Lauren glances at me from the passenger seat and scrunches her face up. "You wouldn't be a third wheel if you found a girlfriend."

"I told you to find me a girlfriend. Not my problem you failed."

"Been there. Done that. Had to listen to too many women cry over the phone about you breaking their hearts. My job as your matchmaker is over. I'd love to say it's been fun, but I'd be lying." She studies me for a few moments. "Do you not want a relationship? Does commitment scare you?"

"It's not at the top of my priority list," I answer with no shame.

Commitment scares the shit out of me. I've never witnessed it firsthand. My mother turns a blind eye to my father's affairs. Every Lane man has been an adulterer. The only man I'm close with who I've seen is capable of staying faithful is Gage.

I'm not against commitment. I'm afraid I'll fail at it.

A hint of disappointment crosses her face before she sets her attention on Gage. "I told you he'd die old and alone." She squeals. "I cannot wait to decorate my beachside villa in ten years." She winks at me before whipping back around in her seat.

"What does my love life and a beachside villa have to do with shit?" I question with confusion.

Gage chuckles. "My girl over here made me bet that you wouldn't have a serious relationship in the next ten years. If you don't, I somehow owe her a beachside villa. Whatever the hell it is, it sounds expensive as fuck."

"You two bet on my love life?" I ask before rubbing my chin. "Better yet, why are you creeps *talking* about my love life? Has your bedroom talk become that boring?"

"Far from it," Gage answers. "Trust me; I couldn't give two shits about who you're banging or marrying, but she wouldn't shut up about it. It's easier to agree, so it's what I did. If you ever do settle down, you'll understand."

Lauren pats his shoulder. "Good man." Her attention bounces to me. "So, keep being a heartbreaking whore."

"Oh, babe, say good-bye to your beachside shit. Kyle will be tied down before then," Gage tells her.

"And how are you so certain?" she asks with a raised brow.

"He's trying to get into his neighbor's panties."

"Neighbor?" Lauren asks. "I need a name."

"Chloe Fieldgain," Gage answers before I get the chance to tell him to keep out of my love life.

"Uh … doesn't she hate your guts?" Lauren questions.

Lauren is unaware that Chloe was writing a story about her being assaulted by her old landlord. So far, with her family's influence and our jobs, we've kept the details to a minimum. People know something happened, but unless Lauren opens up, they'll never know everything.

I grin. "You hated me once, and here we are, headed to a whatever-you-called-it party."

She narrows her eyes. "A *gender reveal* party." She perks up in her seat. "Now, didn't you and Chloe have a thing in high school that went south? Yes! I love me a good second-chance romance." She kisses Gage's shoulder. "Don't I, babe?"

Gage brakes at a Stop sign and stares at her with affection. "I wouldn't call it a thing."

"Fuck off," I hiss.

"People call her the ice queen," Lauren comments. "Like, all she does is hide behind her books and the newspaper she works for."

"I'm trying to break through the frost," I explain.

"You should invite her on a double date."

"He should the fuck not," Gage says. "I'd rather buy you a beachside villa than be involved in Kyle's girl drama like we're teenagers."

That's Gage. He'll tell me when I'm being an idiot, but he isn't one for heart-to-hearts unless it's with Lauren.

"Invite her on a double date," Lauren demands.

Gage smiles over at his fiancée. "The queen has spoken."

———

THE PARTY IS BEING HELD on Lauren's family's property. There's an endless amount of food, and I watch my best friend and his fiancée pop the balloon.

Does Chloe want kids? My guess is yes since it seems like she frequently helps with her sister's kids.

The confetti is pink. The cake is pink.

I'm having a goddaughter.

By the end of the car ride home, I've decided I'm going to ask Chloe on a double date.

CHAPTER NINE

Chloe

KYLE CALLING.

The Ignore button is hit.

I need space to get my head straight before we talk. We haven't done much of that since dinner at his parents'. He still tells me good morning, but it's brief before he leaves for work. His truck was in the drive, but no lights were on in his house when I got home yesterday.

Hours later, Gage's truck pulled up, and Kyle stepped out. When he was unlocking his front door, Lauren yelled his name, ran up the porch steps, and handed him a pink balloon.

He grabbed it, laughed, and hugged her.

My phone rings again.

Kyle Calling.

I hit Ignore.

It rings once more.

Kyle again.

"Jesus, what?" I answer.

"You need to get to Garfield's Grocery," he says in a serious tone.

"Why? I'm working."

"Trey was busted for shoplifting."

"Shit! Give me ten."

"Park in the rear lot, so no one sees you, and I'll let you in."

————

KYLE IS WAITING for me when I pull into the parking lot. I speed-walk his way, and he moves to the side, letting me in without speaking. I curse with every step as I walk down a hallway lined with loaves of bread and pastries.

Damn it, Trey.

Why did he shoplift?

Why didn't he come to me if he needed money?

Kyle leads me into a dimly lit office reeking of mothballs. Trey is sitting in a chair, and surprisingly, he's not wearing handcuffs. Mr. Garfield, the store's owner, is at his side, worry lining his wrinkled face. His wife is sitting in a chair behind an old desk, looking like she's ready to rip Trey's head off.

I cast them a glance of apology, but only Mr. Garfield will make eye contact. Today isn't the first time someone from my family has shoplifted from here. My mom and sister were regular thieves. Mr. Garfield let it slide for a while but eventually started calling the cops. They ended up banned from the store after the tenth occurrence. I haven't been banned yet, but Mrs. Garfield keeps a watchful eye on me. Every visit, I slip extra cash in the tip jars at the registers to make up for my family's theft. Mr. Garfield's soul is kinder than his wife's.

"Seriously, Trey?" I snap with a stressed sigh as soon as the door slams shut behind me.

Regret is clear on his face. Trey isn't a troublemaker, but he's a survivor.

"Your family is filth," Mrs. Garfield hisses. "Thinking they can take whatever they want." Her glare cuts to Kyle. "I don't know why this young man is helping you and that *thief*."

My apologetic face turns cold, and my nails bite into my palms as I clench my fists. *Don't say anything.*

If I lose my cool, she'll take it out on Trey.

"Enough, Mary," Mr. Garfield warns his wife.

Kyle steps to my side and looks in her direction. "Mrs. Garfield, don't act like you've never needed a handout in your life."

I cringe at the word *handout.*

My blood pressure rises. We don't need *handouts.*

"I think they've had enough *handouts,*" Mary answers with a sneer.

"And I think you need to grow a heart," Kyle says.

Mary strokes her throat and grimaces. "No offense, Officer, but you're not the one losing money."

Tears prick at my eyes, but none of them will see them fall.

"Money or not," Kyle says, "he's a kid."

I open my mouth, wanting to say something, but I'm not sure how I can justify Trey's actions. They're inexcusable.

"Kid or not, he's not innocent," she continues. "Her family teaches their kids to become criminals at a young age."

Kyle looks at Trey. "Come on, let's get out of here, so we don't waste any more of their time."

Trey nervously stands up. He looks down in shame when our eyes meet, and my heart hurts for him. That was me so many years ago—surviving by any means necessary. The difference is, I had no one to go to for help. He has me.

"What are you going to do with him?" I ask Kyle, finally gaining the ability to speak before opening my purse. "I'll pay for whatever he took and extra for the inconvenience."

Kyle waves away my offer. "Don't worry about it. I'm not arresting him." He tilts his head toward Trey. "Stay out of trouble, or next time, I won't be as nice."

"What?" I blurt out.

"Officer Lane paid for what your nephew stole and extra

for our troubles," Mr. Garfield explains with a nervous smile. "We won't be pressing charges against Trey."

I let out a huge breath. "Thank you so much. I'm so sorry, and it won't happen again."

"I understand struggle, dear," Mr. Garfield says. "Don't let my wife get you down. She's having a rough day. We both know you're a good girl."

I look at Mary and lock eyes with her, hoping she'll see my gratitude. "Thank you again."

She looks away as if the sight of me disgusts her and snarls at Trey. My anger heightens. I hate being looked at as if I'm beneath someone, but it *really* pisses me off when that disdain is directed at someone I care about.

The three of us rush down the hall, and I don't speak again until we've made it outside.

"What the hell were you thinking?" I yell at Trey as we head to my car. "You could've been arrested!"

Trey looks at me, his eyes flickering with regret and humiliation. "Gloria needed supplies for daycare and food. Mom wouldn't give me the money, so I had to get them another way."

I swallow hard. "Why didn't you come to me?"

"I can't always come to you. You bought us new clothes *and* paid for my football equipment. It's not fair to always ask you for money." His attention goes to the ground, and he kicks at pebbles with his shoe. "It's pathetic enough that Mom always begs you for it and then spends it on booze."

"I would much rather give you the money than her, Trey. I give her money to help you and Gloria. Don't ever feel ashamed about asking me for help. Do you hear me? If you or Gloria need something, you come to *me*. You don't shoplift!"

Kyle clears his throat, and we both look at him. I forgot he was here.

He tips his head toward the corner of the parking lot and focuses on me. "Can I talk to you for a sec?"

"Of course." I grab my keys from my purse and hand them to Trey. "I'll meet you in the car in a minute."

Trey grabs them and walks away. I scrub at my eyes before dragging my hands over my face and meet Kyle. We're facing each other, and his hands settle on my shoulders before he takes a step back, as if he's inspecting me.

"You okay?" he asks.

I nod. "Yes, just a little pissed off. I can't believe Trey would shoplift. I've told him a million times, if he needs something, call me. Instead, he steals, proving to everyone that we're all the same."

He lowers his hands to run them over my arms. "Don't you dare listen to that old bat, you hear me? Block out every fucking word she said to you."

"What she said wasn't a lie," I mutter.

"The fuck it is. The mistakes and wrongdoings of your family don't define you. Who they are is not *you*. What I see when I look at you is a strong woman, a woman who fights for what she wants and takes on responsibilities that aren't hers to make children's lives better."

I don't want his words to make me feel better, but they do.

He's giving me all the feels.

How is this asshole I thought I hated giving me all these good feels?

I inhale a deep breath, and when I move to open my purse, his hands drop, breaking our connection.

"How much do I owe you?"

He shakes his head. "Don't worry about it."

"I can pay for my family's shit, Kyle."

His eyes soften. "I never said you couldn't. It's already taken care of." He whistles and tilts his head toward my car. "Get Trey out of here before Mrs. Garfield comes out with her shotgun."

I frown and hitch my bag up my shoulder. "Fine, but we're talking about this later."

He smiles. "You're always welcome in my home."

CHAPTER TEN

Chloe

Age Fourteen

MY SISTER IS HAVING A BABY.

A baby boy, to be exact.

She won't tell me who the father is, but I've heard her scream at him and demand money over the phone.

Since Claudia doesn't know anything about babies, I checked out books from the library for her, receiving quite the curious look from the assistant librarian. Claudia threw them across the room and said she'd know how to take care of her baby when he got here. So, I took them to my room and read them myself.

Someone in this house needs to be educated on what to do with a newborn.

Sam's visits are limited now. All they do is argue when he comes over. Him not coming around makes me sad. He is nice to me and helps me with my homework. He cares about my interests and never tells me my dreams are stupid. Sam is who I want my father to be.

A month later, Sam stops coming over permanently.

―――――

Age Fifteen

"HEY THERE, STRANGER."

My head flies up at the sound of the voice I've missed.

Sam stands in my doorway, looking clean-cut in a suit and with a ball cap over his head. It's rare seeing him without a hat on.

"Hi," I answer in surprise, unable to hide my excitement. "Long time no see."

He has been nonexistent in our lives for nearly a year. I thought he was gone for good, so the sight of him brings nothing but joy to my face. He's never met Trey, who came into the world three months ago. He did send a care package with no return address. A note was attached, saying he wanted Trey to have the baby essentials.

"Sorry about that," he answers. "Life gets in the way sometimes."

I nod, though I don't understand. Something I've come to learn is, if someone wants time with someone, they make it, no matter what. That means Sam didn't want to spend time with anyone in our home—including me.

Having men come and go isn't out of the ordinary. I've never met my father. My knowledge of him is through old photographs and the few choice words my mother shouts when I ask about him.

Sam steps farther into my room. "Your sister said you're very helpful with Trey."

The baby books I read have been put to good use since I'm Trey's main caretaker. Not his mother. I get up with him at night and change all his diapers, and since she refuses to breastfeed, in fear it will mess up her "good tits," I feed him his formula.

I shrug and hold back the urge to tell Sam that. I want him to be proud of me, but Claudia will kill me. "I try."

He smiles. "You're such a good girl, Chloe. I'm sure she appreciates your help greatly."

I snort. "Claudia doesn't appreciate anything."

"That's the understatement of the year."

I tuck my legs underneath my butt. "So then, why do you like her? Why don't you find a nicer girlfriend?"

It's been a while since I've asked him, but I don't understand how a decent man like him can like her. There must be something wrong with him. Broken people seek out other broken people. I see it every day of my life and wonder how I'm ever going to find someone nice to take on the job of being with someone as broken as I am.

He shrugs. "People like people for different reasons."

"You like her because she's pretty ... and she has sex with you."

He chuckles and slides his hands into his pants pockets.

"You two seem so different," I go on.

"Opposites attract sometimes," he argues.

"Duh," I say with a roll of my eyes. "Opposites have sex with each other, but—"

He cuts me off. "You seem to know an awful lot about sex for someone your age."

I point out my bedroom door. "Uh ... have you seen the people I live with?"

He walks into my room and sits down on the edge of the bed, concern now etched on his face. "None of their boyfriends have ever ... they've never touched you or talked to you inappropriately, have they?"

"No," I rush out.

They've looked but never touched.

"You'll tell me if they do, right?"

"Yes."

"You promise?"

"I promise," I say softly.

He gives me a gentle smile. "You know, you're going to make something of yourself when you get older. I'm certain of it."

His words come out with pride.

They fill me with pride.

"Thank you," I whisper. "I want to be a writer when I grow up."

This spikes his interest. I love when he seems interested in me.

"Yeah? What type of writer?"

"I don't know. I like reading the newspapers."

He chuckles. "Whoa. The pay for the amount of work is chump change."

I frown. "Not everything is always about money."

He rubs his hand over his clean-shaven cheek. "If there's anything you learn from me, Chloe, it's that life is always about money."

CHAPTER ELEVEN

Kyle

A TOWEL IS WRAPPED around my waist after the post-gym shower, and I walk through the living room at the sound of the doorbell. The realization that I'm about to answer my door half-naked doesn't hit me until I'm standing in front of it. I look out the peephole and smile at the sight of Chloe standing at my door, glancing around in annoyance.

As soon as I swing the door open, I lean against the doorframe, leveling my arm above me while a grin plays at my lips. "Hello, my favorite neighbor. Care to borrow some sugar?"

Unfortunately for me, the expression on Chloe's face isn't screaming that she's down for having a good time. Her chin is jutted into the air, and her pretty little lips are pinched together.

A wad of cash is shoved into my chest. "This is for whatever Trey took," she says. "Let me know if it's not enough."

Whoa. Whoa. Whoa.

I shake my head while ignoring the cash. "I'm not taking your money."

"Why?" she snaps.

"I don't need to give you a reason."

"Bullshit!" She inches the cash further. "Now, tell me how much, Kyle."

I wave for her to come in, and surprisingly, she does. She crosses her arms as soon as the door shuts.

"Why'd you do it? Why are you being so nice to me, inviting me to your fucking family dinner, and helping my family?"

"I told you, I'm a nice person."

She snorts. "People don't do things to be *nice*. There's always an underlying reason."

I throw my hands up. "Do I need a reason to be nice to someone? I'm fucking attracted to you, Chloe! I wish I could take what happened between us back every single day. When I see you in the morning, I wonder where we'd be if I hadn't been such a dumb shit then."

This isn't how everything was supposed to go down.

I take a step forward, grab the back of her head, and pull her to me. "Maybe it's time I find out."

CHAPTER TWELVE

Chloe

I CAN'T DIGEST Kyle's words before his lips crash into mine, and I'm pushed against the door. The money slips from my fingers, and I draw in a gasp when his excitement rubs against my thigh over my pants.

I could've thrown the cash at him and walked away. It'd have been the smart response. I might be book smart, but I'm sure as hell not emotionally smart. My emotions have no sense of rationality around him.

So, instead of being smart and fleeing the scene, I walked in, asking for trouble. Our kiss confirms everything I've feared. This is what I want. *He's* what I want, and I'm not strong enough to continue pushing him away.

Sleeping with Kyle doesn't mean we need to have a relationship—or hell, even like each other. The only way sex can happen with us is if it's no-strings attached and with no expectations. With every kiss and touch, I'm allowing him in deeper, knowing I'll be left with emptiness when everything crashes between us.

The gasp escapes me when his tongue dips between the seam of my lips, and his fingers plunge into the base of my ponytail, roughly raking through the strands and then tugging at the ends. This man has fingered me and gone down on me, but those times were always about my orgasm, about him proving he could get me off.

This is different. Our kiss is laced with desperation and urgency, and with tentative fingers, I stroke him over the towel.

He moans into my mouth when I gain the courage to tug on the towel until it falls at our feet.

"Tell me this is happening," he says. "Let me have all of you."

I run my tongue over his bottom lip and wrap my fingers around his bare, swollen length, sliding them along the tip, spreading his pre-cum. "Does this answer your question?"

His chest moves against mine when he chuckles. "So far, it's looking pretty damn promising."

"Very promising," I whisper with a smile.

"There's one problem."

"What's that?"

He knots my ponytail around his fist, forcing my head back, and kisses up my throat. "I'm the only one naked." He licks the curve of my neck before releasing me, and I lose my hold on him when he withdraws a step. "Strip for me."

I steady myself against the door at his command, my breathing ragged, and I take in his naked body in all its glory. The finely sculpted muscles of his chest and arms are no stranger to me, and even though I've given him a blow job, there wasn't much time to take in his swollen, thick cock before.

When my eyes meet his again, I find him intensely watching me, almost daring me to disobey him.

"Strip, Chloe," he demands again. "Get naked. I won't ask you again."

I hold in a breath before grabbing the hem of my shirt and hurriedly ripping it over my head. My heart rapidly pounds against my chest, and it takes only seconds for me to step out of my yoga pants. My attention closes in on him, waiting for approval, but he gives nothing.

I haven't given him all of me yet.

I lock eyes with him, and his gaze turns wicked when I unhook my bra, my breasts spilling forward. Still, not a single word from him. Neither do I get one after dragging my panties down my weak legs and kicking them away from my feet.

This is the first time Kyle has seen me fully naked. My heart is beating wildly, like I was working out for hours, and I've never felt so exposed.

"Take your hair down."

I do as I was told.

He inches closer while drinking me in, his eyes roaming up and down my body. He runs his hand over his face, stopping at his chin, and bites into his thumb.

And, finally—*fucking finally*—he's directly in front of me. "You're beautiful. Absolutely stunning, Chloe." His compliment sparks through me stronger than anything I've felt with another man.

His hand then moves to my chin, and he strokes it. "Can I ask you a question?"

"Uh … yes?"

"Do you want me to fuck you, or do you want to fuck me?"

Holy motherfucking hell.

I gulp, suddenly feeling out of breath. "I want to fuck you."

He smiles in satisfaction before capturing my hand, jerking me into the living room, and then collapses on the sofa. He gestures to his cock and spreads his legs. "Fuck me then."

I eye the cleft in his chin and take a deep breath. *This will change everything.*

It's one thing, giving in to my desire when he's the initiator, but another to climb onto his lap and ride him. To fuck him. He's forcing me to make every decision on whether we cross this line.

Deep breaths expel from his lips while he awaits my next move, and the shock on his face when I fall to my knees at his feet satisfies me.

"*Fuck*," he hisses with a clenched jaw.

It's time for me not to play fair. I waste no time in tightening my fingers around his cock again, and it twitches in my hand. I slowly stroke him, and with deep pleasure, I watch the torture on his face—torture of not being in control.

He hisses through his teeth when I bend forward to rub his cock against my nipple back and forth before releasing it as my mouth waters. I lick up his cock before sucking on the base at the bottom, and then I slide my tongue up, licking and sucking on his tip.

He bites into his lower lip and sucks in a breath. He tilts his hips up, asking for more.

I'm aching for him to be inside me but also throbbing to taste him again. I swallow before taking him fully in my mouth, sliding my tongue along the length, and then I bob my head up and down. My hands rest on his strong thighs for me to get the right angle to suck him perfectly. When I glimpse up at him, I see Kyle with his hands laced behind his neck as he stares at me with desperation.

I feel like I'm on a caffeine buzz, and I'm soaked between my legs.

"Yes, just like that, baby," he groans. "Don't stop. *Fuck*. Don't stop."

I pause. "What if I want to stop to ride your cock?"

His hand drops to massage my cheek, and his face turns soft. "Chloe, anytime you want to ride my cock, I give you permission to always stop what you're doing."

The compassionate look on his face mixed with his dirty words captivates me, and I take a deep breath before standing tall while his cock stands before me.

This is it.

No going back.

I can no longer say I resisted the temptation of Kyle Lane. I'm throwing down the white flag with no apologies.

I can't help but grin at his surprise when I crawl up his lap, grab him by the base, and slowly lower myself down on him, my thighs hitting his with a smack. He fills me up perfectly, like he's always belonged there, already hitting my spots before I've even moved. I use his shoulders for support to lift myself up and then fall down. One of his hands spans over my hip while the other cups my chin, pulling me in for a kiss.

"Fuck me like you said you would," he demands, pulling away before pushing me back against his mouth.

Our kiss is deep, and the hand resting on my chin lowers to my breast, cupping it. He slowly strokes my nipple with his thumb before pinching it. As I set my pace, Kyle uses his hands as a weapon, moving them everywhere—from my hips to my breasts and then to my back.

"You feel so good," he says into my mouth, meeting my thrusts as I ride him. "Better than I imagined."

I circle my hips, alternating between bouncing up and down and then grinding hard, making it my mission to fuck him better than any other woman has.

"Fuck, shit, Chloe," he bites out. "I'm going to come." His finger goes to my clit, and he's rough as he works it.

I crush my mouth to his, his words setting a fire inside me. "Then, come."

My heart slams against my chest as I pull away and wait for it. I want to see. I *need* to witness the evidence of me riding Kyle into an orgasm. For reasons unknown, a surge of pride rolls through me.

I'm good enough to make him lose control like this. I'm strong enough to make him feel this way.

But it doesn't happen. As I wait for it, an arm spans

around my waist, and he clutches my hips, halting me from making another move.

What the ...

"I'm bare," he says in a thick voice. "We forgot a condom, so hop off me before I fill you with my cum."

"No, it's fine," I reply in a comforting tone.

The mood is lifting, cooling down, and I'm afraid it'll burn out.

"I'm on the pill," I whisper with reassurance. "It's fine. I promise." I peel his arm off me and grind on him.

He raises a brow. "You sure you're okay with this?"

"I'm positive."

Is he sure about this?

I'm answered when his hips surge up, his cock hitting me in all the right places.

"I can't believe I'm going to fill you up. *Fuuuccck.* You have no idea how long I've wanted this."

And, as cliché as it sounds, we get off at the same time. He explodes inside me as I arch my back and call out his name. I suddenly feel light-headed before shaking against Kyle as he goes slack. I can feel his heart beating just as wildly. My hands cling to his shoulders as if I can't hold myself up.

"Now, it's my turn to fuck you." He grabs my waist, hauls me over his shoulder, and rushes down the hallway before depositing me on what I assume is his bed.

I watch him from the foot of the bed and rub my legs together. "Let's see if you're as good as you've led on to be."

He's already proven it in his kitchen ... in my office ... on his couch.

"Don't worry, Chloe. I'm about to prove myself to you in every way possible, so you'll never doubt me again."

It terrifies me.

He crawls up my body, and I gasp when his tongue slides up my stomach and to my neck, slowly reaching my mouth.

"I'm going to fuck you how I've imagined every day since I

saw you walk out of your house, wearing one of those skirts I love so much."

"Show me then."

———

I COLLAPSE on my back while working to catch my breath. "Holy shit," I say between pants. "Holy motherfucking shit." I cast a glance to Kyle next to me to find him doing the same.

I just had the best sex of my life. Kyle bringing me to his bed and having his way with me was even better than me riding him. Screw Kent and his half-assed screws. I'll be sending his new wife a thank-you card for their affair. Maybe even a gift card, so she can invest in a good vibrator as a complimentary, shitty sex-stealer gift.

Kyle blows out a strong breath and then chuckles. "That's exactly what a man likes to hear after giving a woman a dozen of orgasms."

I turn my head and glare over at him. "It wasn't a *dozen.*"

Sweat drips from his forehead, and red scratches are visible on his shoulders. He doesn't even seem fazed by my marking him. "Somewhere along those lines, babe."

I lean up on my elbow to look at him, briefly forgetting I'm naked and putting myself on display. I've suddenly become comfortable with him. "Don't flatter yourself."

"I thought you knew me well enough to know that I *always* flatter myself." He stands up, his cock semi-hard with the cum-filled condom attached, and goes to the bathroom to dispose of it.

Even though I'd told him I was on the pill in the living room, he snagged a condom from the nightstand drawer during round two.

He falls down next to me with a wicked grin on his face. "Flattery is the best compliment. If you agree to a dozen, next time, I'll shoot for *two dozen.* It ends in your favor."

"I don't know if we should let this happen again. Don't you think it will make things more complicated for us?"

I'm afraid he'll hurt me, afraid I'll fall for him and get hurt again. If he learns my secret, he'll walk away with my heart and hate me.

He pulls himself out of bed, moves around the room, and snags an abandoned shirt off the floor. "Fine, if it's what you want. I'll get dressed. You get dressed. I'll see you tomorrow morning."

My mouth falls open. "What? Are you kicking me out of your bed?"

He tosses the shirt on the floor while shaking his head, a smile twitching at his lips—his swollen lips a result of me biting into them every time he hit the right spot. "What? You keep talking like us having sex was a mistake. What do you think a man wants to do with that ego booster? Leave me be with my hurt feelings."

I grab a pillow and throw it at him. "I hate you."

"Your moans prove otherwise." He jerks his thumb toward the door. "Now, do you want me to go on an exploration for your panties or stay in here where you will not need them?"

I stare at him in response.

"Answer me. Would you rather me find your panties or your G-spot again?" He points to his watch-less wrist. "Time is ticking, babe."

I shoot him an annoyed look. "Seriously, you're giving me a time limit on my choice to receive an orgasm or not?"

"I am."

I tap the bed. "Hang out here for a sec. You probably need to rest and not search your house at the moment."

"Perfect. Chloe code for fucking her again." He returns to bed.

I hold myself up with my elbow and stare at him. "You don't find this weird?"

He mirrors my stance and gives me his full attention, his

eyes staring at mine and not roaming over my naked body. "No. We're two people sexually attracted to each other. Two people who get along and vibe. Why is that weird?"

I signal between the two of us. "You're *you*, and I'm *me*."

He clicks his tongue against the roof of his mouth. "Good observation."

I push his shoulder. "I never thought ..." I stop to shake my head and don't finish my sentence.

"You never thought you'd give in to the sexual chemistry between us, begging to be discovered since high school?"

I shrug. "Something like that."

He snags my waist and pulls me into him. "I'm still sensing some of that chemistry. Shall we try another go? See if we can fuck it out?"

That's what we do.

———

KYLE HAS BEEN inside me five times.

Five times.

The stamina on this man is unbelievable.

Hell, the stamina in myself is surprising.

We've slept together, shared meals, watched TV, and carried on conversations I never thought we would.

Kyle takes a drink of his water and looks away from his sandwich to me. We're at the kitchen table, devouring the grilled cheeses he made for us.

I shyly look away when I realize he's practically studying me. "What?" I mutter, feeling too on display.

"I like seeing you in my house, in my kitchen, in *my bed*." He shrugs. "I like seeing you here in general. I love you opening up to me and allowing me to see the real Chloe. I like *you*, Chloe. And, even if we weren't sleeping together, if we were sitting in my living room, watching paint dry, I'd still want you to be here."

His words send chills down my body, and goose bumps form on my bare legs. I'm wearing a pair of panties and his tee.

"I don't understand." I shut my eyes, and the next words come out in stutters. "Why? Why me?"

His face scrunches in confusion. "Why *not* you? Why would you ever question why anyone would want to hang out with you? The better question is, why are *you* hanging out with me? Don't sell yourself short on how fucking amazing you are."

I blush while processing his words.

A playful grin is on his face.

"What? Why are you looking at me like that?"

"Watching you blush is sexy."

I cover my face. "Or so embarrassing."

He plucks my hands from my face one by one and caresses my jaw. It seems to be his thing. "Nope. Sexy. I love it. Your pale cheeks turn this rosy color. Your eyes widen. Your lips pucker up. It's why I do everything in my power to make you do it."

I groan. "Stop being sweet. This Kyle is too much for me."

He chuckles. "Never."

I take a bite of my sandwich to hide my smile. "You were born to drive me crazy, weren't you?"

"No, I was born to be a police officer, *but* being able to hang out with you and drive you crazy is a plus. What a perfect life I have." He slides his plate up the table. "Now, what do I need to do for you to take my next question seriously?"

"Not ask it."

He laughs. "Seriously. Don't immediately answer. I know your lips are set to an automatic *no* whenever I ask you to do something."

"Incoming question is now scaring the shit out of me."

He inhales a deep breath. "Want to go on a double date with Gage and Lauren?"

Wow, I was expecting something along the lines of trying anal.

Not that.

Shoot, maybe I'd rather him ask me about anal.

"Uh ..." I draw out. "We're not dating, let alone *double* dating."

"What makes you think we aren't dating? Is neighbor-fucking a regular thing for you?"

"Possibly."

His questions are throwing me off my game.

"Bullshit."

I give him a forced glare. "Excuse me, how do you know what I do with my personal life?"

"I know you."

I snort. "You know nothing about me, Kyle Lane."

His voice softens. "Then, tell me more about you."

"Hard pass."

He laughs. "Looks like we need to work our way up to having a serious a conversation. We've had sex, but God forbid, we get into a too-personal conversation."

"Sounds like a good plan to me."

He groans. "You confuse me."

"Then, let me spell it out for you. This is sex. No dating. You should know this. I've seen the women coming and going from here. You do casual sex. If you want to keep doing *this*"—I gesture between the two of us—"casual is what we have to be. We're casually hanging out, which means no double dating."

"Fine, then have a *casual* hang-out with Lauren and Gage."

I frown. "They hate me." *That should save me from his little group date ... hang-out.*

"They don't."

My frown stays intact. "They should, considering I was going to publish a story about her."

"Lauren doesn't hate anyone, except for any girl who touches Gage and his ex-wife. And you're neither one of those. We never told her about the story. Only Gage knows, and eventually, he'll warm up to you."

"Warm up to me? That's convincing."

"Trust me; he's grateful you didn't publish the story." He tickles my side, causing me to laugh. "So, what do you say, Fieldgain? You. Me. Casually hanging out with friends."

"I'll think about it."

He grins.

"Hey now, that's not me agreeing to it."

He grins wider. "We shall see, dear neighbor."

CHAPTER THIRTEEN

Chloe

Age Fifteen

I TOSS my backpack on my bed and do a happy dance.

I got asked to the homecoming dance.

Me!

The poor girl with the junkie mother, the absent father, and sister knocked up with an illegitimate son was asked to the homecoming dance.

Holy yay!

This weekend, I'm forgetting about my crappy life. This weekend, I won't be the girl living in filth—well, what filth I can't clean. This weekend, I won't be the outsider who yearns to fit in but is unable to afford every puzzle piece.

I wasn't just asked. I was asked by Kyle Lane. The hottest and coolest guy wants to go out with the class loner. I was shocked when he asked. We'd only spoken a few times, and those were to compare test scores.

This is going to be the best day of my life.

———

ALL MY HOMECOMING excitement ends when I tell my mother.

"Why would a boy invite you to the dance?" she snarls, as if it were the most disturbing idea in the world. "He must want to get in your panties."

"Or he might like me," I snap.

She snorts and takes another drink of vodka.

I hate my mother and don't care if I'm judged for it. You don't have to like someone because you're related.

An hour later, my mom passes out in her bedroom, and I play with Trey on the floor.

"I'm sorry about Mom," Claudia says, surprising me. "It's no fun when she treats you like a whore. She's done it to me all my life, too."

I rise up onto my knees. "Did you ever go to a high school dance?"

"A few times, yes."

A twinge of jealousy hits me, and I bite into my bottom lip. "How did you afford the dresses?"

"I stole them."

I briefly consider this.

"You can't pull off shoplifting, Chloe. You're too obvious."

"Maybe I'll find some fabric and make my own."

She reclines in her chair and crosses her arms. "I'll try to pull something together for you, okay?"

I nod, knowing I shouldn't agree to my sister stealing something for me, but this might be the biggest night of my life.

———

I'M SEARCHING the couch cushions for spare change to purchase fabric from the store. Our neighbor said I could borrow her sewing machine. I taught myself to use it a few years ago to fix the holes in my clothes, and eventually, I even made a baby blanket for Trey.

"Hey there, Chloe."

His voice surprises me. I drop the cushion to find Sam with a shopping bag in his hand.

"Hi," I say.

Normally, I'm excited to see him, but he hasn't been around lately, *and* there's not even one penny in the couch. There's no way I'll find enough money for fabric.

"Your sister said you got asked to the dance this weekend."

I brightly smile until I remember my lack of funds. "I did, but I'm not going."

"Why? Isn't every teenage girl's dream to go to homecoming?"

I bite into my lip as tears swell in my eyes. "I don't …" I lower my gaze in embarrassment. "I can't afford a dress."

He holds up the bag. "Lucky for you, I'm here to solve that problem."

"Really?" A few tears fall down my cheek, and I blink them away, making certain this is real.

No one has ever done anything this kind for me.

He hands me the bag. "Go try it on to make sure it fits. Your sister wasn't sure about your size."

I grab the bag, race to my bedroom, and drag the dress from the bag. I run my hands over it and admire the sparkly pink fabric. It feels and looks expensive. I inspect the tag. *Holy wow.* It is expensive. I hold it against my chest and squeal in excitement. Also in the bag is a pair of silver flats decorated with pink stars and a heart necklace.

This will be the best night ever.

I put my dress on, tying it around my neck, and hurry into the living room. Claudia and Sam are waiting for me. She's on the couch, and he's standing in the corner, his hands in his black dress slacks. He never sits down, like he thinks we're contaminated and he'll catch something.

"I love it!" I say, rushing over to him.

He seems surprised when I wrap my arms around him but loosens up and hugs me back, patting my shoulder. "You're welcome."

"Cute. Not my style but whatever," Claudia comments when I pull away.

"Shut the hell up, Claudia," he snaps, taking me aback, and he straightens out his shirt.

Claudia slams her mouth shut and rolls her eyes.

"Thank you so much," I tell him.

"You're welcome." He shoots Claudia a dirty look. "You look very pretty." He points at me. "Remember, boys are bad."

"I'm fifteen," I answer. "I don't need to worry about boys."

Claudia glowers at Sam. "High school boys are never who you need to worry about."

Sam ignores her comment, shoots me a smile, and then leaves.

I jump up and down and smile at Claudia. "Thank you *so, so, so* much for asking him to buy me a dress."

She smiles back. "It's no problem. Don't tell Mom, okay?"

"I won't! Gosh, I wish I had a boyfriend like Sam. He's so cool and nice."

She frowns. "You need to be careful around him, Chloe."

"What do you mean?"

"Sam isn't as perfect as he leads on, okay? We only know him in this trailer. Otherwise, he doesn't exist to us."

I don't ask her what she means. I don't want the moment to be ruined.

———

TONIGHT HAS BEEN nothing short of a fairy tale. I've pinched myself to confirm it's not a dream.

I didn't want Kyle to see where I lived, so I had him meet me at the school instead of picking me up. We went to dinner and then rode back to school in a limo—a freaking *white limousine!* I felt like a movie star.

Kyle introduced me to his friends. I've received a few dirty looks from cheerleaders, but it won't kill my high of tonight. He asked *me* to the dance, not them.

Kyle holds his hand out. "Take a walk with me."

I nod and try to mask the excitement barreling through me.

Looking so handsome in his suit, he can ask me anything right now, and I'll say yes.

Can I have a kidney?

Yes!

Will you sell me your soul?

Duh!

I wipe my sweaty hands down my dress before taking his, and he leads us off our gym's makeshift dance floor. The room is filled with pink streamers, and the DJ has played "Cha Cha Slide" three times too many. Wandering eyes follow our every step as we make our way outside, and I'm surprised when he walks us to the football field.

We don't stop until we're in the center of the field, and he stares at me under the bright stadium lights before taking my other hand, too. "Can I kiss you, Chloe?"

"Yes," I answer with no delay. I lick my lips.

We're going to kiss!

Best. Freaking. Night. Ever!

He releases my hands and steps closer, so close that our lips are already nearly touching.

"Is this your first kiss?"

I swallow. "No."

I don't ask him the same. The stories of his player ways roam through the hallways more than students running late to class, and I've spotted him sucking face with his fair share of cheerleaders. He's experienced. There's no question about it—as experienced as a high school guy can be. I won't put my money on him being Claudia-level experienced.

I play off more confidence than I have. Our kiss will be my second. My first was with Marvin, the boy down the road. His tongue was sloppy, and his breath smelled like Cheetos—not a good time. I should've known a kiss with a boy named after a Martian would be nothing to party about.

Kissing Kyle will be different, not sloppy or gross. The girls I've seen him with always seem to be enjoying themselves and look far from grossed out.

Kyle stares down at me with a genuine smile, and all the anxiousness inside me melts away.

"You're adorable when you're nervous."

"It's *so* not adorable," I mutter. *More like pathetic. Who's afraid of a kiss?*

Goose bumps prick my skin when he cups my chin in his hand and drags my face up until we're making strong eye contact. He grins before tilting his head down, and then he softly presses his lips against mine.

It's perfect.

His lips are like super-soft pillows.

He slightly pulls away to eye me, awaiting my reaction, and when I stare at him, practically panting, he leans in for another kiss. He slides his tongue inside my mouth this time, and I gasp before doing the same.

No Cheetos breath on this guy.

He tastes like peppermint and spiked fruit punch.

I lose track of how long we make out before he stops to sit on the grass and pulls me down with him. My dress hikes up, and I know it's getting dirty. Briefly, I wonder how hard it will be to clean off grass stains because I am *so* keeping this dress for the rest of my life.

He gives me one last kiss before lowering me onto my

back. He moves on top of me, holding himself up with his arm. "Is this okay?"

"Yes," I say in surprise.

I spread my legs for him to adjust himself between them, and my heart races when he lightly brushes strands of my hair off my shoulder. He plants kisses along my neck before dropping his mouth down to my cleavage.

"Your skin is so soft," he mutters, sucking the exposed skin between my breasts before cupping one in his hand.

My dress lifts more, and when I move to situate it, his pants-covered erection slides against my core.

Holy crap.

I've never experienced anything like this, never felt this tingling between my legs. I tilt my hips up to meet his, wanting more.

Okay, maybe he's more experienced than I thought.

He lets out a low moan before pressing against me, and his lips meet mine again.

His hands anchor around my hips. I thrust upward while he rocks against me over and over again as we make out on the field. I slightly pull away when his metal belt buckle hits my core.

"Do you want to stop?" he asks, pulling away and catching his breath.

I shake my head, and with unsteady hands, I unbuckle his belt. I settle myself on my back against the grass when I'm finished and smile. "Much better."

He grins, and our next kiss is rougher. His movements are more hurried as he pushes my dress up to my waist and exposes me, my red panties on display for him. After I fail to lower his pants with my feet, he pushes them down his thighs. We're so close that his breaths are hitting mine. My breathing is ragged when his erection under his boxers slides against my panties. My heart is racing like I ran a mile in gym class.

His fingers hook around the side of my panties, but he

suddenly stops. "Have you done this before?" He peeks down at me with bright green eyes.

Am I that obvious?

"Does it matter?" I whisper.

He flinches and rests his hands on my thighs. "I'm not taking your virginity on a football field, Chloe."

I was so worked up that I forgot we were in public. Not just in public, but at our freaking *school.* Who dry-humps someone at school?

"It's ... it's okay," I assure, struggling to keep my voice strong. *What are you thinking? Your sister was a pregnant teen!* "You have a condom, right?"

He keeps staring, contemplating his next move, and I rock against him to convince him to pop my cherry.

"Are you sure about this?"

I nod. "As long as you have protection."

"I do."

I miss his touch when he pulls away to grab his wallet, and the sound of him opening the condom cuts through our heavy breathing.

Then, that sound is overtaken by shrills of laughter.

"Holy fucking shit, ladies and gentlemen! Get a load of this! Lane is about to fuck Little Miss Trailer Trash!"

Kyle jerks my dress down and stands to pull his pants up before holding his hand out to me. I glare at him before moving my attention to the crowd around me. My chest tightens with embarrassment. My fellow classmates, clad in their formal attire, are pointing and laughing at me. They're holding their cell phones in my direction, no doubt recording my humiliation. The flashes of cameras nearly blind me.

I'm collapsed in the middle of the football field in a wrinkled, dirty dress, and the condom Kyle planned to wear while taking my virginity is lying beside me. There will be photographic evidence of this forever.

Tears prick at my eyes while the insults continue.

"I can't believe you'd touch her!" a girl yells. "Haven't you seen her sister? She has, like, ninety STDs. You can get them from sharing a toilet, you know."

"Now, I know why he asked her to the dance!" another shouts.

"We knew you could do it, man! See, there's no stick up her ass, only your cock!" adds another.

More laughter erupts.

I cover my face in embarrassment, forcing myself to breathe, and tears stream down my cheeks. I kick off my flats, jump up, and sprint away from them with Kyle on my trail, screaming my name. When we're out of earshot from the mocking crowd, I whip around and face him.

"Chloe," he says, taking a hesitant step forward.

I bend down at the waist and catch my breath while holding my hand out to stop him. "You stay away from me."

"Let me explain."

"No. You're like the rest of them."

I push him, and while he catches his step, I take off running in the opposite direction. I go this way to school every day, so I can walk it with my eyes closed. When I hear his steps and voice still calling my name, I duck behind a bush. I wait until I only hear the leaves rustling with the wind before standing up and starting the walk home.

I sniffle and wipe my eyes with every step.

I'm naive and stupid.

The loser never gets the fairy tale.

She gets the nightmare.

———

I'M ten minutes away from home when a car pulls up behind me.

My back goes straight while I contemplate whether to take off running or turn around.

This is it.

Straight out of a horror movie, this will be the night of my death. I say a silent prayer when I hear a door slam. Even if I wanted to make a run for it, my feet don't want to move.

"Chloe!"

I whip around and zero in on the man headed in my direction. My heart pounds, but as he moves closer, I grow more comfortable.

"What are you doing out here?" he yells when he's steps away. "You're going to get yourself run over!"

I wipe away my never-ending tears, and my body trembles when I blow out a shaky breath. "I ... I don't want to talk about it."

Sam stops and stares down at me. "What were you thinking?" He takes me in. He shoots a glance toward his car running, and then his attention moves back to me. "Come on. I'll take you home, but you can't say a fucking word. Do you hear me?" His face is laced with concern, but his voice is harsh.

I look past him toward the car, and my eyes widen. "I don't need a ride."

A head pokes out of the window. "Who is she?" he yells.

I squint, taking in the people in the vehicle before dragging my eyes to Sam. I'm just as confused as the voice asking who I am. "Who are those people?"

"It doesn't matter," he barks. "Now, do you want a ride or not?"

My lower lip trembles, and I want to wrap my arms around him. I want to tell him how terrible my night has been because Sam is my only friend. But I don't. I don't because, right now, this isn't the Sam I know, and I'm not getting into a car with those people.

"No, I'm okay."

"Chloe," he warns.

"I'm fine," I snap.

He stands tall. "This is the last offer I'm giving you."

"I appreciate the offer, Sam, but I'm okay."

He leans down to whisper in my ear, "Don't say a word about this. You never saw this. You never saw me *or them*. Do you understand me?"

I nod, and the tears continue to fall.

I don't start walking again until he pulls away.

When I get home, I throw the dress in the trash.

———

WHEN I RETURN TO SCHOOL, I'm no longer the class loner no one pays attention to.

I'm the joke. They laugh and point at me. I'm called the same names my sister is called. A photo of yours truly is plastered against my locker. The pain hits me as I take in the picture of me on the football field, and I cringe at the horror on my face in the photo.

"Chloe Fieldgain gave pussy on the football field," is chanted down the hallway.

I slam my locker shut and flee to the restroom, locking myself in a stall as I cry *again*.

I've lived up to my family name because of him.

After the bell rings, I wipe my eyes and leave the restroom, unsure of what my next move will be.

Do I leave or cut class?

I round the corner to find Kyle waiting for me.

He's in his football jersey, his hair is messy, and his green eyes are wide. He halts, glancing to each side of the hallway, and then moves closer.

"Chloe," he draws out.

"You stay away from me," I warn.

He takes another step until he's standing in front of me. "Let me explain ..."

The few people lingering in the hall gasp when I smack him across the face. "Go to hell, Kyle."

I whip around and start walking away.

"Dude, she smoked you!" I hear a guy say to him in the background.

"She came to me, begging for a second round, and was pissed I told her to kick rocks," Kyle says. "They always come back, wanting more."

I freeze in my step, and my heart nearly explodes out of my chest. *Is he kidding me?*

"Dude, you'd better go get checked after that one."

I hear someone smack him on the back.

"I always wrap it up," he replies.

I cringe and ball my knuckles into fists while I talk myself out of turning around and punching him in the face this time.

I go home and vow to hate Kyle for the rest of my life.

As time passes, I learn to ignore the names, the rude gestures, and the condoms stuck to my locker.

I'm now known as the girl who gave it up to Kyle Lane on the football field.

CHAPTER FOURTEEN

Kyle

I ADMIRE Chloe in my bed like a stalker from a Lifetime movie. The sheet is pushed up her chest as she faces me, sleeping. I'm pushing a strong eight on the creep scale. I don't stare at women like this.

She's beautiful—drop-dead fucking gorgeous.

The first time I saw her was in elementary school. She was front and center of the classroom, sitting there before anyone else arrived, with her attention on the book sitting on her desk. She was a stranger. I'd never seen her at any birthday parties or playdates. I was nervous when I took the seat next to her, but she never once glimpsed in my direction.

Her social isolation continued into middle school. Anytime I attempted to strike up a conversation, I was given short responses, and then she would go back into her shell of solitude.

Then, high school hit, and she talked to me. It wasn't the conversation I had been hoping for. It was about grades. We held the top GPAs in our class, and grades were something she took seriously. She studied her ass off. Her attention was always focused on school, and everyone knew her end game was to be valedictorian. She wanted it enough to step out of her comfort zone and ask me to compare test grades.

She needed to become valedictorian more than me. You didn't need to know her backstory to know she wasn't as fortunate as I was. She walked to school, her off-brand sneakers were always in poor condition, and she never attended a field trip. She needed the scholarships more than me. I was headed to college whether or not I had them, so at times, I'd answer questions wrong to lower my test scores.

I liked her. I wanted to know more about her. She was naturally beautiful, both inside and out, and intelligent. She was kind to everyone, not just to those she deemed worthy, like most kids in my circle.

I finally gained the courage to ask her to the dance after Gage told me to stop pussyfooting around. He knew I crushed on her, and like me, he didn't give a shit about outside influence. When she said yes, I was ecstatic. Sure, a few assholes made snide comments, but I didn't care. I wanted to know more about Chloe Fieldgain, about the girl who seemed to be a shining star among others who dimmed with nothing.

Then, everything fell apart. I hate myself for how it went down.

After the dance, I had no way to contact her. She had no phone or email, and all anyone knew was that she lived in a trailer court on the west side.

It got worse when she came back to school and gave me the smack I deserved. I was pissed, my friends were making fun of me, and I was a stupid-ass teenager, so I lied. I joked at her expense because of my embarrassment that she wanted nothing to do with me.

Over time, we became rivals. I led her to believe I was vying for valedictorian while still throwing tests. On the day of graduation, when she shyly gave a short speech, I grinned.

Chloe isn't just an attractive woman. I liked her before I

knew about sex or relationships or status. I wanted her to be my girlfriend then. Now, I want to make her more. After having all of her, there's no way I'm letting her go this time.

I've never touched skin as soft as hers or experienced a connection so strong with someone—both inside and outside of the bedroom. I've never had sex without a condom or wanted to keep a woman in my bed, like I do her.

Fuck me. My feelings for her are stronger than I thought.

She stirs when I press my lips against her cheek.

"Good morning," I whisper.

Her eyes don't open, but she releases a sleepy laugh. "Fuck off."

"As much as I love our porch routine, I love this one *so much* better. Say fuck in this bed as often as you like."

Her eyes stay closed, and she grins.

"Call into work today," I say when her eyes flutter open. Correction: I fucking plead.

She yawns and keeps her head rested on the pillow. "As much as I'd love to, I can't. Neither can you. You need to stop the criminals."

We're facing each other, our eyes locked and cheeks against pillows.

"I work second shift," I say, stretching forward to brush back a strand of her hair. "Did you decide about *hanging out* with Gage and Lauren? They're going to the city for a night and invited us."

"Are you sure they didn't invite *you*, and you're asking me to tag along?"

"Babe, I doubt they'd invite me out on the town as a third wheel. They want you to come."

She pulls in a breath, and I take in the beauty of her blonde hair against the pillowcase and the light freckles sprinkled across her nose. "I don't know."

"Give me your reasons for not wanting to go," I challenge.

"People are already gossiping about us hanging out. Imagine what they'll say when we *double date* with your best friend."

I want to say, *Let them talk*, but don't. She's Chloe, and Chloe overthinks.

"It's out of town. No one will know us. Trust me."

She bites into her plump bottom lip.

"Come on," I tease. "It'll be fun."

She throws her head back. "All right, you've talked me into it."

My eyes widen. "You do know all right means yes?"

She laughs. "Yes, I'm well aware of what all right means. Why are you so shocked?"

"You said yes to double-dating with me."

She points her finger my way. "No, I agreed to double *hanging out* with you."

"It's a date. Admit it."

She holds in a smile while shaking her head.

I slide out of bed. "I'm going to shower. Care to join?"

She turns on her back and stretches. "A hot shower sounds amazing right now."

I walk around the bed to her side and hold out my hand. "I'll be nice and share my shower with you on one condition."

She rises up. "What's that?"

"Admit we're going on a date. I'll share my shower, wash your hair, and then, if you're good, give you an idea of what to look forward to on our double date."

She sits on the edge of the bed and stares up at me. "Maybe I'll shower when you're done."

"I'll be sure to run *all* the hot water out. If you like taking cold showers, it'll be all yours, babe."

She stares at me with reluctance.

"Say it," I tease. "You know you want to."

"Fine. I'll go on a *double date* with you."

I grab her around the waist and throw her over my shoulder. "All right, since you insist, I'll go on a double date with you!"

————

"I TOLD you I'd make you breakfast in bed one day," I say, shooting a glance over at Chloe. "I have a future breakfast lover in my bed."

Plates with pancakes and eggs are balanced on our sheet-covered legs, and our backs are resting against the headboard.

"Maybe I don't want to be a breakfast person," she comments, turning to grab her cup of coffee from the nightstand and taking a drink.

"What's your beef with breakfast, huh?" I ask. I cut into my pancake, smother it in syrup, and take a bite.

She sets her cup down and shrugs. "It's not my thing. Sometimes, I'll grab something while on the go, but it's not a meal I've ever looked forward to. My mom didn't bother with feeding us well-balanced meals, and we were stuck with what the food pantry handed out. Most of the time, it was plain, generic cereal that I grew tired of."

If there wasn't a plate of food on her lap, I'd drag her to my side and collect her in my arms. I wish I could've helped her when we were younger, given her someone to ask for help when she needed a cheeseburger or a friend. I should've never taken the broken girl to the football field and shattered her more. I never planned for us to hook up, and contrary to what Chloe believes, I never meant for anyone to follow us. All I wanted was to kiss her, but one thing led to another, and the horny teenager in me was game for whatever she'd allow.

"I will make you breakfast every morning in exchange for you not telling me to fuck off." I playfully elbow her. "Deal?"

She glances at me sideways and points to me with her fork.

"I'll get back to you on that, Officer." She takes a giant bite and nods while chewing it up. "And, since you're always asking me for favors, I have one to ask of you."

"Lay it on me. Getting a yes from me will be more effortless than getting one from you."

She nervously looks away.

"Spit it out. You asking for my firstborn?"

I've come to realize Chloe never asks anyone for anything. This must be important to her.

She takes in a quick breath. "Trey has a football game tomorrow. He asked me to invite you."

That's it? She's nervous about a football game? The fuck?

"I'll be there."

She squints at me. "What? That was too easy."

"Did you want it to be complicated? He has a football game. I don't have plans. Why would I say no?"

She shrugs. "Kent never wanted anything to do with Trey or Gloria." She frowns. "Sometimes, he acted like they were more of an inconvenience."

I like kids and consider myself a good big brother. Trey seems like he can use a good big brother influence.

"You *still* haven't realized that Kent is an asshole? Him bailing on Trey's games isn't a surprise," I say. "I don't blame him for bailing. He didn't like being reminded of how he couldn't catch a football to save his life."

"Oh my God, you're terrible!"

A piece of pancake falls from her mouth when she snorts, and I laugh as she stares at me in horror. I shrug it off, not wanting her to feel uncomfortable about it, and she grabs her napkin to clean up her mess.

"In the beginning, it was a healthy relationship. He was a good boyfriend," she says. "He wasn't a cheater or so self-centered. Maybe it was a game to him. Men seem to enjoy games." She throws me a dirty look.

"A boyfriend who can't give you an orgasm isn't a good boyfriend," I counter.

"It wasn't like that *every time*, only a few. Women don't *always* get off, Kyle. Google it if you doubt me."

I grab her empty plate, set it on top of mine, and place them on the nightstand. I don't regularly leave dirty dishes in my bedroom, but I'll take care of them as soon as we're done with this stupid conversation about her lame-ass ex.

"A few times he didn't give you an orgasm or a few times he did?"

She scowls and folds her arms across my tee she's wearing. "I'm not talking about my old sex partner with my new sex partner."

I hold my hand up. "Please do not refer to me as your new sex partner again."

"Then, what would you like me to refer to you as? My booty call? My neighbor dick?"

I start counting out the names on my fingers. "The guy who gives you the best orgasms. Your favorite dick. The guy you are *kind of* dating but don't want to admit it. Refer to Kent as your sex partner all you want—your inadequate sex partner —but not me."

She rolls her eyes. "Don't be so mean."

"Don't defend a chump, and I won't be."

"He was the only guy who'd speak to me after what you did, you know."

I gape at her. "Wow. Did you know he never once stood up for you in the locker room? In fact, not to hurt your feelings, but he cracked plenty of jokes at your expense. Plenty."

She waves off my information. "He was a stupid high school boy. We didn't start dating until after college."

"He gets to be a *stupid high school boy*, but I'm fucking Satan?"

"The rumors started because of you." She fixes her stare on me but isn't as pissed as she normally is when we talk about this. Hurt is clear on her face, but now, there's a thin layer of understanding. She's lowering her walls, trusting me, and finally giving me a chance to explain myself. "You could've changed everything and stopped your friends and *girlfriend* from making my life miserable."

I suck my cheeks in. "You wouldn't speak to me!"

"Why would I?" she snaps. "You set me up!"

I repeatedly shake my head. "I never set you up. That's bullshit."

She snorts. "Oh, come on. We're hooking up, and then, *boom*, your asshole posse of friends shows up to take humiliating pictures of me. I used to think you were this amazing guy. I can't even explain how excited I was when you invited me to the dance. It was my first dance and turned out to be utter hell—because of you, Kyle. I was stupid enough to believe you liked me."

Whoa. What?

I glance at her and refuse to continue our conversation until her eyes meet mine. Hers are sad. Understandably, this conversation hurts her, but I'm glad we're finally talking this out. There's a thickness in my throat when I respond. Even though I couldn't stop them from finding us, she's right that I could've attempted to stop their teasing. Chloe hurt me, and I let my stupid male ego stand in the way of realizing I could've stood up for her.

"Chloe," I gently say, "I would've never asked you to the dance if I didn't like you."

She scoffs as an attempt to hide the hurt. "You invited me as a joke, as a prank."

I wince. *She thinks it was a prank?*

"Chloe, I swear to you, me inviting you to the dance was not a prank. Should I have taken you to the field? No. I wanted to kiss you, and it sounded better, maybe even romantic in my teenage eyes, than in some supply closet or a bedroom at an after-party where my friends were taking their dates. I never brought you there to put on a show for the school. They also took pictures of me with my pants down."

"Which made the girls want you more," she cuts in.

Shame fills me. It's true.

"Why would I take you as a prank? I could've had anyone go with me."

She throws her hands up. "Oh, wow, everyone. Let's welcome Kyle's ego to the conversation."

"I didn't say it to brag but to make a point. I sincerely liked you. You intrigued me. You were smart and fucking gorgeous, and your personality was genuine. You never said a distasteful word about anyone, and you worked hard for everything you had." I blow out a stressed breath. "Did it piss me off when you wouldn't even let me explain myself? Yes. Did it piss me off when you slapped me in front of my friends? Yes. So, I decided, *Fuck it. If she wants nothing to do with me, then it is what it is.*"

"You let them make my life a living hell," she grinds out.

I situate myself, so I'm sitting in front of her when I notice tears slipping down her cheeks. *Shit.* I don't want to make her cry, especially in my bed.

She attempts to look away and hide her swollen face and tears, but I don't allow it. Her eyes dart toward the bathroom door and then the hallway, searching for an escape plan so that I don't see her without her armor on.

"Fuck," I hiss, cupping her face with my hands. "Please don't cry. I'm sorry. Tell me what I can do to make it better. You want me to put an ad out in the paper? Wear a tee with an apology letter on it?"

She sniffles but is no longer trying to pull away. I still haven't earned eye contact yet though.

"It doesn't matter. It's over with."

I grimace and soften my tone. "If it still hurts you, then it matters. I'm sorry, Chloe. I was a stupid little prick who didn't think about where my actions would lead. I'm sorry."

She inhales a few calming breaths before releasing a nervous laugh. "Thank you. Even though we can't go back in time, I'm glad we talked about it. It was long overdue, and I should've come to you about it. You also should've grown some balls and made an announcement or even put out a stupid ad, you prick."

"If it counts for anything, I broke up with Becky Binds after she wrote *slut* on your locker. Oh, and I punched Daniel Moore for asking me if I'd put in a good word with you for him to get into your panties."

"Wow, that makes sense now. While I appreciate the attempt and your intentions might have been pure, you breaking up with her made her hate me more."

"Shit, that sure backfired on me, didn't it?"

She nods.

"I can still put out an ad now, you know?" I stretch forward and grab my phone from the nightstand. "Let me call Melanie and see who's in charge of advertising in *The Blue Beech Register.* I'll ask them to draft up something." I hold my phone up. "Do you think we can have it in this week's paper?"

She snatches my phone from me. "Oh God, no! I was kidding!" She points it at me. "Swear to God, if there's *anything* with my name in the paper tomorrow, I'm killing you. I can see Melanie being sneaky and allowing you to do it."

"So, you're done hating me now?" I attempt the best look of innocence I can manage.

"No matter how I feel toward you now, I will always hate you for it." A smile plays at her lips, and she pinches two fingers together while shutting one eye. "A little less now."

I grip her waist and draw her toward me. "Let me fuck all that hate out of you, and you can work on loving me."

We both flinch at my words.

Oh fuck.

That was the worst thing to say.

I have feelings for her but can't love her.

We hardly know each other.

I've never been in love with a chick.

In high school, I thought I was in love a few times, but again, I was a dumb fucking teenager.

I act like the words never came out of my mouth and kiss her, hoping my dick will help her forget them.

CHAPTER FIFTEEN

Kyle

"WHAT ARE YOU DOING HERE?"

I turn around to find a woman I vaguely recognize. I know her from somewhere but can't pinpoint exactly where. Her blonde hair is teased, her top is low-cut enough to show me her push-up bra, and hints of red lipstick decorate her front teeth.

"And you are?" I question.

"I'm Claudia, Chloe's sister," she answers with a snarl.

Ah, yes.

I've arrested her a few times. She's called me every name in the book and then some I've never heard before. Chick might be a junkie, but she's creative as fuck with her insults.

"You need to leave," she demands with a hostility I don't understand.

Chloe said her sister hated my guts, but damn, this is overboard.

We're in a crowd of people, and my hands are full with concession stand snacks. This isn't the best place to hold this conversation.

"I'm here for the same reason you are," I answer. "To watch the football game."

Her shoulders slightly relax, but her tone is still louder than necessary. "Trey said you got him off the hook for stealing from that Garfield bitch."

People stop at her words, and they glance at us with curiosity, some even with disgust.

I lower my voice, hoping she'll do the same. "I helped him out, yes."

"Why?"

"I like to help people."

She takes a step toward me. "Is that what you're doing? Helping my sister like you're goddamn Superman? Do not use my children as a pawn to fuck her." She shakes her head. "I know your type. Your stuck-up wife who can't suck dick properly bores you in the bedroom, so you come to us *trash* to entertain you instead. When you're finished getting your rocks off, we get thrown away."

Fuck, the shit Chloe has to put up with from this woman.

No wonder she's always stressed the fuck out. This chick has raised my blood pressure after a five-minute conversation. I can't imagine what it's like to live around her. I need to help Chloe remove some of her sister's weight off her shoulders, maybe help out with the kids.

"Sorry to burst your bubble, Claudia, but there's no boring housewife sitting at home, so I don't understand what you're talking about," I reply with a smile. "And I doubt I'll ever grow bored with her."

She winces and takes a moment to come up with a response. She didn't expect my answer. "You'll have one eventually and then throw my sister away. I'm here to stop that."

"It won't happen, so do yourself a favor and stop worrying about Chloe. Pass your worries onto your children. Now, let's go enjoy your son's game."

I walk away before she can respond and head toward the bleachers where Gloria and Chloe are waiting. I hand them their goods and take a seat next to Chloe. Minutes later, Claudia and a man sit down in the row behind us.

"Kyle," Chloe says, gesturing to them, "this is my sister and her friend—"

"My *boyfriend*, Roger," Claudia corrects.

"Right, Roger," Chloe replies.

I give them a nod. "It's nice to meet you."

Claudia gives me a cold glare. "Really, asshole? You going to act like we didn't share words back there?"

Chloe earmuffs Gloria with her hands.

"No, I wasn't going to mention you going nuts on me, but fine." I move my gaze from her to Chloe. "Your sister is convinced I have an imaginary wife and need to stay away from you."

Chloe's face shades in embarrassment. I didn't need to say her sister's words for her to understand.

"Claudia," she warns, "this is not the place for one of your scenes."

Too late for that.

"I don't want him or his stuck-up family around my children," she snarls.

"Relax. He wants to help Trey stay out of trouble. Trey didn't get a shoplifting charge because of Kyle. You should be thanking him instead of giving him a rough time."

"Roger can help Trey stay out of trouble."

I can't stop myself from laughing, and I hold my hand over my mouth to hide it. I don't do it well though. I can tell Chloe is biting her tongue from doing the same. Roger is the last person I'd want as a role model for my son. I've picked him up for petty crimes. Dude also has sticky fingers.

Claudia leans forward and sticks her head between Chloe and me. "He thinks he's better than us."

"No, *he* doesn't," I correct.

"He doesn't. Kyle is trying to help," Chloe says. "Like I said, this isn't the place."

"It's never the place to state my opinion with you. No one is allowed to embarrass precious Chloe and her perfect reputation." She lets out a sarcastic laugh and fixes her attention on me. "Oh, wait, some asshole already tarnished your reputation. Now, you're fucking him and making a fool of yourself. Don't come running to me when you find out he's using you for pussy."

She sure puts a somber mood on shit.

Claudia was kind enough to raise her voice louder than the announcer, so all eyes are now on us. Chloe is pulling her jacket tighter around her body, and her eyes won't meet mine —no doubt, out of embarrassment.

I stand. "I'll go."

Chloe brings her hand up to stop me. "No." She glances over at Claudia. "Trey wanted Kyle to come. Let's not disappoint him more than we already have, okay?"

"Wanted him to come?" Claudia says, appalled. "Okay, whatever." Her glare turns to me. "Stay away from my children. This will be the last time my son will want to hang out with you after I tell him what you did to his aunt." Her glare goes back to Chloe. "Here I am, trying to show up and be a good mom, and you do this."

I ignore Claudia and focus on Chloe, forcing a smile before leaning in so that only she can hear me. "I'll stay, but I'm going to watch from somewhere else."

"Thank you," she whispers.

I ignore Claudia's shit-talking as I walk away. As I'm looking for a new seat, I spot Gage and Lauren in the stands. They exchange a confused glance when I sit down. I failed to tell them I was coming.

"I see you party animals are enjoying your Friday night," I say. "What are you guys doing here?"

"Dude, what better way is there to spend a Friday night than watching high school kids kick ass in football?" Gage replies with a grin.

"The better question is, what are you doing here?" Lauren says. "Normally, you spend your Fridays at Down Home with the guys."

I nod toward the field. "Chloe said Trey asked for me to come."

"Trey as in Chloe's nephew?" Gage questions, the words slowly leaving his mouth.

"Yes."

"You're so damn screwed," he mutters.

"She agreed to a double date," I inform them. "So, please act normal for once."

Lauren fakes offense. "What? I'm always normal."

Gage snorts while I chuckle.

She rolls her eyes and slaps Gage on his shoulder, resulting in a laugh and kiss from him.

I sit back and watch the game.

Trey is the JV quarterback and has talent. I watch him play while also keeping my eye on Chloe. She's trying but not doing a great job of hiding how miserable she is with her sister and Roger.

"PIZZA! I LOVE PIZZA!" Gloria sings while skipping into the pizza shop with Chloe at her side.

Trey's team won. After the game ended, Chloe texted, saying Gloria was hungry and cranky, so they were leaving, and she thanked me for coming. As soon as I saw them get up, I jumped up from my seat and followed her down the bleachers.

Not in a stalker way, I swear it.

I stayed to the side while Chloe and Claudia talked near the entrance, but Claudia's loud mouth made it possible for me—along with everyone around—to hear her every word. From what it sounded like, she was skipping out on Trey's celebratory pizza dinner in exchange for having a drink with good ole Roger. I'm a drinker. I don't care who else drinks, but don't ditch your kid who played his ass off for a few beers.

Because crazy Claudia bailed, I had the opportunity to invite myself.

So, here we are.

Pizza-ing it up.

Gloria and Trey squeeze into one side of the booth while Chloe and I do the same across from them. I rub my hands together after ordering drinks and study the menu even though I've eaten here hundreds of times. It's the only pizza joint in town.

"So," I say, setting the menu to the side, "your aunt Chloe said we're getting extra anchovies on our pizza."

I'm good with kids. We hold events and fundraisers at the station all the time, and when my siblings and I were growing up, my mom insisted we do our fair share of charity, most of them involving children from bad upbringings.

"Heck no!" Trey exclaims, shaking his head. "I'm not eating that nasty crap."

Gloria peers up at me, her blonde hair back in French braids and finished off with red bows. "What are anchovies?"

"Dead Nemos," Trey replies.

"Trey!" Chloe warns. "Not funny."

"What?" Trey questions. "I'd prefer not to enjoy Nemo with my extra cheese."

Gloria appears close to tears.

Shit. Maybe I'm not good with kids anymore.

She's thinking we're devouring cartoon characters tonight. "But ... but I love Nemo."

Chloe shoots Trey a stern look. "Your brother is kidding, honey." She slides crayons to her. "Now, show me how well you color."

Chloe's attention moves to entertaining her niece and taking her mind away from eating striped fish.

"You played a good game tonight," I tell Trey.

He grins and perks up in his seat. "Thanks, dude. I'm hoping they move me up to varsity. It'd be awesome!"

"Kyle played varsity," Chloe says, bumping my shoulder.

Whoa. Is this about to finish with a compliment or a smart-ass comment about jocks?

"Cool!" Trey says with wide eyes. "What position did you play?"

I scratch my neck. "Quarterback."

"I bet you got laid all the time," Trey comments.

"Seriously, Trey," Chloe says, gesturing to Gloria.

He shrugs. "It's the truth. Dudes on varsity get so many chicks, and considering there's not much else going for me, I need all the help I can get."

Chloe flinches next to me at the same time I frown.

"What does that mean?" she snaps.

Uh-oh.

Trey plays with the straw in his drink and looks down in shame when answering, "Come on, you know our family and where we live. Girls don't want to date guys who come from the trailer park or ones with no money. So, if I make it to varsity, they'll like me more."

I open my mouth to assure him it's not true, but a response coming from me isn't appropriate. I hate he's going through it, but I've never experienced that struggle. The best person to tell him not to look at himself that way and ensure it gets better is the woman sitting next to me—a woman who was raised in it, struggled with it, and then rose from it. Chloe is living evidence you can't control the cards you're dealt, but you can control how you play them.

Hurt and resentment are clear on her face, but her voice is soft when she speaks, "That's not true."

I wait for her to say more, but there's nothing. Maybe it's a sensitive subject for her. Shit, *maybe* is an understatement. I've talked to children who live there, and their lives aren't pretty.

I point to Trey and decide to brighten the somber mood the best I can. "I'd suggest not pursuing a girl who dates you because you either made it to varsity or have money. She's not the type who will end up being a good girlfriend."

"Plus," Chloe adds before Trey can reply, "I thought you were dating a girl from the neighborhood?"

He shrugs. "I was."

"And?" she questions.

"She's not ..." He pauses to shake his head, as if he's debating whether to continue. "People make fun of her. People make fun of *me* for hanging out with her."

I look over at Chloe in fear for myself. Her attitude is sexy but can also be scary as hell. Her eyes are closed, and a mixture of pain and fury flashes across her face. Trey's attention goes to his drink. He's taking loud sips, realizing it's better to keep his mouth shut sometimes.

"Let me guess," Chloe finally snaps, and she peeks over at Gloria before continuing her ass-chewing. "Earmuffs, sweetie."

Gloria drops her crayons and places her hands over her ears.

Chloe clears her throat, lubricating her impending lecture. "Let me guess; she's called trailer trash for where she lives— side note, which is also where *you* live—and for her parents being poor. She doesn't own brand-name shoes or have the extra funds to go on class trips, so they sneer at her in disgust, as if she were scum beneath their shoes." She focuses on him in disappointment. "Don't you dare judge or hurtfully treat a girl—better yet, *anyone* for that. Do you hear me?" She rests her elbows on the table, leans in, and lowers her voice. "Let me tell you something. I was that girl they're teasing. Do it again, and I will ground you for so long; you'll be eighty before you see a varsity jersey."

Da-yum.

Chloe came in with the kill shot.

Trey struggles for a response. "I … I didn't mean it like that."

"Yes, you did," she says within seconds.

He looks at us, embarrassed. "It's hard here." He shakes his head. "Forget it. Remind me not to talk about my girl problems with you."

"You can bring up your girl problems with me anytime," Chloe says. "I'd prefer it, so you don't make decisions like that again."

"Or ask me," I add. "I happen to be very educated on the ladies."

Chloe elbows me. "He is not very educated on the ladies, hence why he's still single." Her eyes focus on Trey. "Don't be an asshole to her, you hear me? I will make it my mission to check up with her regularly to make sure you're not."

"I understand," Trey says. "I know it's wrong. I'll talk to her tomorrow and apologize."

Chloe leans forward to remove Gloria's earmuffs.

Dinner has taken a sad turn. I frown. Chloe's reaction hit a chord. A thickness forms in my throat for not treating her better or for not sticking up for her, so she wouldn't feel like *that girl.*

"Now that that's over, let's change the subject to rainbows and butterflies, okay?" Chloe says, her mood turning the opposite in seconds. She grins at Gloria and starts coloring with her again.

We order our food. I talk football with Trey while Chloe and Gloria color until our pizza comes. Pepperoni, no anchovies.

The mood lightens as we eat. Gloria talks about how much she loves her preschool teacher and how her class loved the pink boots Chloe had gotten her. Trey talks about his grades and how he aced his last few tests.

They're good kids.

Good kids limited on opportunity because of their background.

And that fucking sucks.

Being a police officer has matured me and opened my eyes to how others aren't born into privileged lives like I was. I see these kids who go without. If it looks like they need food, I'll buy them something at the diner, or I'll slip them some candy. But I've never heard their stories like this.

This dinner has enlightened me.

———

TREY SLAMS my Jeep door shut at the same time I get out, and we walk over to Chloe's house from my drive. He asked to ride with me after pizza. It's unfortunate the people in this town label kids like him as delinquents without knowing their stories. Trey isn't trouble. He's a kid who needs direction and a good role model, and I'm up for helping anyone I can.

"Dude," he says next to me. He's a teenager and already nearly six feet tall. "You'd better be coming over and hanging out with us tonight."

We walk up the porch steps where Chloe is jamming her key into the front door lock while Gloria stands next to her, holding a doll sporting ratty hair.

"I'm not sure about that, buddy," I answer. I have no problem with coming over uninvited when it's just Chloe home but not when the kids are over.

"Come on," Trey argues with a face full of determination. "I have the best Netflix watch list. Plus, it's not like you old folks have anything better to do on a Friday night. You're going to go home, get rid of the corns on your feet, and then clean your dentures."

Trey is a little smart-ass.

He reminds me of myself at his age.

Chloe helps Gloria inside the house and starts flipping on

lights when we walk in. "Hey now," she calls out to Trey, "we are not that old."

"You two are freaking ancient," Trey continues before glancing at me. "There's no way you're going to bed this early."

I peer over at Chloe and wait for her permission. Yes, fucking wait for her permission like I'm the same age as Trey.

"Yes, Kyle, you don't want them to think we're *too old*," she replies in a playful tone. "Let's show these youngins that we can totally hang."

"Never say *totally hang* again," I say, winking. "You're already making us look old."

Trey slaps me on the back. "I'll be on popcorn duty. Kyle, make yourself comfortable!"

Gloria plops down on the couch and situates her baby next to her. "*The Grinch!*" she squeals. "I want to watch *The Grinch!*"

I sit down in an abandoned chair across from her. "*The Grinch?*" I question. "It's October."

"Gloria requests to watch it every day of the year," Chloe says around a sigh. "Netflix won't take it down." She sits down and starts carefully unbraiding Gloria's hair. "It's your bedtime, honey. How about we put your pajamas on, and I'll read *The Grinch* to you before bed?"

"Okay!" Gloria says with excitement. "Can I wear my princess pajamas?"

"Of course." Chloe peeks over at me. "Let me get her situated for bed. I'll be back."

I nod. "Take your time."

I've never seen this side of Chloe. I've seen the competitive, pissed off side of her. All she cared about was her grades in high school, so they called her the ice queen. She went to one school dance—the one with me. She didn't attend field trips, parties, games—anything. From the looks of it, she had no social life. Also, from the looks of it now, she still doesn't.

Trey returns with drinks and a large bowl of popcorn. "Here, dude." He tosses me a can of Coke. "This cool?"

I pop open the tab. "Sure is."

He takes Gloria's abandoned seat. "Aunt Chloe's ex was a Coke drinker, too, which I liked."

I raise a brow. *Not sure why the kid is bringing up Kent the Buzzkill.*

"Dude, you're way cooler than him," he quickly adds, as if reading my annoyance. "What I meant was, I like hanging out with someone who can have a good time without drinking beer and getting wasted—like all my mom's boyfriends do. I've drunk beer a few times. It tastes like cow piss." He peers at the hallway, making sure Chloe isn't within earshot. "Now, vodka, on the other hand …"

Shit. How do I tell this kid not to drink vodka when I was chugging the shit in high school? Fuck, I am not ready to be a dad yet. But, as a cop, I've given the same speech numerous times. Bonging a few beers didn't affect me when I was younger, but I can't say the same for others.

"This is much more satisfying than alcohol, I promise. Not to mention, safer."

He chuckles, shaking his head. "You have to say that as a grown-up and cop."

I lean back in my chair. "I'm not trying to be a dick, but look at your mother's boyfriends. Are they who you want to be like?"

He points his Coke to me and grins. "Good point."

I hold up my can in a cheers gesture.

He props his feet up onto the coffee table. "Thanks for coming to my game tonight."

"No problem. I had fun. Thanks for inviting me and letting me crash your pizza party."

"Crash our parties anytime, dude."

He pulls his phone from his pocket when it rings. "Shit," he whispers under his breath when he glances at the screen.

"What?" *I mean, watch your mouth.*

All playfulness is gone. "It's my mom."

He hits the Ignore button and shoves it back into his pocket. Can't say I blame the guy.

What seems like a minute later, Chloe returns to the living room with a ringing phone in her hand.

"Let me guess," Trey huffs out. "It's her."

Chloe's smile is gone. "I'm sorry, buddy," she replies with a strained voice.

"Ignore it, like I did," he replies.

Her face falls. "We both know what happens when I do that." She repeatedly shakes her head while moving out of the room and heading back down the hallway.

"What happens?" I ask Trey when she's gone.

He scrubs his hand over his chin, debating on whether to tell me. "Mom shows up here with her boyfriend of the week, and it ends up turning into some big drama-fest."

"Ah. No one likes drama-fests."

He uneasily glances around. "I hate her."

I wince. *Damn.* "Now, that's harsh."

He shrugs. "Maybe it is, but I do."

"I understand, but parents make mistakes, and eventually, maybe she'll learn from them."

"No, she won't." His voice is tense.

The little guy hates his mother. Even though my relationship with my father is strained, I love my parents. I have a good fucking mother who'd do anything for her children, whose world is wrapped around her children. It saddens me that he doesn't.

"Sorry, guys, but your mom wants you to come home," Chloe says, coming back into the room.

"Seriously?" Trey groans. "We just got here, and it's not a school night."

"I tried explaining, but she said she had plans for you in the morning," Chloe answers.

Trey rolls his eyes. "Yeah, right. Plans for us to make her and her boyfriend breakfast." His breathing shakes. "No. She chose not to go to dinner. Tell her we're staying here tonight."

Chloe looks at him in devastation. "I'm sorry, buddy. I tried. Now, grab your bag. Maybe I can pick you up tomorrow and we can do something, okay?"

She turns around, walks down the hall, and returns with Gloria in her arms.

"I'll drive you," I say, jumping up from the couch.

She shakes her head. "You don't need to do that."

I start following them outside. "I want to."

She sighs. "It will be a pain in the butt to move the car seat."

"Then, we'll take your car." I wink. "It won't be the first time I've driven it."

She shuts her eyes and sighs, as if she's lost all energy to carry on our conversation. "*Fine,* but I'll drive since I know where it is. You can ride passenger."

Her giving in so easily surprises me. "Works for me."

The four of us load into the car, and everyone is quiet as she makes her way out of town. I've answered police calls in this neighborhood plenty of times. Sadly, it's where most of our crime comes from—the outskirts of Blue Beech.

Chloe parks in front of a run-down brown trailer, unbuckles her seat belt, and then glances at me. "I need to go in and make sure everything is okay."

"What do you mean, make sure everything is okay?" I ask before she gets out.

"She needs to go in and make sure Mom isn't drunk, or it's an unsafe situation for us to be in," Trey answers for her.

She looks back and gives him a look, saying he shouldn't have said that.

I clutch my door handle. "Let me come with you."

She grabs my shoulder to stop me. "Definitely not a good idea. It'd make things worse. Stay here. I'll be back."

I don't settle in my seat. "The fact that the three of you could possibly walk into an *unsafe* situation makes me uncomfortable, and there's no way I can sit here. I'll stand on the porch, out of the way. No one will even know I'm there."

She opens her mouth to argue, but her phone starts ringing. I see Claudia's name on the screen.

"Fine," she says with a groan.

She helps Gloria out of her car seat while I grab her bag, and we walk up the creaky porch steps. I hand Trey Gloria's bag, and a whiff of cigarette smoke and mold hits me when they open the door. I stand out of view and watch through the torn blinds. Claudia is sitting on the couch with a cigarette in her hand, talking to Chloe about needing money for food. Roger is spread out next to her with a beer in one hand and a slice of pizza in the other. Claudia must be too dumb to realize that asking for food money when there's an open pizza box in front of him isn't helping her case.

"You've tapped me out this month," Chloe says with a stressed breath.

"Don't act like you've forgotten who took care of you when Mom didn't," Claudia snaps.

"I took care of myself, but thank you for the reminder," Chloe replies.

Claudia puts out her cigarette while Trey helps Gloria out of her coat. "When will you have it then?"

"I will go buy you groceries in the morning," Chloe says.

"I like doing it myself. You buy too much healthy stuff for our liking."

"I'll drop off groceries tomorrow, Claudia. I'm not arguing with you tonight." Chloe kisses Gloria and then Trey on their heads. "Good night, guys. Call if you need anything."

"They won't need anything, *Chloe*! I'm their mother. If they do, they can ask me," Claudia shouts to her back.

Chloe nods and walks out the door.

I rest my hand on her back as we walk down the steps to the car. I get into the driver's side while she takes passenger. She doesn't fight it. I see the defeat in her eyes.

I blow out a breath as I pull out of the neighborhood. "Chloe, I don't know how you do it."

She peeks over at me. "Do what?"

"Deal with her."

"I do it for the kids. Not her."

"I'm surprised she didn't let them stay. She seemed like she didn't want to spend another minute with them at the game."

"Trust me; it wasn't her wanting to spend time with them."

"What do you mean?"

"When she called, she asked me to borrow a few hundred dollars. I told her I didn't have it. She demanded I bring the children home, or she was calling the cops."

Wow. The nerve of her sister. "Babe, in case you haven't realized it, I am the cops. Did you tell her there was already one there?"

She gives me a look. "I don't want to drag you or any other law enforcement into my family's drama. Not to mention, people talk. She already causes enough problems for me, just being her. There doesn't need to be record of endless police visits to my house."

"Maybe you should take her to court and fight for custody."

"I've tried, but there's nothing I can do. She's passing drug tests. I have no power, and if I take it too far, the kids might end up in foster care before the process of adoption goes through. *If* I'm even able to adopt them. It's complicated. The system wants to keep children with their parents. Claudia uses it to her advantage with me."

"You ever walked into something you'd refer to as an unsafe situation with Claudia before?"

"A few times, yes."

"And?"

She fiddles with a ring on her finger. "I threatened to call the cops if she didn't let me leave with the kids. Claudia is not a fan of the police," she says, glancing over at me.

I grip the steering wheel. "Shocker."

"Big time."

"I need you to make me a promise." It's dark in the car, so I can't see the expression on her face.

"What's that?"

"Anytime you go over there, to make sure the kids or you aren't walking into a dangerous setting, you call me to come with you."

"I'm a big girl, Kyle," she replies with a thick voice.

"I'm well aware that you're strong as fuck, Chloe, but you're not invincible. Neither are those children."

"Okay."

I briefly scope her out. "Okay, what?"

"I'll call you before visiting any seedy trailers."

Her giving in without another argument surprises me.

When we get back to her house, I follow her into the kitchen where she grabs us a few waters from the fridge and then leads me back into the living room. I sit down next to her on the couch, and she tucks her feet underneath her ass, slightly facing me.

"If you also don't mind me asking, where's their father?" I ask, grabbing some popcorn from the bowl Trey brought out earlier.

Chloe shrugs. "They have different ones, and to be honest, I don't know."

"You don't know who they are or where they are?"

"Last I heard, Gloria's was in prison, and Trey's was a deadbeat asshole who chose not to be in his life." She rolls her eyes. "Exactly my sister's type."

"Has it always been this way? Her running to you every

time she needs something? Being neglectful and expecting you to fix the problem?"

"For as long as I can remember."

I rest my arm on the back of the couch and study her. "If you ever need help with them, let me know."

She gives me a small smile. "They'd probably enjoy it, to be honest." She takes a long drink of water and rubs at her bottom lip. "Trey likes you, and I think you'd be a good influence on him."

I smirk arrogantly. "What's there not to like, babe?"

She shoves my chest.

"Maybe I'll ask him to put a good word in for me with his aunt."

"Hmm … you might already be putting in a good word for yourself," she whispers.

Surprising me again, she straddles my lap and circles her arms around my neck. I shut my eyes as she slightly grinds against me, her core rubbing against my now-growing cock.

I smile and run my fingers over the slit between her lips. "You know, I've realized something."

"What's that, *Officer?*"

I massage her breasts over her top, moving in a circular motion. "You haven't introduced me to your bed." I drag my fingers through her soft hair. "It seems unfair since you've become so familiar with mine."

My cock throbs when she slides off my lap and holds out her hand.

"Let me introduce you to it then."

My attention stays plastered to her ass, and I'm surprised I don't run into a wall as she leads me to her bedroom. The room brightens with the switch of the light, and she wastes no time before undressing. Chloe needs this tonight—needs to forget, to let loose, to be free of her problems.

What better way to make her feel good than with my fingers, my tongue, my cock?

I open my mouth to disclose all the dirty things I'll be doing to her body tonight when a thought pops into my head. *Yes*. Instead of my original plan of throwing her on the bed and devouring her pussy, I head to her nightstand while she stands, watching me.

She stops mid-unsnap of her bra. "What are you doing?"

"Oh, nothing. Proceed as you were," I answer with a grin, my attention staying on the drawer. I push away panties and bras until I find what I'm looking for. Her face reddens when I turn around and hold up her vibrator. "I want you to show me how you use this, Chloe."

She stands frozen, catching her breath, as the blush on her face grows redder. "What?" The word stutters from her plump lips.

I hold out the vibrator to her. "Show me what you like."

Her mouth falls open, and she rakes a hand through her hair. As she moves, her bra falls to the floor, and I lick my lips at the sight of her perfect breasts. I want to suck on them, suck on her, *fuck her*, but the urge to watch her play with herself overrides all those cravings—for the time being.

I inch forward, and she shivers when I run my hand over her hip.

"Chloe, I never want you to feel uncomfortable with me. I'll never judge you for what you like and don't like in the bedroom." I turn the vibrator on, rub it up her stomach, and then lower it to her core, running it over her panties. "If you want to show me, I'd love it. If not, we can do anything else you want."

I use my free hand to cup her breast, sliding my tongue against her perky nipple before wrapping my lips around it while continuing to stroke her with the vibrator. I lose my hold when she rips it from my hand and steps back. She's hesitant as she climbs up her bed, but as she watches me stare at her with desire, her confidence builds.

Fucking yes.

"Shit, Chloe," I say. "You are so fucking sexy, baby."

My words give her more courage, and she slips her panties down her legs, kicking them off her feet. I grab the ottoman sitting in the corner of the room and slide it in front of the bed, taking a seat and preparing for the most spectacular show I'll ever see.

"I've been dreaming of this."

It takes me seconds to unbuckle my pants, and my hand is wrapped around my cock before they even fall to the floor. She opens her legs and puts herself on full display for me—*for motherfucking me.* I'm close to exploding before giving myself the first stroke. How I got lucky enough for a sight and experience like this is beyond me. She caresses her clit with the vibrator first, then her slit, and then slowly plants it inside herself. I throw my shirt off and keep my eyes glued on her.

"Yes, God, that's so fucking hot," I pant.

I'm hypnotized, watching her pleasure herself. I keep the same pace, jerking myself off. It's torture to stop myself from coming. She rocks her hips up, her back arching, and I know she's close.

My voice falters when I tell her to stop.

I have to do it with her.

I want to do it with her.

On her.

A wild grin is on her face when she crawls to the end of the bed. She arches a finger, gesturing for me to come forward, and my cock twitches. I lick my lips, and my cock aches when I stop stroking it. She situates herself on her knees when I reach her and wait for her next move. Her gaze locks on mine when she rubs the vibrator along my lips.

"I've never done anything like this before," she whispers before handing me the vibrator and spreading her legs.

I caress her clit with it and then slide it inside her. Her hands grip my shoulders as I fuck her with it.

Her nails dig into my skin. "Have you ... ever watched

another woman do this?"

I drag away the vibrator, rest my palm on her stomach, and push her back before meeting her on the bed, my body over hers. "Nope, and don't care to. Only you." I groan when I push my cock inside her. "Only you, Chloe."

She whimpers as I stay in place, not moving, and I stare down at her. We make the strongest eye contact I've ever experienced.

Tonight was a big step for Chloe. She's never opened herself up like that to anyone else, not even to men she's opened her heart to.

I shiver when she runs her hands up and down my arms. "And trust me; you will be the only man who's ever watched me."

"Thank fuck."

Her confirmation sets me on fire. I grab her thighs, situate them on my shoulders, pull out, and thrust back into her. We find our release, and I fall down next to her.

I roll off and catch my breath as she rests her head on my chest.

"Thank you for everything tonight. For going to Trey's game, for the pizza party, and for giving me an orgasm." She snuggles tightly into my side. "And for tagging along to Claudia's. I feel safe with you."

I squeeze her tight. "And thank you for tonight—for letting me crash your party and be there for you, for fucking yourself in front of me and then letting me fuck you." I sigh. "And, even if you hadn't agreed, I would've followed you to Claudia's."

She holds herself up to look at me in question. "Why didn't I know you were this sweet?"

"You were too busy telling me to fuck off to give me the chance to show you the real me."

She laughs. "Oh, yeah, right."

Her lips meet mine through a smile.

CHAPTER SIXTEEN

Chloe

KYLE WALKS into my living room and frowns while eyeing me. "I have to say, I'm a little disappointed."

"What? Why?" I question.

I peek down at myself. I appear the same as I did when I left his house this morning for work. Sleepovers at his place are now an everyday occurrence, and instead of saying good morning from his porch, he says it from next to me in bed.

"I was hoping you were dressed up."

I throw him an annoyed expression. "And what are you? Where's your *sexy* cop costume?"

"At my house. I'm saving it for later." He winks. "When I handcuff you to my bed."

I can't hold back my grin.

"Yes, handcuffing you to my bed is definitely tonight's plan."

Gloria stomping into the kitchen ends our flirt-fest. "Look at me, Aunt Chloe!" she squeals. She gives Kyle a lopsided smile when she spots him. "Can you guess what I am?"

He settles his finger on his chin. "Hmm … are you … the Tin Man?"

Gloria laughs and shakes her head. "No, silly!"

Kyle squints at her. "Are you the Cowardly Lion?"

Her smile widens. "No!"

"Then, you must be Dorothy!"

She hops up and down. "Yes." She holds her basket up and snatches the stuffed dog inside. "And this is Toto."

Kyle kneels, so he's eye-level with her. "Hello, Dorothy and Toto. It's nice to meet you." He shakes her hand before petting Toto on the head. "I'll give you extra candy when you stop by my house later."

"Yay!" She claps her hands. "I can't wait for all my candy."

"All right, Dorothy," I say, resting my palm on her back. "Let's do your pigtails."

We gather in the living room, and I sit down on the couch while Gloria plops onto the floor in front of me.

"What made you be Dorothy?" Kyle asks Gloria, resting in a chair. "Is that your favorite movie?"

Gloria nods. "My favorite in the entire world!" She kicks her feet back and forth, showing off her sparkly red shoes. "Do you like my shoes?"

"Very much," Kyle answers before lifting his leg. "Much cooler than these Nikes I'm sporting."

Gloria squeals. "What's your favorite movie?"

He glances around the room. "Promise not to tell anyone?"

Gloria holds her pinkie out. "I pinkie promise to infinity."

He leans in as if telling her a secret and then loops their fingers together. "It's *The Wizard of Oz.*"

She claps her hands again. "Yay!"

I finish her pigtails at the same time Trey walks in, wearing his football gear.

Gloria frowns at the sight of him. "Where's your costume? You're supposed to be the Scarecrow!"

Trey's shoulders slump. "I told you, I'm not trick-or-treating this year."

Gloria crosses her arms and sulks. "And I said you have to."

"Sorry, but I'm too old for trick-or-treating," Trey answers.

She hops up and looks close to tears when she stomps her foot. "That's not fair!"

I stand and drape my arm around her. "Let's have a girls' Halloween night."

She sniffles and scowls at Trey, shooting him a stare that'd force me to cave in seconds. "You always come with me!"

He offers her an apologetic smile. "Sorry, Glor-Bear. Aunt Chloe said she'd take you though."

"Fine, I don't want you to come anymore," she declares, hiding her face in my waist.

"What about this?" Kyle comments. "I'm handing out candy at my house." He signals between Gloria and Chloe. "You two trick-or-treat it up." He winks at Gloria. "Save me the Reese's Cups, and Trey can hang out at my house. I made tacos, so come over when you're finished."

Trey gives Kyle a glance. "You made tacos?"

"Sure did."

"His mother made tacos," I correct with a smile.

"Your mom still cooks for you, bro?" Trey asks. "That's lame."

"For your information, *I* made the tacos tonight. My mom only makes my date-night meals," Kyle argues.

"That's even lamer," Trey comments. "You're supposed to impress chicks."

Trey goes to Kyle's, and Gloria and I go trick-or-treating for a good hour before we go to Kyle's for tacos. Trey might be too old for trick-or-treating, but he has no problem with raiding Gloria's candy bag.

Claudia picks the kids up late, and then I let Kyle use his handcuffs on me.

"I LOVE THIS PLACE," Lauren sings out, skipping into the restaurant. "Oh, the memories here will last a lifetime."

A prominent magazine I'd kill to write for has chosen Clayton's as one of the finest restaurants in Iowa for the past four years. I came here with Kent for all of our celebration dinners—our birthdays, anniversaries, and promotions. The restaurant is an hour out of Blue Beech, and we're staying in a hotel in the city for the night. It's nice, not worrying about nosy people gawking at you.

"Yes, such romantic memories." Gage chuckles before kissing Lauren.

Lauren glances at me while we make our way to the hostess stand. "When Gage came home, he followed me here. He also brought a date in a desperate attempt to make me jealous."

Gage ruffles his hand through Lauren's hair, resulting in a glare from her. "Why don't you elaborate on the story, babe? Tell her how you deceived me into thinking you were having an affair with a married man. Come to find out, you were here, celebrating your friend's birthday with his husband."

"Wow," I say while laughing.

I envy Lauren and Gage's relationship. They were high school sweethearts, and even though they broke up and he moved away, they reconciled. Now, she's pregnant, and they're engaged.

Lauren is wearing a red dress, her baby bump on display, and her black heels don't bring her close to Gage's stature. Her dark hair is down in curls, and Gage's is messy as he protectively settles his strong arm around her.

I'm dressed in a simple black dress with black heels. My blonde hair is straightened, and the only makeup I'm wearing is a bright red lip. Kyle is sporting a white button-down shirt with a hint of color on the collar and cuffs and dark jeans.

Like his uniforms, the shirt perfectly fits him and showcases his broad shoulders and muscles.

In high school, I had no friends. All my dinner companions tonight were in the cool crowd. I never spoke to Gage. He spent most of his time with Kyle, and anyone who hung out with Kyle was an enemy. Lauren was always nice to me and once even picked me as her Chemistry partner when she realized I was always picked last.

Kyle wraps his arm around my shoulders. "Come on, let's grab a drink from the bar."

I stop him and nudge my head toward Lauren.

She waves away my concern. "Don't worry about me. I take notes of all the delicious-looking martinis and will come back when there isn't a little one in my stomach. I'm totally cool with you guys drinking without me."

Kyle takes my hand and leads me to a small open section at the bar.

"The bartender is not even paying attention to us," Lauren whines.

"You're pregnant and at the bar," Gage says.

Lauren glares and then kisses him. "Go get the bartender's attention, Kyle."

"Be right back," Kyle tells us, giving my side a squeeze. "He's giving the other side all his attention."

I lean forward and rest my elbows on the bar while observing him move around the bar. I bite into my lip when I catch women staring at him as if they want him as their dessert. There's a bridal party assembled around the bar, attempting to capture his attention, but he ignores them. I beam with pride. He's overlooking them because of me. He wants me.

"Wow, you're here with *him*?"

I tense and immediately know who said that.

"With fucking Kyle Lane?" Kent snarls.

I turn to scowl at him and notice his wedding ring. There's

no bitterness. Kent stands in front of me, and I feel nothing toward him, not hurt or regret.

He sets his drink on the bar and nudges closer by bumping the person next to me. "I need not go into details about why being around him is a vile fucking idea."

"And you cheating on me with another chick was a vile fucking idea, but you did. Now, you're *married* to the woman you swore you weren't touching while I'm sharing a meal with the man you warned me away from. Oh, how the motherfucking world turns," I snap with no hesitation.

He snatches his drink up and chugs it before slamming it down. "Don't come running to me when he screws you over."

My eyes narrow his way as we form strong eye contact. "Trust me; don't concern yourself with that. Go back to your wife. Maybe you can be a not-so-shitty partner to her."

I tense up when I see Kyle approach us. He doesn't look threatened my Kent's presence. Kyle slaps Kent on the back, bumps his shoulder when stepping around him, and places our drinks on the bar before dragging me into his side.

A hard expression spreads across Kent's face.

"Good to see you, man," Kyle addresses him. "I hope you're doing well. Thank you for cheating on Chloe to give me the opportunity to make her happy—*very* happy."

"Fuck you," Kent scowls.

Kyle laughs coldly. "Nah, I'd rather have fun with Chloe. Appreciate the offer though."

"Why do you even care who I'm here with?" I ask Kent.

"I still care about you! I don't want to see you get used by this"—he tosses his hands out to signal Kyle—"asshole who has already hurt you once. Don't trust him. You think he'll ever want to be with you? Look, he took you out of Blue Beech for your date, so no one would see you together."

Kyle's fingers curl around my waist. "Fuck you. Don't assume shit you know nothing about."

Gage steps between them. "Enough. Both of you, walk away, and we'll all enjoy a nice dinner."

Kent furiously shakes his head. "Go ahead, Chloe. Let him treat you like the whore he always made you out to be. I guess your little nickname suited you." His nostrils flare.

My cheeks redden in embarrassment.

Kyle settles me behind him, blocking me from Kent. I attempt to go around him to give Kent a good ass-kicking, but it's too late. One second, my ex's mouth is talking shit about me, and the next, Kyle's fist is hitting it, preventing him from talking more shit about me.

People step out of the way when Kent cries out and holds his nose.

"That's assault!" he screams. "You assaulted me!"

"It was a love tap, Kent," Kyle replies with annoyance, as if he were scolding a child. "No damage was done."

With that, Kyle grips my hand and leads me toward the exit. As we pass the restrooms, I bump into Kent's wife, and she blinks a few times, as if she were imagining me. When she realizes I'm real and I'm unable to move, her attention then swings to Kyle, and I grin.

I pat her shoulder. "Thank you so much for stealing Kent away from me, Lacy."

"Screw you, Chloe." An evil smirk stretches across her lips. "Maybe I'll be able to give him babies, you barren bitch."

Oh, this bitch.

Hell no.

Sadness and rage consume me at her words. At this moment, two things can happen: I could burst into tears or punch Lacy. I raise my hand, ready for a catfight, but Kyle grabs it and leads me out of the restaurant while I attempt to jerk away.

"Hey," I yell, swatting at him when we make it outside to the valet. "Why are you allowed to hit someone, but I'm not?"

He whips around to look at me, his face filled with irritation. "That can get you into tough shit."

I tap my heel against the ground. "Uh, in case you forgot, you're a *police officer*. That can get you into some tough shit."

His hand leaves mine when he holds up a finger. "First, if it does, it does." Another finger goes up. "Second, I made sure not to do any damage."

"Damn it, Kyle, you couldn't wait to punch him until *after* we ate?" Lauren yells, stomping her feet and shaking her head until they make it to us.

Kyle rubs the back of his neck and throws Lauren an apologetic look. "My apologies. Go yell at Kent for not waiting to talk shit until *after* we ate."

I wipe away the tears over Lacy's words, and my mouth goes dry as I stare at Lauren. "I'm sorry."

Lauren glances at me. "No, don't you apologize." She points to Kyle with her chin. "Now, you need to be sorry, stupid. You're a cop. You can get in serious trouble for that."

"I'm sorry," Kyle states. "You two go eat. We'll figure something out."

"Nah," Gage cuts in, looking indifferent. "It's too busy in there anyway. Where's our next choice of food?"

"I have an idea," Kyle says, chewing on his lip. "How about we hit that arcade in the mall?"

"What are we, twelve?" Lauren asks.

"No, smart-ass," Kyle replies. "At night, it turns into adults only. They serve food and alcohol. It's a good time."

"I'm game," Gage responds with a shrug. "It'd be nice to do something different and low-key."

"We need to stop by the hotel, so we can change then," Lauren says. "These heels are killing my feet. I live in scrubs, so I need jeans ASAP."

"Totally agree," I say.

Lauren gives me a bright grin.

———

WHEN WE WALK into the hotel's lobby, Kyle heads to the counter for our room keys.

"I know the night is still young and all," Lauren says around a groan when she stops next to me while Gage joins Kyle. "But can it be young for only you and Kyle? I'm a prude who wants to order room service and go to bed."

I frown. "I'm sorry about dinner."

She waves away my apology. "Girl, don't worry about that. I feel terrible, so you did us a favor."

The guys come back with key cards and grab our luggage.

"Change of plans," Lauren tells Kyle. "Gage and I are going to our room, calling room service, and passing out."

Gage strokes her back and seems fine with not going out.

Kyle offers a warm smile. "Tell them to charge it to my room."

Lauren starts to object, but Gage smacks Kyle on the back.

"How kind of you to offer. I'll be sure to inform them." He glances at Lauren. "My girl is eating for two, so I apologize in advance for the bill. You two have a nice night and don't get in too much trouble."

We crowd into the elevator, and our rooms are next to each other. After Kyle unlocks our door, I toss my bag on the bed, collapse on it, and unstrap my heels.

"My feet are killing me." I drop them to the floor when I'm finished. I open my suitcase and select a pair of flats. "So, we're going to an arcade?"

Kyle nods.

"One where you play Skee-Ball, win tickets, and select cheap prizes?"

Kyle sets his bag down and grins. "It'll be fun. I promise."

"Is it weird that a woman pushing thirty is excited to go to an arcade?"

"As weird as it is that a guy pushing thirty is excited to go to an arcade." He snags a shirt and flashes me a look. "Excited to go because of who his company will be."

I change my clothes in excitement.

———

I THROW my arms up and jump up and down. "Winner, winner, chicken dinner!"

We came, ate arcade food, drank, and now, we're playing games.

There's been a gleam in Kyle's eyes all night. We've had a blast, and I'm thankful we came. I would've never gone if he hadn't recommended it.

"I'm officially wiped out." I yawn as my buzz flutters through my belly.

"Let's cash in our tickets." He snags my hand in his. "My guess is, you won enough for a new car."

Kyle let me win all the games. I had no idea what I was doing while he explained them. We leave the mall where the arcade is, and the chill of the night smacks into us. The mall is down the street from our hotel, so we walked.

I hook my arm through Kyle's and skip forward as if I were Gloria's age. "Thank you, thank you. I had so much fun!" I scrunch my nose up. "The arcade part, not the Kent part."

He chuckles while dragging me closer, and I inhale the masculine scent of him.

God, I love his smell.

"You having fun was my goal for tonight, so that makes me happy."

I peek up at him. "You know, I've never acted like a kid before. It was freeing, not worrying about everything and having fun. I don't remember the last time I did that."

He tightens his hold, and we stroll past a couple making

out. "We can go back whenever you want. Next time, we can bring the kids. They'd have a blast."

My heart flutters, and we don't lose contact.

"Why are you so good to me and my family?"

"Family means everything. My brother, my sisters, my mom—they mean the world to me. I like you. That means, I like your family." He clicks his tongue. "With the exception of your sister—no offense."

I laugh. "We can't love them all."

I love that he thinks about that stuff, that he thinks about Trey and Gloria being like me—children never given the chance to do anything like go to an arcade. Sure, I give them more than I had while growing up. We've seen movies and gone to fairs, and I've taken them shopping but never anything like the arcade.

This, I would've remembered as a kid.

This, I'll remember as a grown-up.

I realize three things as I walk down the street with him.

1. I never want Kyle to leave.

2. I'm falling for him.

3. I'm terrified of losing him when he learns my secret.

———

I KICK off my shoes when we make it back into the hotel room and collapse on the bed. "Kyle Lane, you let me drink too much tonight," I sing—no, slur. "I will be placing all blame on you for tomorrow's hangover grumpiness."

He chuckles and heads over to our luggage. "Hey, you're the one who insisted on three margaritas while we played Whac-A-Mole. That's all on you, babe."

I glare at him with just one eye. "Don't blame a girl for having a good time."

He grabs our bags and sets them on the luggage rack. "Trust me; I love watching you enjoy yourself. Now, what do you want to sleep in tonight?" He unzips my bag and shuffles through it. "Did you pack pajamas?"

I drag myself up to look at him. "Huh?"

He continues searching through my bag until he pulls out a pair of pajamas. "You sleep nude when we're together, but what about when you're traveling ... not naked?"

I jerk my head toward the pajamas in his hand. "Those."

He tosses them to me.

"You're okay with me sleeping in these?"

He stops going through his bag to look at me. "I'm sorry, am I okay with what?"

"With me not sleeping nude," I clarify.

He blinks. "I'm still not following, babe."

"We're usually naked when we're in bed together."

He inhales a deep breath when he understands what I'm saying, and he tosses the shirt in his hand back into his bag. "Chloe, what the fuck? I'm not hanging out with you for sex. If I only wanted quick pussy, I could get it anywhere, at any time."

"Full of yourself much?" I mutter.

He stares at me with frustration and hurt. "Not saying it to pipe my ego. I'm saying it to prove my point to you." He signals to the pajamas at my side. "Sleep in those. Sleep in my sweatpants. Sleep in a fucking Halloween costume. Either way, it won't change my mind about being next to you."

His response shocks me. At first, I played it off as a joke, but deep down, it's been bothering me, not knowing if that's all he wants. From the beginning, we've made it clear this is sex and then we go our separate ways. And I said the same. I was adamant on no double dating or getting too close.

The truth keeps hitting me tonight. I was afraid of expressing myself and wanting more in fear of Kyle hurting me again. I didn't want him in case he didn't want me.

But it seems like ... he does.

My life gets more complicated.

"Now …" he says, breaking me out of my thoughts. He's holding up a pair of his sweats when I look over at him. "Are these okay for me to sleep in?"

I flip him the bird. "Funny."

I grab my pajamas, and he comes over to play assistant while I struggle to get undressed.

So, it is about sex, I wonder when he drops to his knees and drags my pants off. I'm thinking the same when he helps me with my shirt and bra, my boobs bouncing free.

So, maybe it isn't about sex, I wonder when he grabs my pajamas and dresses me.

He returns to our bags to grab our toothbrushes from *his* bag. My drunken lips curl into a smile. He texted me, asking what my favorite color was after my first weekend at his house. The next day, there sat a new toothbrush of the same color on his bedroom vanity. Neither one of us mentioned it, but he smiles and winks every time I pick it up.

"You need me to brush yours?" he asks, handing mine over.

I laugh and lead us to the bathroom. "Hopefully, I can manage this one by myself."

"Tell me if you change your mind. I've never brushed anyone else's teeth, but I don't mind getting that personal with you."

We share the sink and brush our teeth in silence. Next, we floss. He leaves when I ask him for my makeup wipes. He drops them off and then goes back into the bedroom. When I walk out, he's already changed into sweatpants with no shirt on and in bed, his back against the headboard.

Sharing a bed with him and not for sexual reasons makes my stomach flip-flop. Sure, we sleep in the same one during sleepovers, but that's after sex. This is different. This is comfortable. This feels like we're in a relationship.

I shake my head. *Quit questioning this. He'll probably jump on you as soon as you get in.*

I wouldn't object to it.

He taps the spot next to him. "Come here."

When I crawl in, he pulls the sheet to our waists, snatches my hips, and drags me to his side. I rest my head on his shoulder.

A pained breath leaves him. "I want to tell you something."

I perk up in his arms. "What's up?"

His voice turns gentle. "Kent's words ... they keep creeping up on me."

"Kyle, he was mad and talking shit."

"He said I'd treat you like a whore." He leans us forward, so he can settle his arm behind me, and then he runs his fingers through my hair, untangling the mess. "I never want you to feel like that, Chloe. I've never and I will never think of you that way."

"Kyle," I cut in.

"No, let me finish."

I shut my mouth.

"If you ever, for even one second, feel like that, you tell me ... and slap me in the face. I'm not only here for sex. You're not my whore. I'm a fan of dirty talk, yes, but us having sex isn't what this is all about."

My heart races at his confession, and I struggle for words while staring at him. "So, this isn't just casual sex between two neighbors?"

His lips tilt into a smile.

I give him a cheesy smile in return.

"Absolutely fucking not. Again, I can find sex anywhere." He squeezes me.

If I could see my heart, it'd be glowing.

I make myself comfortable, and he rests his hand on my waist. The warmth of his skin relaxes me.

The room turns quiet, the TV he turned on the only

noise, and he scratches his jaw before speaking. "Can I ask you a question?"

"Depends on what it is," I mutter.

His hand moves and begins stroking my shoulder. "Hey, don't blame a man for being curious about the woman in his bed."

"I'm close to drunk, so ask away."

"What made you decide to be a writer?"

I gulp. I hate being asked that question, and I normally lie. I don't to him. "Because of Trey's dad."

He tenses. "The deadbeat asshole?"

I nod. "He was the only guy of my sister's who was nice to me." I hold a finger up. "Correction: he was nice *then*."

He tightens his hold, expecting a bad story.

"He helped me with my homework and talked to me about my goals. I only got books from him or the library, so when I was running low, I read the newspaper. It was a national paper, and I loved reading the articles. He told me writers got paid pennies and to choose a better career path. I won't lie and say I didn't change my mind, but then he broke my heart. I went to my journal and wrote about him, wishing I could publish it so that everyone else would know, too. I signed up for the newspaper to spite him, not caring if I'd make money, and I fell in love with it."

"What did he do to hurt you?"

I rub my forehead, and the memories of fear and hurt play through my mind. "He was the same as all her other boyfriends. He was better at putting up a front. He hurt me, he hurt Trey, and I'll never forgive him for that."

He grits his teeth. "What do you mean, he hurt you?"

"No, no, nothing like that. More like hurt my feelings."

He presses his lips to my cheek, then my nose, and then pulls back with a gentle smile. "I'm sorry that happened."

I duck my head down. I hate talking about Sam. "Why were you so hell-bent on not going into law and politics?"

"I was expected to grow up in my father's shadow. Instead, I decided I wanted to be a police officer. It pissed him off, but I didn't care."

"I like that you followed your heart."

"I'm glad you followed yours. Fuck Trey's dad." His chest moves when he chuckles. "When you became editor of the school paper, Ms. Sanders allowed me to read your unapproved articles."

Embarrassment and shock trickle up my spine. "What?"

There's playfulness in his tone. "I was her TA, and she talked about how you wanted to create controversy with your articles. You never cared about speaking the truth, no matter how many toes you stepped on."

"Nope. The truth will set you free."

"If I recall, you wrote an interesting article about me."

My face reddens. *Shit. Shit. Shit.* "No, she didn't."

"She did."

"Isn't that against code of conduct?"

"Like it mattered. She let me do whatever I wanted."

"Oh my God, did you sleep with our teacher?"

"Why would you think that?"

"She was young and hot, and why else wouldn't she have approved my articles about you?" I elbow him. "That's against the law, you know. My next article will be about Ms. Sanders, the woman married to the principal, who was biased against my articles because you were banging her."

He holds his hand up. "Whoa, hold on, killer. She wasn't breaking laws and banging me."

I snort.

"We slept together once *after* I graduated and was eighteen. She wasn't married then."

"Eh, whatever. I'll be digging up dirt on her. I can't believe you didn't kill me for writing up the article."

"Sweet Chloe, who would want to be upset someone wrote an article about them being a bully?"

"I never said your name."

"The description fit me to a tee. A *young athlete* with a father *in power* receives favor from the principal and teachers and drinks underage at parties."

"Why didn't you say anything?"

"It didn't get published, did it?"

"It could've."

He shrugs. "I like that you thought about me enough to write an article." He kisses the top of my head. "You're a skilled writer. I read everything you wrote. Don't think I'm a stalker."

"Really?"

He nods. "Everything that did and didn't get published."

"Why? Some of them were boring as shit."

"I won't deny that." Quick breaths leave him. "You've always intrigued and interested me, Chloe. You wrote from the heart, whether people liked it or not. Gage gave me so much shit for reading them. You hated me, but those articles allowed me to learn more about you."

I see the sincerity and honesty in his eyes.

He's not lying.

He blows out a breath. "We've been drinking, so I'll do a drunk confession, and if you don't like it, maybe you'll forget about it in the morning."

"How about we make this a night of drunk confessions?" I stupidly reply.

His next words leave his mouth seconds later, as if he was waiting to release them. "I don't think I like you anymore. It's more than that now. Stronger than that. I'm fucking falling for you faster and harder than I have with anyone." He grabs my face, rubbing small circles with his finger on the top of my cheek. "Please tell me if you feel it, too."

My heart hammers against my chest, and fear sets in. "I do … I feel the same way."

He grins but still looks concerned. "You can ruin me. Please don't."

It's weird, seeing Kyle like this, so open, vulnerable, and not the strong, joking guy he always is. His feelings for me scare him.

"I won't."

And, just like that, I lied straight to his face.

CHAPTER SEVENTEEN

Chloe

THE MORNING SUN beams through the curtains. We're at the hotel, and I don't want to leave this room, where we poured more secrets in one night than our entire relationship.

Relationship.

Is that what we are?

In a relationship?

The idea of us being more than casual fuck buddies is exciting, but what happens when we return to the reality of Blue Beech?

What happens when what I'm hiding comes to light?

My back is against Kyle's chest. We stayed in this position all night, and today feels different from any other morning we've woken up side by side.

His fingers lace around my stomach, and the sound of him yawning hits my ear. I somehow manage to twist in his arms through the tight confinement he has me in until I'm facing him, chest-to-chest, our mouths inches apart.

I love the view of his handsome face in the morning. His hair is unruly. Day-old scruff sits on his cheeks of perfection. He's so carefree in the morning. Hell, he's so carefree in life. That balance is nice because I am so the opposite. Kyle puts me at ease when the rest of the world tears me down. The corners of his eyes crinkle when he notices me studying him.

"Good morning," I whisper.

"Good morning, gorgeous girl," he answers with a smile. "As much as I love saying those words to you, it's nice to hear them first. How did you sleep?"

I respond with an easy smile. "Perfect."

He rubs his hand over his scruff before leaning in to kiss me. "Any hangover signs yet?"

"So far, so good."

Except for my word vomit last night.

He chuckles. "Your chest of secrets feel lighter this morning?"

Yes. No. Maybe.

"For the most part, yes."

He snorts. "Only you would say *for the most part.*"

"What do you mean?"

"You're a glass ball of mysteries and secrets, but soon, you'll let me crack each one open. You'll see."

"Pretty sure of yourself, aren't you?"

"How many things did I say would happen between us while you stayed adamant they wouldn't? All of them. Us in bed together—*check.* Serving you breakfast in bed—*check.* You opening up to me"—he playfully squeezes me—"in more ways than one—*check.*"

I slap his arm. "Eventually, you'll need to buy my place in order to house your entire ego."

I shiver at his hand sliding up and down my arm.

"Fine by me. How about you stay at my house and my ego takes residence at yours?"

"Are you still nervous to have sex?" I ask teasingly.

"I'm not *nervous* to have sex with you. What's worrying me is what your dumbass ex said."

"You don't make me feel like a whore, I promise." With

that, I grab his cock over his sweats. "In fact, maybe you should worry about me treating you like *my* whore."

We drag our pants down at the same time. His nails bite into my waist when he thrusts inside me.

"I see no problem with that."

I moan at his first thrust. We're close—*so close*—and I've never had sex like this before. He cups my ass to yank me deeper into everything that is him before dragging his hand to my breast, cupping it.

Then, he stops me. "Can I ask you another question?"

Jesus. This man and his goddamn questions.

I attempt to move, but he doesn't allow it. "Let's save the question for when your cock isn't inside me." It's never fair on my end.

"Why? I'm much more persuasive when my cock is inside you."

I'm well aware.

"That's where you're wrong," I lie.

"That's untrue. My cock was inside you when I asked if you wanted me to fuck you harder. You said yes. My cock was inside your mouth when I asked you if you wanted me to fuck your face harder. You said yes. My cock was inside you—"

I dramatically tilt my head back. "All right, all right, I get your point. Spit it out."

His hand rides up to my back as he lightly caresses it. "Dallas Barnes, Lauren's brother, is tying the knot next weekend. Want to be my wedding date?"

I've heard about the wedding. It's had bigger buzz than my ex's. Dallas and Willow's story is more beautiful than my ex's. No affairs present in their situation. Dallas lost his wife to cancer. It was tragic. I went to the funeral, and he was devastated. Willow saved him and his daughter from a lonely life.

I shove my face into his neck. "I don't think that's such a good idea."

He pulls out of me, and I fall to my back as he hovers above me, making strong eye contact. *"Au contraire,* I think it's a great one."

I bite into my lower lip. "People will talk."

"Hopefully. I doubt anyone will be up for a mute wedding, but I'll put in a request if it'll make you more comfortable. Do you know sign language?"

I smack his shoulder. "You know what I mean."

"No, I don't."

"You're you ... and I'm me," I stutter out.

"Yes ... I didn't know you weren't aware of that."

"You're a Lane. I'm a Fieldgain. We don't go together."

He slides back inside me and raises his hips, resulting in a gasp from me. "Wrong. We sure seem to go together pretty damn well right now."

"To the outside world, we don't go together." *And to me.*

His hand reaches up to cup my breast, lightly squeezing it, and then his lips head to my ear. "Why do you care so much about what the outside world thinks?"

I caress his chest. "Says the guy who the entire town loves."

"Says the girl this guy is falling for."

My heart flutters, and my breathing is heavy as I smash my mouth to his.

All wedding talk disappears as he takes me away into another world, both physically and emotionally.

———

I'M EXHAUSTED.

We're back at my house.

We ate breakfast with Gage and Lauren before leaving the hotel early this morning. It's nice having a social life. Before Kent, it was nonexistent and went back to that after our breakup.

Kyle grabs my foot in his lap and massages it. "This weekend was fun. Thank you again." He smiles. "Let's figure out a weekend we can take the kids."

I love that he thinks of things like that.

That's when it hits me.

Kyle is great with kids. I saw it with Trey and Gloria. He'll be a great father to lucky kids someday.

"Do you want kids?" I rush out before I lose the guts to ask.

His hand on my foot stops, and he uses the free one to scratch the back of his neck. "Maybe. Possibly. If it happens, it happens. Maybe adoption is a good idea for me."

His answer seems rehearsed, as if he conjured up the right words for when I asked him. Sure, he most likely does get asked if he wants to be a father, *but* what guy says he wants kids but is considering taking the adoption route? A guy who's had to think about it.

Anxiety twists in my gut. "Don't bullshit me."

He winces at my response and peers over at me in confusion. "What?"

"You heard Kent's bitch wife call me barren."

He nods. "I did, but it's not my place to bring it up. It's a personal issue for you, and when you're ready to trust me with it, you'll come to me." He squeezes my foot. "I don't mind waiting for you to reveal all parts of yourself to me. Do it piece by piece; that's cool with me."

"I can't have children," I whisper. I told him I was on birth control the first time we had sex because I was afraid of telling him this.

People aren't sure how to respond when they hear a woman say infertility. Hell, before, *I* wouldn't have known how to respond with that statement.

He nods again, processing what I said without showing an ounce of emotion. Lowering his voice, he says, "You love children."

"I do," I answer with a choked-up voice, and my anxiety rushes harder as the tears start.

"I'm sorry, Chloe." He grabs my arm and pulls me onto his lap.

I stare down and gulp. "That's why you said you were up for adopting, isn't it?"

He delves his hand through my hair before lowering it and using the tip of his finger to drag my chin up. "Hey, you don't know that. Maybe I've always wanted to adopt."

"Always as in the last twelve hours after you heard what Lacy said?"

I sniffle, and my breakdown is coming. My hurt normally comes when I'm alone, and no one's here to judge me. They can't see my pain—not my doctor, not my mother or sister, not Kent.

It's thrown in my face—by my mother, by my sister when I ask her for the children, by Kent when we broke up. Pissed off people never fail to throw other's misfortune in their faces.

He wipes away my tears. "That doesn't matter."

I keep my gaze on him. "So, you did say it because you knew there was a possibility of that. You said it, so you wouldn't hurt my feelings."

"True, but I also said it because I *mean* it. I see a future with you. Shit, I want a future with you." He places a hand over his heart and gives me a smile. "If adopting a child is how we have children, then I'm down."

I wind my arms around his neck. "I guess I'll have you."

He gives me a gentle smile, grabs my hand, and kisses it. "Do you want to tell me why you can't?"

"I have endometriosis," I tell him. "It's a health condition that can cause infertility in women and issues that can result in having their uterus removed. I was one of those women."

He rubs my back as compassion crosses his features. "I'm so sorry."

I'm not sure what starts it, maybe because I'm *finally*

opening up to someone, but all my emotions, all my thoughts, suddenly spill out—in front of a man I'm finding myself trusting more than anyone. "It kills me," I say around a groan and a sob. "I see so many women, my sister being one, who don't deserve—" I pause to correct myself. "That's mean of me to say. I see these women who don't *want* to be mothers or take care of their children, and it kills me to see them take it for granted." Sadness overcomes me. "God, what I'd kill for that."

"Babe," he says, continuing to rub my back.

I wipe away the tears while Kyle stares at me, giving me his undivided attention with a concerned face. Shame corrodes my insides. "It's what a woman was created to do, right? Our bodies are made to bear babies. As little girls, it's what we look into our future for, hoping for. I remember when I took care of Trey when I was fifteen. Sometimes, I'd act like he was *my* baby. I couldn't wait to be a mother someday." Pain grips my chest as my throat thickens with sobs. "All that was taken from me by a simple diagnosis. Sometimes, I don't even feel like a woman. Sometimes, I hate my body for being this way, for doing this to me."

Kent's mother helped me post-surgery. She was kind but couldn't hide the sadness in her eyes that I wouldn't be giving her a grandbaby. Coming to terms with my infertility is hard enough, but seeing the disappointment and judgment on others makes it so much worse.

Kyle is quiet. He never cuts me off, never tries to justify what I'm feeling. He listens and takes my pain in. "Don't you dare base your worth off your ability to have children. You're still a woman—a strong, compassionate, sexy woman who gives out unconditional love for so many people. Why aren't you giving that same love to yourself?" He strokes my face, collecting all my tears with his fingers. "You, along with other women, weren't put here for that. Period. You're over here, helping Trey and Gloria and taking a job that pays half of what it should. Anyone who makes you believe any different shouldn't be in your life."

I gulp, unable to produce any words. I'm not withdrawn from him like when I told Kent.

"There are alternatives," he goes on. "Adoption. Surrogate. Don't let your diagnosis stop you from being a mother if it's what you want."

I nod. Adoption crossed my mind, but worry set in that it'd be selfish for me to bring a child into a single-parent home. I grew up without a father, and it hurt. I want to give a child that perfect life—mother, father, stability, white picket fence, all that. Right now, I can't.

Kyle isn't finished speaking. My honesty with my confession opened up the emotional floodgates. He doesn't blink as we make steady eye contact, and my body feels weak as he looks at me with … I'm not even sure *what* it is.

His voice is rich with emotion when he finally talks. "Chloe, last night, we wanted alcohol in our systems to speak our sober thoughts, but speaking honestly, no bullshit, I'm falling in love with you. I'll say it drunk, sober, today, tomorrow, and every day for the rest of my life. I want to make this official. I'm done pretending like we're just casual sex friends. I want you to be mine, and in the future, if we make it there, we can adopt all the babies in the world."

Kent never talked about it with me; he'd shut down when it was brought up. He was pissed about his life plan changing drastically. It scared me to hear another person call me a failure, so those wounds always stayed with me.

Kyle wanted this conversation with me.

Kyle will never put me down for flaws I can't control.

He'll stay by my side, exploring every alternative.

Kyle will stand by my side always … until he learns my lie.

CHAPTER EIGHTEEN

Kyle

I'VE BEEN on shift for three hours. So far, we've settled a domestic dispute with exes fighting over custody of their golden retriever and handled another where a woman slapped a man for rear-ending her car.

I'm thankful the crime rate in Blue Beech barely exists, and because of that, there's a great deal of downtime during our shifts. Gage is definitely grateful for it. He worked for Chicago PD before returning to Blue Beech and had no downtime on the job. I've considered moving out of Blue Beech and taking a job where I can save more lives and make a bigger difference, but I could never leave my family.

Gage thrums his fingers against the table and smirks my way. We're at the diner, having dinner. We're regulars here when our shift is slow, and we need a bite to eat. If we receive a call, Shirley will sometimes keep our food and heat it up when we come back.

"Why are you looking at me like that?" I question before taking the last bite of my cheeseburger.

He tilts his head to the side, as if he's studying me. "Lauren ordered me to inspect you."

The fuck?

I raise a brow. "Inspect me?"

"Yes. She's curious if you're looking or behaving differently."

I scratch my head. "Why is your girlfriend worried about me looking or behaving differently?"

"She enjoyed our little double date and believes you and Chloe will make a good couple."

I snort loudly. "You two bailed before the night started."

After the Kent drama, the four of us went to breakfast the next day. I'd woken up with a sense of relief that morning. My talk with Chloe had answered questions I'd wondered about since our night at the bar.

I joke about sex and our relationship, but deep down, I want more. My feelings for her build the more she lets me in and opens herself up to me.

We shared more in one night at the hotel than we had in weeks. I had been outraged when Kent accused me of using Chloe as my whore. Sure, in the beginning, we'd shared orgasms more than feelings, but sex isn't all we're about; it wasn't ever what I wanted us to be all about.

"We were doing you a favor," Gage says.

"Or you two are lame," I counter.

"Yes, my *pregnant* fiancée was tired, but she wanted to give you two alone time since you hadn't been out much. When you'd suggested the arcade, she'd found the perfect opportunity for you to have fun without worrying about the curious eyes of Blue Beech residents. If we had been there, it would've interfered."

I grab my napkin and wipe my mouth. "I wasn't aware they taught relationship expertise in nursing school."

I appear uninterested but have always appreciated Lauren's advice about women. She's played a role in successful relationships in our town.

"She has statistics to back up her claims. Dallas and Willow had town gossip issues. She was an out-of-towner, pregnant with Blue Beech's attractive widower. It helped their relationship when they got out of town." He shrugs. "Plus, Lauren offered room service, crime TV, and sex. I was down for whatever she suggested."

"You're always down for whatever she suggests."

"Welcome to being in love, man. Get ready for it."

I snort.

"I almost shot Lauren's landlord in the head after he hurt her. You punched Kent after he insulted Chloe. A man only interested in sex doesn't fight over a chick he's not falling for. You like your neighbor, and for Lord knows what reason, she likes you. Happiness and possibly *falling in love* looks good on you, man."

I grab my water and suck the rest of it down. There's no disputing his claims. Even though Chloe and I haven't labeled our relationship, every token of us having one is there. We spend all our free time together, have expressed our feelings toward the other, and aren't interested in dating anyone else.

There's no denying it now.

Chloe Fieldgain is no doubt my motherfucking girlfriend.

I can't help but smile.

Now, I need to convince her to let her guard down and realize it, too.

Gage yawns and goes for his coffee, but the static of our portable radio stops him. The dispatcher reports a public disturbance call. Gage flashes me a concerned look, and my stomach knots when she states the address.

He tells her we're on it, and I throw down cash to cover our bill before we jump into the car. Gage flips on the sirens and races toward my neighborhood while I fish my phone from my pocket and dial Chloe's number.

No answer.

Dial it again.

No answer.

"Any idea?" Gage asks, his eyes not leaving the road.

"Her sister gives her trouble sometimes," I answer.

"Domestic problems—my favorite," Gage grumbles.

A beat-up truck is in Chloe's driveway, and Claudia and Roger are standing in her yard. Chloe is on the front porch, her arms folded in disdain. All attention deviates to us, and I'm positive this calm scene isn't what it was five minutes ago.

"The sister, I take it?" Gage asks.

My eyes harden, and I nod.

"I've picked up the guy a few times."

"It's her boyfriend."

I draw in a steady breath and step out of the car. My anger heightens the closer we get. Roger is pacing in front of the house. Claudia flicks her cigarette onto the ground and lights another.

"What's the problem here?" Gage asks.

Roger laughs coldly with bloodshot eyes when he sees me. "You've got to be shitting me! The boyfriend has arrived to play hero. What a fucking joke."

"Not here to play hero." I glower. "Only here to do my job."

If I wasn't in my uniform and on the clock, my answer would be different. We're steps away, but Roger reeks of alcohol as if it's a second skin. A public intoxication arrest might be in the works. Roger and Claudia not fleeing is odd. Most arrestee regulars avoid contact with us at all costs.

I'm grinding my teeth when I dart up Chloe's porch stairs to be with her. "What is going on?"

She shakes her head in agitation. "This is so damn embarrassing," she rasps out. "You, my neighbors—everyone in this godforsaken neighborhood is being treated to a front-row seat to my family drama."

I nod in understanding but have to do my job at the same time. "Give me the details, so I can get this figured out for you."

Claudia has the right to take her kids, and there isn't a

damn thing Chloe can do. In fact, I'd have to break her heart and let her take them from Chloe's home.

"I want my goddamn children!" Claudia shouts before Chloe can answer me, and she signals to Chloe with a snarl. "That's illegal, you know." Her attention turns to me. "I'd like to report her for kidnapping."

Jesus Christ.

Exactly what I was afraid of.

When I said I wanted less downtime, I wasn't referring to dealing with Claudia's crazy-ass antics.

Chloe tenses, and I can't stop myself from stepping closer to her, my hips meeting hers.

I tip my head down to whisper in her ear, "She's right."

Chloe blows out a series of short breaths before shouting to Claudia, "You've been drinking. Our deal from day one has been I keep them when you've been drinking. I don't trust you to make responsible decisions!"

"I had two beers!" Claudia screams. As much as I want to dispute it, she's not displaying any signs of being overly-intoxicated. "I'm not drunk!"

"I'll be right back," Gage cuts in.

He knows the easiest solution to our problem. Everyone is quiet while he walks to the car and then comes back with a Breathalyzer test in his hand.

"Let's make this easy, so we can all be on our way. If you're under the legal limit, you're good to go." His gaze cuts to Chloe, and he delivers the news with apology. "And I'm sorry, but unless there's a court order, she can take the children with her."

Chloe clenches her fists when Gage tests Claudia first. We are silent as she blows into the tube and wait for her results.

Gage inspects the numbers. "She's good," he calls out.

Chloe curses under her breath. She's so pissed. I wouldn't be shocked if she marched down the stairs and fought Claudia.

"Told you I'm not drunk!" Claudia yells to her.

I drape my arm around Chloe's waist in case she makes an attempt to charge Claudia.

"Not drunk doesn't mean you haven't been drinking *or* that the kids won't be around your hotheaded boyfriend who tends to get angry after drinking too much," Chloe screams back, all worries about neighbors listening be damned.

Roger steps forward while Gage prepares the test for him. "Fuck you, you dumb bitch!"

Gage reaches out, his arm hitting Roger's chest, to stop him from advancing our way. Roger retreats from Gage and sends us a poisonous glare, mainly focused on Chloe.

He then angles his eyes toward me. "Dude," he spits out, "do you know how stupid you look, protecting her?" He's now screaming at the top of his lungs. "She is *using* you! Has she told you her little family secret?" His glare moves back to Chloe. "Of course not. Otherwise, he wouldn't be at your side, you dumb bitch!"

"Kyle," Gage draws out in warning, reading my mind to stop me from impulsively punching Roger in the face harder than I did Kent.

"Shut your goddamn mouth, Roger," Claudia warns, rushing to his side in alarm. She throws down her new cigarette and attempts to pull him away.

Roger doesn't allow it. "Why? The bitch has done nothing to help you."

Gage says my name again as I loom closer to Roger. I'm gulping down my anger, but it's growing more difficult.

Curiosity creeps through me when I peek at Chloe. Her hands are cupped around her mouth, and her face is paler than usual.

Roger uses the back of his arm to wipe his nose before pointing at me. "You sure you don't want to walk in the house, so you can take care of your little brother?" He lets out a sinister laugh. "*Or* maybe it's time your father steps up and supports his bastard son better! Maybe you can be the one deciding who Trey goes home with, considering you're just as much family as Chloe is!"

What the fuck?

My eyes return to Chloe in question. "What is he talking about?"

She's staring at me, shocked and speechless.

"He's drunk," Claudia says, attempting to shoo Roger back to the truck. "Don't listen to a word he says."

"Listen to every word I say, man," Roger replies. "I'm the only person you'll get the truth from, not these two! They've been blackmailing your father for years, ever since Trey was a baby, and accepting checks from him in exchange for their silence!"

I'm not dumb. It's clear what Roger is insinuating. I wouldn't believe a word falling out of his mouth if Chloe didn't look like she was close to passing out and if Claudia didn't appear close to a panic attack.

"Come on, Roger," I say with annoyance. "Stop hinting around the bullshit. Are you saying that Trey is my father's son? That he's my brother?"

They all appear shocked that I was so up-front in questioning his allegations.

"I, uh …" Roger stutters out, suddenly realizing the consequences of his fuckup.

Gage's jaw is dropped open, and he's repeatedly looking from me to Chloe to Roger.

"You need to leave," Chloe croaks out loud enough for everyone to hear. "The kids are sleeping. You've done enough damage for one night. Call me tomorrow to pick up the children."

Claudia and Roger turn around to leave, and Claudia slaps Roger in the back of his head. "You stupid idiot! If I'm cut off, you'd better get a job to make up for the money he gives me!" She hits his back next. "Congratulations! Your big mouth fucked up our lives!"

Gage waits until they leave, Claudia in the driver's seat, and eyes Chloe with a scowl. "I'll be in the car," he informs me without granting Chloe another look.

I wait until he's in the car before turning to start my cycle of questions. "I take it what Roger claims is true? My father is Trey's dad?"

She scrubs her hands over her eyes. "Kyle, it's complicated."

"No, it's really not," I fire back in seconds. "It's a quick yes or no answer."

She nods slowly. "Yes."

I stare at her in disbelief. So much damage to our relationship has happened in ten minutes.

How did I miss this? How didn't I know?

"And why did you keep it from me?"

She's silent as she racks her mind for the best answer, her face unreadable. Chloe is an expert at hiding every emotion flowing through her.

My police radio beeps with a call.

I hold my hand up to stop her. "I need to go. It seems like you need time to come up with your answer. Don't worry about it. I don't fucking care."

With that, I turn around and walk away.

———

GAGE'S FACE is contorted in what almost looks like disgust when I slip back into the car. "Wow," he draws out, as if, like Chloe, he's at a loss for words. "I'm not sure what to say to you right now, except for I'm fucking sorry and I'm here for you, man."

I only nod.

The rest of our shift passes in a blur.

No one gets arrested.

Gage doesn't bring the conversation back up until he pulls into my driveway when our shift ends.

"What are you going to do?" he asks, shifting into park.

My mind races with the endless questions I have for people—Chloe, my dad, my mom, Trey.

"I have no fucking idea," I mutter.

He rubs the back of his neck and moves it from side to side. "Maybe there is a reason she kept it from you."

I scratch my cheek and give him a silent look.

"You know why Lauren kept her secret from me."

"That's different, man. She lied to protect someone you love."

"Chloe lying saved your mom from heartbreak and humiliation," he adds. "There had to be a reason for it."

I scoff. "That'll change tonight. Roger might as well have shouted it from a microphone. People will know, and if Chloe had been up-front with me, we could've talked about it. Roger wouldn't have seen the confusion on my face, and the chances of him running his mouth would've been lower." I shake my head. "I can't be with a liar. I've given her nothing but honesty since we've been together and received nothing but lies and walls up from her. And, not to mention, her taking money from my father in exchange for her silence." I shudder.

He nods. "I understand. Let me know if you need anything, okay? And keep me updated."

"I will."

I open the door and step out, and a heavy feeling knots in my stomach when I glance at Chloe's house. The living room light is the only one on. I contemplate whether to talk to her, but my phone rings, breaking my thoughts, and I tug it out of my pocket.

"Good job with selecting your girlfriend," Sierra yells on the other line when I answer. "Word has already spread about Dad's love child. Cassidy said Mom's crying in her bedroom."

Shit.

My anger flares, and I scowl at Chloe's before walking into my home. "Call Dad and yell at him."

My father cheating on my mom with Claudia—how the fuck that happened is another story in itself—isn't Chloe's fault; I'm well aware of that. Him impregnating Claudia isn't Chloe's fault. I can't be pissed at her for any of those things, but I can be pissed for lying, and I can be pissed that her actions caused my mother pain.

If I hadn't been there, Roger would've never said it. If I hadn't forced myself into her life, this wouldn't be happening. If she had told me, I could've figured out a better way to relay the information to my mother.

But no.

Now, we're in a shitshow.

Roger was told but not me.

How the fuck was he trusted over me?

"Trust me," Sierra says, interrupting my thoughts. "I've called him fifteen times. He's not answering. My issue isn't with Chloe particularly. It's the fact that she came to our house and looked our mother in the eyes without caring about her hoe sister being a homewrecker."

I toss my keys in the bowl and go straight to the fridge for a beer but stop myself. Tonight calls for something stronger. I snag a bottle of Jack, grab a Coke, and make myself a nice, strong drink. "I know. I know. Any advice?"

She blows out a frustrated breath. "It depends on how much you like her. Me? I don't know if I could forgive a guy whose cracked-out sister's boyfriend did what he did. Not to mention, the cracked-out sister's boyfriend said that they'd been blackmailing Dad for money. That's not cool. I need answers. Get answers from her, Kyle."

I grit my teeth and grip my drink as I go to my bedroom to change out of my uniform. "I'm carrying too much anger to ask for answers from her or him at the moment."

She releases a stressed breath. She's as protective of our family as I am. "Understandable. I will blow his phone up all night and am prepared to sit in his office if need be."

I put her on speakerphone to remove my gun from the holster. I slip it in the nightstand drawer and throw on a tee and sweatpants. "Doubt he'll come home tonight."

"He has to eventually."

I down my drink. "Maybe I should join you."

"Not happening. We can't add the mayor's son giving him an ass-kicking on top of the mayor having a love child all in one night."

I make another drink when we end the call.

My next incoming call is from my mom.

I chug my whiskey and pour another when she asks me to stay on the phone with her as she cries and rants about how much she hates my father. I stop myself from throwing the glass across the room.

CHAPTER NINETEEN

Chloe

Age Fifteen

I DIDN'T GO to school today.

I *never* miss school if I can help it.

Today, I couldn't help it.

Couldn't *mentally* survive another day of the taunting.

I made it through yesterday, tears blinding my eyes as I walked home, and cursed Kyle Lane with every step I took. I ate lunch in the restroom and sped to my classes before anyone could see me in the hall. I haven't seen Kyle once after I slapped him.

A few days off from school will prepare me for becoming the target of my bullying classmates.

Kyle has made everyone believe we had sex and that I wanted a *round two*. Heck, I'm glad we never made it to *round one*. Giving him my virginity would've been a giant mistake on top of going to the dance with him.

No more dances or school functions for me.

I slapped him and he deserved it. He had taken me to the dance as a prank straight out of a '90s chick flick—ask the geek to the dance as a joke and then publicly humiliate her.

I'm in my bedroom, reading to Trey, when I hear the front door slam shut. Fear spirals through me. My mother is at her boyfriend's for the week, and it's too early for Claudia to be out of bed. I drop my book at the sound of roaring footsteps and scurry to the corner of my room where a baseball bat is hidden. I settle Trey into the closet behind my clothes and tell him to shush. My sister hangs out with sketchy people, and I've prepared myself in case she pushes one to flip their lid and hurt us.

My door flies open, and Sam stands in my doorway.

"Chloe!" he shouts. "What were you fucking thinking?"

His face is red, fury in his eyes, and a vein in his neck is twitching underneath the skin.

This isn't the Sam I know.

No.

This crazy, irate man isn't him.

"What ... what are you talking about?" I stutter.

"Going to the dance with my son!"

Whoa. What?

"Wait ... Kyle is your son?"

He winces. "How could you not know that?"

I shrug. "I've never seen you two together."

"His mother was in the car with me," he grinds out.

I met Kyle's mom when we went to his house to take pictures before the dance. I didn't notice she was the woman in the passenger seat of Sam's car, but I knew there was one *and* children in the backseat. None of them were Kyle, so I had no idea they were his siblings. I'm not dumb. As soon as I saw them in the car, I knew Sam's secret. He has a family. I said nothing to Claudia, in fear of her flipping out on me or anyone else.

Sam is the least of my worries at the moment.

Well, he was ... *until* now.

I gulp. "I didn't know he was your son."

Sam shakes his head and continues to talk, frustration

lining his features. "You know now, and I know why he's been depressed, wallowing around the house with a broken heart. I'm sure it's over you and the fact that I saw you walking home in the middle of the night for who the fuck knows what reason." He snarls. "Looks like the apple doesn't fall far from the tree with us interested in trailer trash."

I flinch at his words.

Sam has never made me feel ashamed of where I live. That's something I always admired about him.

The tears falling down my face seem to shake off some of his temper.

He bends down in front of me on one knee. "Chloe, I don't want to be mean, but keep your mouth shut about me and your sister. It could end harmful to you."

I silently stare at him.

"You've never seen me here. Got it?"

"I'm sorry …" Tears fall faster with each word. "I didn't know!"

"What the fuck is going on?" Claudia yells, stomping into my room. She stops with her arms crossed. Her eyes turn cold and suspicious when she notices Sam next to me. "What the fuck are you doing in my sister's room?"

Sam stands and wipes his hands down his pants. He points to the closet and keeps his attention on me, ignoring Claudia. "Trey, the whimpering baby you're trying to hide in the closet, *I'm* his father." His finger swings around to the corner of the room where I keep all Trey's essentials. "You see those diapers? *I* pay for them." He gestures to my bedroom. "You like your home?"

Not particularly.

"I'm the one who helps pay the bills here," he says louder before pointing to my sister. "I'm the one who takes care of her *and* puts food in this house."

"You son of a bitch," Claudia yells.

Sam leans back down to meet my eyes. His tone is softer,

but his eyes are full of warning. "Chloe, if you say one word about me ever stepping foot inside here, you'll regret it. You and your entire white-trash family will regret living in this town. Same goes for Trey. If you want him to be safe and well taken care of, you'll keep to yourself. The only times you'll go to school is to learn, and then you'll come back home. Stay away, or you'll be put away."

My heart slams against my chest. *What is going on?*

"I thought you were a good person."

"Here's a quick life lesson for you, Chloe: quit thinking people are good. All you're going to get is let down."

He steps away, bumping into my sister while walking out of my bedroom, and I jump at the sound of the door slamming. I run out into the living room to make sure he's gone.

"Good job, you dumb bitch!" Claudia screams behind me. "Whatever it is he's pissed about, you keep your goddamn mouth shut about it, okay? Sam is someone you don't want to cross. He'll ruin our lives and take Trey from us. Do you want that to happen?"

I shake my head, blinded by tears. "No ... no, of course not."

"Then, what you saw, you take to the grave. Understood?"

"But ... but—"

"There are no *buts*. Now, go to your room and read or whatever the fuck you do." She pauses. "Hold that thought. Watch Trey for a while. I need to blow off some steam after the problems you caused today."

CHAPTER TWENTY

Chloe

ANXIOUSNESS CRAWLS through me when I lock my front door and take small steps over to Kyle's.

It's four in the morning, and I can't sleep. All I can think about is where his head is, though I'm not sure I'll be able to sleep even when I find out.

I want to kick Claudia's ass for telling Roger about Michael being Trey's father. Roger's outburst cost everyone so much. When Michael finds out people know about his secret child, he'll cut Claudia off. She no longer holds any leverage over him. No longer will the *I'll call your wife and expose you* threats work. Michael has supported Trey since his birth, supported our family, and all that will be gone.

Eventually, I came to learn that Sam wasn't Sam's real name. It was Michael. *Mayor Michael Lane*, to be exact. I was shocked at first, but it taught me a valuable lesson—not to trust anyone.

Michael's attorney signed and sent out all payments, so there'd be no trace of Michael being involved. His money put food on the table, gave Trey what he needed, and paid our bills. He promised this in exchange for our silence. When I turned sixteen, those checks were no longer made out to

Claudia. My name was on them, and I cashed them with guilt.

After I graduated from college and started making decent money, I stopped accepting his money. Claudia's threats never stopped, so the checks went back to her.

I can grasp Kyle's anger. I was searching for the right time to tell him. With every call, hang-out, and touch, the desire to unmask the truth was like a knife to my throat. It wasn't my life I would be hurting if I opened my mouth, so it was too risky. Kyle would've confronted his father.

He sees me as a liar and someone who blackmailed his father for financial gain.

"I know it's late, but we need to talk," I say as soon as he answers the door.

I smell the liquor on his breath when he steps to the side to allow me entrance. His glossy eyes confirm that not only can't he sleep, too, but he's also wasted—something I've never seen from him.

There's a glass in his hand, and he takes a drink before replying. "There's nothing to say, Chloe."

I stop, knowing I need to be careful with my words. "If you'll let me explain ..." I should've thought this through before coming over.

"Let you explain?" he shouts, his voice cold and callous. "Let you explain how I spent an hour on the phone with my heartbroken mother, how she's embarrassed the entire town knows, how you chose to keep it from me, *or* how you've been blackmailing my father for *fourteen fucking years*?" He scoffs. "Unless it's to explain any of that, I don't want to hear shit from you." He downs his drink and sets it down. "Were you ever going to tell me?"

I bite into the edge of my lip. "I ... I think so."

"You think so?" he repeats slowly. "When? A year? Two? Never?"

Tears glisten in my eyes. "I can't answer that because I don't know."

"You've been lying this entire time."

I shake my head. "When you asked who Trey and Gloria's father was, I never said I didn't know. I never lied."

His upper lip curls. "Wow, really? I didn't find it necessary to specify *my father*, but I did ask who his dad was."

He did, and I was careful with my wording for this reason.

"I told you he was a deadbeat asshole. That's the truth in my opinion—no offense."

My answer isn't met with approval.

"You also said you didn't know where he was."

Again, I was careful with my words.

"At the time, I didn't know where he was." I press my lips together.

My response only pisses him off further. "Bullshit, Chloe!"

"I never lied to you." I fight to keep my voice strong.

"You selectively left out details."

"I still didn't lie."

He glares. "You've had years to tell me."

Anger surfaces, and I push through the incoming tears. "There was never a reason to tell you! I hated you!"

He lifts his chin. "So, when you were in my bed, you hated me. While I was going to *my brother's* football games, you hated me. When you told me you had feelings for me, it was all a lie, and you hated me?"

I press my finger into my chest. "You came to me, Kyle! I didn't come knocking on your door, asking you to hang out." I swallow hard, and tears are streaming down my face. "I did hate you. I never pursued you in the beginning."

"And perusing you was a big fucking mistake!"

I jump when he throws his glass across the room, and it hits a picture of his family, shattering it.

"One big fucking mistake!" He points to the door. "Leave, Chloe. I don't want you here, and I don't trust you."

I wipe away tears, forcing myself to not give up yet, to not give up on us. "Can you please hear me out?"

"Like you heard me out years ago?" He deepens his tone. "Please, Chloe, it took you years to finally *hear me out.* You had all this time to say something, anything, and you said nothing." A cold laugh rumbles from his throat. "And here I thought, I was falling in love with you." He holds up a finger. "I thought *we* were falling for each other. I'll never trust you again. Mark my fucking words. My father confessed everything to my mother. You and your sister blackmailed him for years, accepting over a hundred thousand dollars, and it didn't stop when we began dating. That's where you crossed the goddamn line. Now, get the fuck out of my house."

"*Please,*" I beg. Salty tears hit my lips, and my chin quivers. I've never been so terrified of losing someone in my life. I inhale a pained breath. "I'm sorry, I really am, but I was protecting my family."

"And that's what I'm doing." He glares at me. "My guilt for what happened in high school is gone. Looks like you got your revenge. Con-fucking-gratulations. Now, you can fuck off."

CHAPTER TWENTY-ONE

Chloe

I NEVER THOUGHT I'd miss Kyle telling me good morning.

It's been two days since we talked. After our four a.m. conversation, I left with tears in my eyes. He was drunk, and there was nothing else I could say to change his mind. I stayed positive, hoping he'd calm down and we'd talk the next day, but nothing.

Claudia is furious, and I'm sure Roger got an ass-kicking when they got back to the trailer. You don't mess with Claudia's money. She told me she'd been blowing up Michael's phone but hadn't heard back from him. I'm surprised he hasn't paid her a visit about her boyfriend spilling the beans. Michael made it clear from day one that, if a word was muttered, his checkbook was closed.

His silence means the Bank of Michael is out of business.

I ignore the looks and whispers when I walk into my office building, but there's no ignoring Melanie. As soon as she sees me, she demands I tell her everything. I do. At least someone will hear me out.

———

I ANSWER the phone when I see Trey's name flashing across the screen.

"Hey, buddy!"

"I hate you!" he screams on the other end.

"Whoa," I say. "What is going on?"

"How could you know and not tell me?" Hurt is clear in his voice.

If I could see his face right now, I'd be in tears.

"How could you not tell me who my father is … that Kyle is my big brother? How could you?"

I open my mouth to speak, but he cuts me off. "I had to find out at school where everyone is calling my mom a homewrecker. I didn't believe it until Cassidy came barreling down the hall in tears, calling Mom the same thing." His voice breaks. "You listened to me ask about my father for years when I was younger, and you told me he was gone. He was in the same town. I could've known him all along."

"I'm sorry," I choke out.

"Did Kyle know?"

"No. He's just as mad."

"Tell him I never want to see him again. He and his family are terrible. And, right now, so are you."

The line goes dead.

———

THE SOUND of my phone ringing drags me away from the article I'm writing. I stretch across the table to grab it.

Kyle Calling.

Maybe he is drunk and wants to remind me of how much he hates me.

Or maybe he's ready to hear me out.

I take a deep breath of courage before answering, "Hello?"

"We have a situation."

A crappy situation from the tone of his voice.

"Jesus, did Trey get busted shoplifting again?"

"It's your sister."

My blood runs cold anytime those words are spoken. "What?"

He groans, and I can imagine him running his hand along his forehead like he does when he's stressed.

"She got picked up for possession. With her record, she's most likely not going home tonight." He pauses as faint yelling comes from the other side of the phone. "She wants to talk to you."

Of course the screaming maniac is her.

Her inebriated voice suddenly slurring on the other line stops me from telling him I have nothing to say to her.

"Chloe! Tell your boyfriend to get me out of this hellhole!"

Oh, now, she wants me to date Kyle.

"He's not my boyfriend," I answer flatly. *Unfortunately.*

"Your fuck buddy. Whatever," she counters with urgency.

I frown. She's saying this in front of people in the station. *Perfect.*

"Where are the kids?" is all I answer.

"The kids? You're worried about them when I'm about to go to *jail*! What kind of sister are you?"

Jesus. This chick. How are we related?

"Yes, I'm worried about your children. I need to pick them up, considering you won't be able to," I reply, not bothering to answer about helping her out. Let her sit there all night or longer for all I care. She's not my main concern.

"They're at school," she finally answers.

"It's too late for them to be at school."

"Then, I'm not quite sure where they are at the moment. You know their schedule better than I do."

"Jesus. I need to go. Hand the phone back to Kyle."

"No! Not until you fix this for me!"

I hang up.

A few minutes later, my phone rings again.

"This'd better be Kyle, or I'm disconnecting the call again."

"It's me," he answers. "Never thought I'd hear you say that on the other line."

"Me either," I mutter. "So?"

"She won't see a judge until tomorrow, concerning her bail … if she'll even receive one. The guys who arrested her said she asked her boyfriend to look after the kids."

"So, she knows where the kids are. She just wouldn't tell me."

"Or she doesn't remember. She's drugged out of her mind. I'm surprised she knew who *you* were. Roger somehow wasn't carrying anything. My guess is, he gave it to Claudia, so we couldn't book him, too. You and I both know that dude isn't someone I'd trust with my children. Call Trey and pick them up. Gage can go with you if you're concerned about your safety. I'll have someone keep you updated about Claudia."

"Don't worry about sending Gage. I'll be fine and figure everything out."

"Good luck, Chloe." His tone isn't one filled with intimacy. He's concerned but still cold. He's doing his job, treating me as he would anyone else in this situation, but it's not the man who told me he was falling in love with me. He's no longer the man I was falling in love with.

"And, Kyle?" I say, hoping to catch him before he hangs up.

"Yes?"

"Thank you."

"I'm not doing this for you. I'm doing it for the kids, and it's my job."

I grab my purse and keep my phone to my ear while walking to my car. "Right … I guess." I stop to find the right words. "Do you ... do you think you can stop by and talk tonight or tomorrow?"

"There's nothing to talk about."

And it's his turn to end the call.

———

I CALL Trey as soon as I get in my car, and he answers with the first ring.

"Where are you?" I ask.

"Mom's," he mutters.

"Who's there with you?"

"No one. We got back from the Y a few hours ago."

Claudia and I set up a schedule where we take turns picking them up from school or the after-school program.

I start the car and reverse out of my driveway. "How did you get home?"

"We walked."

I'm going to kick Claudia's ass. She could've at least asked me to pick them up.

"Why didn't you ask me for a ride?"

"I don't want to call you all the time, and I'm mad at you at the moment."

"I'm coming to get you. Your mom has to go out of town for a few days, so you get to stay with me."

He sighs and lowers his voice. "I already know she was arrested." His voice is filled with disappointment, and I have a feeling it's more for me lying to him *again* than Claudia's arrest.

"Yes, she was arrested. How did you find out?"

"It was here in the trailer park."

"You were home?"

"No, but everyone told me when we got home. Roger said we're supposed to stay with him and not to call you. He left for a beer run about ten minutes ago."

"I'm on my way. Get yourself and Gloria ready."

When I pull up, they're waiting for me outside with bags in their hands. I wish I could say this was the first time we'd done this, but it isn't. Call it a routine for us Fieldgains.

"Mommy's boyfriend told us not to leave!" Gloria says when I get out of my car.

"Yeah, well, Mommy's boyfriend can get over it," I tell her, scooping her up in my arms.

I turn around and notice the squad car pull up across the street. I see Gage on the driver's side.

I strap Gloria into her car seat while Trey gets in.

"Give me a sec," I tell them before heading over to the squad car.

Gage rolls down his window. "He's not here, if that's what you're wondering."

I shake my head and lie. "I wanted to say thank you."

His face turns neutral, but his words are harsh. "You should've told him, you know."

I sigh. "It's complicated."

He nods. "I understand complicated. I've told him to talk to you, but he's stubborn. Don't give up though."

"Aunt Chloe!" Trey yells.

I turn around to look at him.

"We'd better get going before Roger gets back!"

I nod and then glance back at Gage. "Thank you —again."

———

TREY IS SITTING in my living room, throwing a football in the air and catching it, when I walk in after putting Gloria to bed.

He sets the ball aside. "So, uh … the mayor is my dad?"

I tighten my sweater around my chest and slump down on the couch.

I called Trey after he hung up earlier. He's young and confused. He didn't answer my call, but he did text, saying he was okay but needed time to clear his head and had a test to study for. I told him okay, but I'm still not prepared to have this conversation.

"Yes," I reply.

He slowly shakes his head in disbelief. "How? I don't understand. He's ... *him* ... and Mom is *Mom*."

"Trust me; you're not the only one confused."

When I was sixteen, Claudia got drunk and opened up about her relationship with Michael. They'd met at a job fair. Claudia's probation officer had forced her to go look for a job. Instead, she sat in the back parking lot and smoked. That was where she met Michael, who was sneaking out to do the same. They'd talked, hit it off, and exchanged numbers.

He hesitates before asking his next question. "Is it true you made him pay you money not to tell anyone?"

I grimace. "I don't think this is an appropriate conversation for a teenager."

He appears annoyed at my response. "I already know you did."

"It sounds worse than what it was. We didn't hold a gun to his head. He'd offered. He wanted to make sure you were taken care of."

That's the truth. Michael paid Claudia from the beginning, but she took it upon herself to demand more with the threats. With how much money he's given her, I'm surprised he hasn't gone bankrupt.

His face scrunches up. "Is Kyle mad that I'm his brother?"

"Of course not," I assure with a soothing voice. "Everyone was just taken by surprise."

"Did you break up because of it?"

I suck in my cheeks and tilt my head toward his book bag on the floor. "You need to do your homework, and we'll talk about this another time. It's been a long night."

"Kyle was a good dude. Too bad he couldn't be my big brother when I was growing up."

I clutch my sweater around myself tighter, nearly ripping it. "I'm sorry for keeping it from you."

He only nods, grabs his book bag, and pulls out a notebook. "What happens next ... with the whole Mom situation?"

Ease pumps through me for him not asking more Michael-related questions.

"You'll stay here until we figure something out," I state.

His face brightens and then falls. "Roger said Mom told him we could only stay with you if you paid her bail and got Kyle to drop the charges on her."

"I can't convince anyone to drop drug-possession charges."

A flicker of a smile passes over his lips, but he attempts to hide it. "Maybe, we can stay with you now."

CHAPTER TWENTY-TWO

Kyle

SO MUCH HAS HAPPENED in the past few days.

The town is torn on their thoughts about my father. His scandal is nothing out of the ordinary with politics, so him having an affair and illegitimate son won't affect him professionally, but those secrets will alter his public image—our family's public image.

My father left town *for a conference* and won't be back for a few days. He hasn't answered my calls but did take Sierra's. She was a daddy's girl growing up, and I think his affair has hurt her more than the rest of us children. He apologized profusely.

When I visited my mom, she was in the kitchen, and stacks of papers sat in front of her—legal documents, receipts of money transactions, and papers covered with texts. She demanded the documents or threatened a divorce. My father surprisingly had his attorney drop off everything. When I asked if she was leaving him, she only shook her head and grabbed another piece of damning evidence against Chloe.

I sat down and skimmed through them with her, grimacing with every check made out to Chloe for thousands and thousands of dollars. My mom hasn't commented on my involvement with her, but I won't be inviting her to dinner in my mother's home again. *Shit.* Inviting her to dinner, *period.*

When I went back to work, all eyes were on me. People had questions but were too timid to ask them. Then, Claudia was brought in, making everything worse. She talked shit to me the entire time the arresting officers booked her. She announced I was having sex with her sister and threatened to release more family secrets if I didn't get her out of trouble.

I didn't.

Her threats only sped up her booking process.

———

"GIVE THEM TO ME, you stupid cunt!"

The loud voice wakes me. I throw some clothes on, grab my gun, badge, and phone, and rush outside to find Roger standing in front of Chloe's house, throwing rocks at it.

Not again.

I look away from him to see Chloe standing on the porch in her robe, begging him to leave.

I walk closer, and it's no surprise Roger is wasted off his ass. He drops the rocks in his hand when he notices me approaching.

"What's going on here?" I ask.

"He's trying to make me give him the kids," Chloe shouts, worry clear in her voice.

Roger takes a step forward, causing me to do the same and block him from getting closer to Chloe.

"I told the little shitheads not to leave," Roger slurs. "Claudia said they couldn't stay unless she bailed her out. She didn't, so I'm here to collect the brats."

"They're not going anywhere with you," Chloe answers, her hands going to her hips. "Keep throwing rocks at my house all you want. I'll call the cops."

"Why *haven't* you called the cops?" I ask her.

She shrugs. "I didn't know what was going on at first. I came out here, saw him, and figured asking him to leave would be easier than involving the police and having every town bigmouth talking about it tomorrow."

"Roger, you need to call someone to pick you up," I demand. I want him gone, but he's too drunk to drive anywhere.

"Fuck you, dude," he spits. "Go back home. You have nothing to do with this. Don't you hate her now?"

"I'll call one of my friends and ask them to pick you up then." I grab my phone. "You can keep your girlfriend company."

He lets out a cruel laugh. "At least my girlfriend doesn't keep secrets from me."

I freeze up at his words.

I can't help but laugh at myself for my stupidity.

I pull out my phone and call the station while making my way up to Chloe's porch. Douchebag can't say or do anything. Dude is dumb but not dumb enough to fuck with a police officer.

The police cruiser pulls up five minutes later, and they arrest him for public intoxication and disturbing the peace. Chances are, he'll be out tomorrow if he makes bail.

―――――

"THANK YOU," Chloe says when Cliff and Pete leave, Roger in the back of their cop car.

Standing on her porch, I nod in response. I should walk away and go back to my house, but for unexplained reasons, I can't. The need to make sure she's okay, not shaken up, is there ... and so is the need to be near her.

I'm so fucking conflicted, and I'd be lying to myself if I said I didn't miss her.

Fuck, do I miss her.

I miss our mornings, both before and after we started a relationship, our arguing, our sex, the conversations that somehow convinced her to open up to me.

I miss Chloe Fieldgain, but I fucking hate her at the same time.

The porch light shines over us as she leans back against the front door, and I take in the fluffy pink slippers on her feet.

"Are you ready to let me explain myself?" she asks, letting out a breath. "I gave you that chance."

I slip her a glare. "You did, after a goddamn decade, so I'll call you when that time comes."

She grimaces. "Grow up, Kyle, and let's act like adults about this, okay? We've both made mistakes."

"What's there to explain?" I snap back. "It's clear as motherfucking day. I pissed you off in high school, so you got your revenge by blackmailing my family."

She advances a step from the door into my space. "You think that's why I cashed the checks *he offered* us? Over teenage heartbreak?"

A chill hits my core. "I want you to be honest with me."

"Always," she says with no hesitation.

Liar.

I decide against calling her out for it. "Were you ever going to tell me?"

"I don't know. The more I trusted you, I think, yes, I would've eventually." She peeks up at me with a sad face. "Thank you for controlling Roger."

"I did it for the kids," I halfway lie.

"I'm sorry for all this, you know. I never wanted to hurt you or your family. That was never my intention. My feelings for you have been pure from the very beginning. It's going to kill me to watch you walk away from me."

She stands up on her tiptoes and presses her face into my

neck. I can't stop myself from cupping her ass and shifting her close. Her teeth tug at my earlobe, and I don't hesitate to follow her when she leads me into the house to her bedroom.

CHAPTER TWENTY-THREE

Chloe

I HAVE no idea what I'm doing.

I don't seduce men.

I mean, I didn't until now.

A lamp shines in the corner of the room next to my bed, giving me a good view of him. I place my hand over Kyle's mouth as soon as he shuts the door behind us and push him against it. I'll prove to him in every way possible that our feelings are real and not to walk away.

He removes my hand. "You're the screamer, babe. I'll be the one forcing you to be quiet."

Facts.

I smile in return. He doesn't do the same. The stare on his face is packed with pain and desire. He wants me but doesn't. He believes me but doesn't. He wants to work this out but doesn't.

Everything I'm reading on Kyle is confliction.

Let me prove it to you.

I sink to my knees, hastily undo his pants, and lick the length of his cock the moment it springs free. A deep groan leaves his mouth before he catches himself and bites into his lower lip, masking the sounds of his pleasure. It's a shame. I want to hear every word and moan leaving him, but the kids can't hear us. I capture him in my mouth, sucking hard, and hope to erase the hate he has for me. He's smooth as I attempt to use his dick to deep-throat my way back into his heart, as pathetic as it sounds. He won my forgiveness by orgasm; maybe I can do the same with him.

He grows harder with every stroke from my mouth. I get lost in the act and don't tear myself away until he speaks. "Stop, Chloe. This isn't going to finish with my cock in your mouth."

When I stare up at him, he's taking me in with cold eyes and a guarded look. That's when I realize he hasn't touched me. His hands aren't in my hair. This is the first time he's never touched me. Instead, he's made this impersonal, as if I were a random chick he was about to fuck in the restroom of a bar.

I need to give him more.

I rise up on my knees, gripping his thighs, and kiss up his chest—over his tee, his neck, his jaw, moving my way toward his lips. He subtly turns his face away from me.

"Kiss me, Kyle," I embarrassingly plead. "Touch me." *Forgive me.* "Fuck me."

My last two words do the trick. He grips my waist and kisses my hair before crashing his lips to mine. He breaks away to remove his shirt and then palms my breast over my robe.

"Is this what you want?" he whispers into my mouth.

"More than anything," I reply.

He wastes no time before pushing me back toward my bed. My shoulders tighten as he takes me in, and I lose a breath when he harshly tugs the ties of my robe, releasing it, and then tosses it across the room. My panties are torn and flung in the opposite direction.

He twists me around, my back facing him, his broad chest pushing up against me. My knees hit the bed, and I shiver when he reaches out and tucks my hair behind my shoulder.

"You always seem to get what you want, don't you, Chloe?" he hisses in my ear before running his tongue along the lobe.

I gasp when he grips my waist and rubs his hard cock against my ass. I press against him at the same time he guides us up my bed. He lifts himself on all fours while I stay on my stomach, and he lightly feathers a finger down my spine.

"Chloe, how you've ruined me," he says, his finger still skimming my skin.

My hips are raised, and with no warning, he slams inside me before lowering me so that I'm flat on my stomach again. Our legs tangle together, and I'm already close to getting off as he balances himself over me. Our bodies rub against each other's with every stroke, and I don't have the power to move. He carries our weight as he slams into me.

I shove my face into my pillow to mask my moans. I've never had sex like this before. It's angry. It's raw. It's rough. This is a pure hate fuck.

I move my head to the side and bite into his arm as I grow closer, and his hands grab mine, squeezing them as he nears his release.

"Yes, fucking mark me," he grinds out.

He grips harder, and I bite deeper with every push and pull from him.

My pussy constricts against his cock as waves of pleasure hit me, and then I shudder out my orgasm while his hips continue to slam into me until it's his turn to come. When it's time, he pulls out and releases on my back, like I'm some random whore he only wants to come all over.

He falls to the side of me as we fight to catch our breaths, and I already miss the heat and sweat of his body when he rolls off the bed. I start to turn around to see him but jump when he slaps my ass.

"Thanks for the fuck, neighbor," he comments. "I've needed some release."

I jump up to my knees. "Excuse me?"

He grabs his shirt from the floor and then his pants.

"You're not spending the night?"

He throws his shirt over his head without glancing in my direction. "I'll pass. Like I said, I appreciate the fuck. This was fun. Next time you want a quick, meaningless fuck, you know where to find me."

"You're an asshole," I hiss.

"You thought I was an asshole then? Just wait." He leans onto my bed with his palms on each side of me. "You know what's funny? You're exactly like him. A manipulative liar."

With that, he turns around and leaves.

———

I STOMP into my office with fury in my eyes. Fury in my *sleepy* eyes. I was up all night, pissed about Kyle.

"Whoa, killer. Who's on the murder list today?" Melanie asks.

"Kyle motherfucking Lane," I grit out. "I hate him!"

She holds her hand up to stop me and narrows her eyes at me in confusion. "Hold up. Last time we talked, you said you wanted him, and he hated you. Now, you hate him, too? What happened?" She leans back in her chair. "This is getting *very* interesting."

"He came over last night, and we had sex," I confess.

She tilts her head to the side. "Isn't that what you wanted?" She stops to study me for a moment, as if she's missing something. "Was it bad sex or something? Did he leave before getting you off? Start some kinky shit you weren't okay with?"

"No! It was amazing sex!"

"Good boy," she comments with a pleased smile. "So, what's the problem then?"

"The *problem* is, after we finished, he slapped my ass, said thank you, and then left!" I throw my hands up in the air and throw my bag onto the floor. "Who the fuck does that?"

"I told you, hate sex is the best sex," she replies. "Nothing beats pent-up frustration like rough sex that ends with someone telling the other to fuck off." She chews on the pen in her hand as if this isn't a big deal.

I grab my bag from the floor while still looking at her. "Remind me why I talk to you about my problems. Hate sex might be *the best sex*, but the after-party of hate sex fucking sucks."

She shrugs. "Look on the bright side; you guys are making progress in the shitshow that is Kyle and Chloe's relationship. Yesterday morning, he wanted nothing to do with you. Now, he's jamming his cock into your vagina. Things are looking up, my friend."

"No. Things are looking more along the lines of homicide. Be prepared to finally get a new job because I'll be in prison."

She laughs before her face turns soft. "Give him time, Chloe. Was it a dick move? Absolutely. The man is pissed, and his ego is bruised."

"I'm not giving him shit, except sliced tires, so do you have any better advice?"

"At the moment, no, but let me drink some coffee, answer some emails, and take a two-hour lunch break, and then I'll get back to you."

"I'm screwed," I mutter before walking into my office.

CHAPTER TWENTY-FOUR

Chloe

CLAUDIA CALLING.

I hit Ignore.

It's her fifth call in a row.

I don't have time for her bullshit games today.

My phone beeps with a text.

Claudia: Quit ignoring my calls!

They released her from jail days ago. Surprisingly, the judge had granted her bail. Also surprisingly, Roger had paid it. She hasn't seen the kids or picked them up from my house, but the weekend is over. Claudia always waits until the weekend ends to threaten me with seeing them if I don't give her money.

An hour later, Claudia comes storming into my office with Melanie on her trail.

"I tried to stop her," Melanie says, shooting Claudia a scowl before looking at me. "But I figured you'd frown upon me tackling your sister to the ground."

A smile twitches at my lips. *Right now, probably not.*

"I appreciate that."

Melanie isn't a Claudia fan, and this isn't the first time my sister has barged into my office, barking out demands.

Melanie throws Claudia another dirty look before leaving and makes sure to shut the door behind her. Claudia tends to get loud during her visits.

Claudia plops down on the chair in front of my desk. She's sporting the hungover look, complete with dark circles under her blue eyes and last night's makeup smudged across her face.

"Your secretary is a bitch," she snarls.

I fold my hands together, set them on my desk, and lean forward. "No, she isn't. Now, what's so important that you felt the need to visit me at my work, which I've asked you numerous times not to? This is a public office, not a place for me to handle my family issues."

Claudia has never taken my job seriously. Oftentimes, it seems like she *wants* me to lose it.

She rolls her eyes. "I need money."

I cut her off before she can elaborate. "No."

She winces. "But—"

I interrupt her again. "I said, no."

"You're a goddamn bitch," she seethes. "I hate you."

The feeling is mutual.

I shrug. "If that's how you feel, then that's how you feel."

She bows her head. "I'm in trouble, and Michael still isn't answering my calls."

"That's nothing new, Claudia. You're always in trouble, and your reasoning for needing money is never-ending, dramatic, Shakespearian bullshit. If Michael isn't giving you money, go back to the job you quit."

She lifts her chin and glares at me while I'm fighting with myself not to cave in. I'm a habitual pushover when it comes to Claudia. Eventually, I grow tired of her pleading and give in. That's not happening today.

She lowers her voice. "Roger and I owe some men money." She continues before I get the chance to confirm she won't receive a cent from me. "Roger borrowed additional money on top of our debt to pay my bail!"

"How precious of him," I mutter. "He lives in your home, rent-free. He should help you."

"They're dangerous, Chloe. They can hurt me!"

"You are adults and capable of paying your own debts. I'm done bailing you out of your messes. Last time, when I said it was the last time, I wasn't lying." I push my hands forward before doing a scraping them clean motion. "No more."

"What about the kids then, huh? Are you not concerned with their safety?"

"They are safe at my house."

"*Please*, Chloe." She's close to tears, and I'm close to caving. It happens every single time. She knows what works on me. "*Please.*"

Don't do it. Don't do it.

"I've given you thousands of dollars to help you, and you've done nothing but blow it on booze and taking care of your deadbeat boyfriends. No more. Nothing."

"My kids need to eat," she grits out before pushing her fingers through her greasy hair.

"Then, I will buy them food."

"They need heat and electricity."

"I have both at my house. They can stay with me."

"What about me, huh? Do you not care if I'm cold and hungry?"

"If you need to sleep in my spare bedroom, you can, but you'll be pulling your shit together. No drugs. No Roger. There will be rules." I shut my eyes in dread. Babysitting Claudia is harder than babysitting both Trey and Gloria.

"I don't want to live with you," she snaps.

I fix my stare on her. "That wasn't a friendly invite. It was a desperate offer."

She jumps up from the chair and wags her finger in my direction. "Fuck you, Chloe! Fuck you! Expect not to see the kids this week *or ever*!"

My blood pressure rises with every second we're speaking. "Don't make the children suffer out of spite and deprive them of a life we wanted when we were children."

Her hand splays across her chest. "Are you saying you'd be a better mother for them?"

I rub my forehead. "I'm not trying to be their mother. I'm trying to give them a better life—whether it's as their aunt or even their friend. They are my number one priority, and they will always be my number one priority. *Period.*"

Her lipstick-messy lip curls up as she releases a hard laugh. "God, you're so desperate for children that you'd even take someone else's."

I slam my hand down on my desk and stand. "Now, it's my turn to say fuck you." I jerk my finger toward the door. "Leave my office."

She scrambles back, and regret flashes across her face. It takes her a few moments to plaster on a fake smile. "Sorry, that was wrong of me to say."

I shake my head and keep my finger pointed. "Save your apology. You meant it. You've meant it every time you've said it. Shove that apology up your ass."

She uses both hands to flip me off, dropping one momentarily to open the door, and then puts them back in the position as she walks backward out of my office, and from the sound of Melanie's laughter, I'm assuming she's doing the same to her.

I'm still standing when Melanie wanders into my office minutes later.

"You should've let me tackle her, babe," she says before circling around the desk to droop her arm over my shoulders. "You are one strong-as-hell woman, and I'm so fucking proud of you for not letting her walk all over you." She squeezes my shoulder before stepping back. "If you need help with the kids, I'm here." Her head tilts to the side. "None of them are in diapers, right?"

"One hundred percent potty-trained."

"Perfect. If you need help with the kids, you let me know."

I smile. "Your bad humor is always what I need on stressful days."

"I'm here all day, folks." She stops to correct herself. "Or at least until five."

She scurries away at the sound of the front desk phone ringing, and I snatch up my phone to text Trey. It's his lunch hour, so hopefully, he has his phone.

Me: I'll pick you up after school today.

My phone beeps with a response seconds later.

Trey: Mom said to go with Roger.

Me: I'll deal with your mom and Roger.

They're always tardy, picking them up from school. If Claudia wants the kids, she'll come to my house. Today isn't the first time Claudia has said her life is in danger. Normally, when she says that, I grab my wallet. Even though I don't one hundred percent believe her, doubt is still in the back of my mind, and I worry about the kids' safety. Hell, I'm *always* concerned with their safety.

Let them come to my house.

I'll be ready for that fight.

––––––––

I'M NOT surprised when Roger and Claudia show up at my doorstep hours after school let out. Their breath reeks of alcohol, and the dilated pupils and scabs on Roger's face confirm my suspicions that he's using more than alcohol for getting high.

"I want my goddamn children," Claudia screeches as soon as they come in.

I cross my arms. "Tough shit."

I gulp and stand straight even though my heart is pounding when Roger lunges my way. Him coming closer results in Trey stepping to my side. Claudia scoffs, and a cynical laugh leaves Roger at Trey's protective gesture.

This isn't going to end well.

"Look at this badass," Roger barks out, signaling to a fuming Trey.

Trey's jaw is clenched, and his hands are knotted into fists. There's a *finally fed up* expression on his face. Roger pressing him will make things worse between everyone.

"Fuck you," Trey bites out. "We don't want to leave with you." His attention swings to Claudia. "I refuse to stay with you and your"—he tips his head toward Roger—"piece-of-shit boyfriend. You'll have to drag me out."

"That can be arranged, you little asshole," Roger grits out before lunging toward Trey.

I kick my foot out, tripping Roger, and the floor vibrates when his body hits it. I use Trey's shirt to pull him to the other side of the room while Roger gets up, and I rush to my purse.

"Stop!" I yell. "I'll give you the fucking money. Hold on!"

The angry look on Roger's face is why I'm giving in. I'm not risking the kids' or my safety.

"Twenty-two hundred dollars," Claudia demands, kissing Roger's cheek in celebration of their win. "We'd prefer cash, but a check will do if you don't have that much on you."

"I'm not giving you twenty-two hundred dollars," I say, shuffling through my bag until I find my wallet.

"If you want to keep them, that's how much I want," Claudia replies. "Take it or leave it."

Trey takes a step forward and scowls at his mother in repulsion. "Whoa, whoa. Are you *selling* us for twenty-two hundred dollars?" He peers over at me with disbelief. "Is that what you're giving her the money for? So we can stay here?"

Instead of answering him, I collect all the bills from my wallet, step forward, and shove it into Claudia's chest. "There's three hundred dollars. That's all I have and all you're getting. If you take it, you'll leave and let the children stay here. You will not come tomorrow, begging for more money. This is your one chance. Take it or leave it."

Roger snatches the money from her hand, counts it, and motions to the door.

"Fine," Claudia draws out. "But I want them for the holidays."

I nod. "I'll let them spend a few hours with you."

"I'm not spending a minute with her!" Trey screams.

"I don't want to spend the holiday with your selfish ass," Claudia spits out. "I only want to see your sister."

"I want to see Mommy!"

Our attention goes to the hallway where Gloria is standing.

Perfect.

Hopefully, she didn't witness too much of what just happened.

"Of course, honey," Claudia says, leaning down and gesturing for Gloria to come over. "I'll be here to pick you up."

Gloria barrels down the hallway, right into her arms, giving her a hug. Claudia wraps her arms around her and squeezes her tight. It's moments like this: where Claudia attempts to be a decent and loving parent that I somewhat feel bad for her, but then I remember how she operates. She'll promise Gloria everything under the sun and then disappoint her. Then, I'll be the one to pick up the pieces.

Gloria is the only person who says good-bye when they leave.

CHAPTER TWENTY-FIVE

Kyle

Two Weeks Later

UNLESS FIREWORKS ARE INVOLVED, holiday shifts are uneventful.

So far, this Thanksgiving, there hasn't even been a failed deep-fried turkey attempt, so for the past two hours, Gage and I have been sitting idle in the car, talking shit to each other.

"Go talk to Chloe," Gage says, repeating the same thing he's said daily. "You look like hell."

I take a swig of my coffee and settle it in the holder before answering him. "I look like hell because I had to survive a family dinner where the table conversation involved my ex-girlfriend's family blackmailing my father out of thousands of dollars."

He nods in understanding, but his words are the opposite of that. "A—quit being so dramatic. I know it fucking hurts to be lied to, but it happened. B—listen to her side of the story. You've only heard your father's, who's a man you can't stand, by the way." He sighs. "Do you remember what happened when Lauren hid secrets from me and wouldn't explain herself?"

"Yes, you skipped town for years." I grab my coffee and bump his shoulder with the side of the cup. "Is that what I'm supposed to do?"

"No, that's what I don't want to happen. Skip that part. From experience, I can tell you, it's miserable. Talk to her. Maybe you can work shit out."

"Even if we do work shit out, what am I supposed to tell my family? They hate her."

"Your family is understanding and forgiving."

"And you're usually not, so what gives? Why are you all of a sudden Team Chloe?"

"Let me make this clear; I'm always Team Motherfucking Kyle. *Always.* As for that, I see this is tearing you apart. You liked her, or still like her, but won't listen to her side of the story. No matter what, you owe her that." He inhales a deep breath. "When everything came to the surface with why Lauren did what she did, a heavy weight was lifted off our shoulders. It was the push we needed to move on and be happy. Be grateful Chloe isn't making you wait years." He blows out a breath. "I'm not telling you to get back with her. All I'm saying is, clear the air. You're pissed, I get it, but all of this is because of your father."

"I hate when you're right," I grumble. "Maybe—" I'm interrupted by the dispatcher's voice on the police radio, informing us of a car accident report.

"On it," Gage replies to her. "We're only minutes away from the scene. Call the medics just in case."

He flips the lights, and the car sirens blare through the dark streets and pouring rain. It becomes difficult to see once we hit the unlit back road.

"There," I say, pointing to the view of bright headlights.

He swerves over to the side of the road, and we both jump out as soon as the car is in park. An old sedan is crashed into a tree, the lights shining bright, and smoke is coming from the hood. We sprint through the field to the car, hostile rain showering down on us.

I'm there first, and I shine my flashlight into the driver's side to find a woman. She's motionless, her forehead resting on the steering wheel. A bottle of opened vodka and drug paraphernalia is in the passenger seat. I hold the light while Gage manages to open the door.

He rushes to take her pulse. "Still alive."

A rush of relief hits me. "Thank God." I move my attention to the backseat. "There's a passenger."

I'm soaked, blinking away the drops hitting me, and the door creaks when I open it. I flash my light on the backseat, and fear twists through my stomach. A chill colder than the icy rain pelting my face runs through my veins. My heart sinks into my stomach while an intense pain hits me.

"No!" I scream with a shaky voice while crawling to the body slumped against the backseat. She's half off the seat, and her cheek is resting against the floor. "No!"

"Motherfucker!" Gage yells behind me, and I hold a breath before checking her pulse. "Kyle, talk to me!"

I cradle the body in my arms, my chin trembling, and I look back to see EMTs running our way with a gurney.

"Here!" I scream at the top of my lungs. "Here now! Help me!"

I crawl out and carefully help them pull the limp body from the car.

The EMT looks at me with dread and confirms what I already know. "DOA."

I step in front of them, and my breathing is ragged as I attempt to do CPR.

Gage comes to my side, grabs my elbow, and stops me. "Brother, don't."

"No!" I yell, my hands going back to her chest. "Let me try! I can fix this!"

"I'm sorry," the EMT says. "Even with CPR, which will do more damage to her body, there's nothing we can do to save her. There's severe blunt force trauma to the head, and she's lost too much blood."

She looks at me with wide eyes filled with sadness. "Trust me, if there was anything I could do, I'd be fighting for it right now."

I scrub my hand over my face and scream before looking at the EMTs helping the driver onto another gurney.

"You stupid bitch!" I yell, advancing toward her.

All my morals dissipate in this moment, and it's scary to say there's no doubt in my mind that I could walk away from this scene without giving the driver a second look.

Gage throws his arm out to stop me while the EMTs look at me as if I've lost my mind. "Kyle, calm down!" He tilts his head toward the EMTs moving the passenger up the hill. "Help them get her into the ambulance!"

I nod, turn around, and run up the hill. Even though putting her in the ambulance won't stop the outcome of tonight, she deserves to be out of the rain, deserves a lot more than this. I don't slide into the warmth of the car after I help them. They shut the door in my face, the sirens wailing through the unlit road.

Gage helps the medics with the driver when the second ambulance leaves shortly after the first. We silently stand there, soaked, staring at the scene, wishing we could've changed it, that we could've driven faster, run faster, saved her.

"You need to go, Kyle," Gage finally says. "The investigators are on their way to the hospital, and I'll meet them there to tell them everything. If they need any additional information, they'll call you."

"No," I grit out. "I want to be there."

"You're too pissed to go there, and the investigators will immediately make you go home out of conflict of interest.

Monroe is on his way here, and we're driving to the hospital. You have somewhere else to be."

I get into the car, drive home, and sprint to a porch that isn't mine.

The door swings open.

"Kyle?"

CHAPTER TWENTY-SIX

Chloe

I BLINK a few times as if I'm imagining Kyle standing in front of me. Water drips from every inch of him, and my stomach knots at the sight of his trembling hands. Anguish covers his face like a blanket while he stares at me with fear-stricken eyes.

What the …

This is unexpected.

"Chloe. Can I come in?"

His question snaps me to my senses. "Of course," I answer, moving aside to allow him room to step into the entryway. "You must be freezing." I shut the door behind us. "Let me grab you a towel." I'm stopped when he reaches out and closes his cold hand around mine.

"I don't need a towel." He squeezes my hand, and water falls along my bare toes when I look into his damp-lashed eyes. "We need to talk."

This isn't a courtesy visit.

"What's going on, Kyle?" I question.

Do I want to know?

Instead of answering me, he lightly touches my shoulder with his free hand and brushes away a strand of loose hair fallen from my ponytail. "Let's sit down."

Dread falls upon me as he leads me to the couch, and I sit on the edge of the cushion. "Please tell me what's going on," I stammer out. "You're scaring me."

He retreats a step and casts me a terrified glance. "There was an accident."

The tone of his voice heightens my panic. This *accident* will affect me. I don't speak. I wait for him to continue. I wait for him to break me down more than what I already am.

He drops to his knees only inches away and clears his throat. He blinks away tears before using his arm to wipe them away again.

He stares up at me with a pale face, and his voice cracks as he prepares to deliver bad news. "Your sister ..." He pauses, as if searching for the right words. "She hit a tree while driving."

I jerk my head back. "What? Is she going to be okay?"

His jaw clenches. "She's on her way to the hospital right now."

A burst of relief hits me. "Thank God." That relief suddenly filters into dread. "Gloria ... Gloria is with her tonight. Is she at the hospital with her? Is everything all right?" I pull away from him and jump up in search of my purse. "I need to go get her."

Kyle stands. "Chloe ..." He says my name in caution, as if I were about to walk off a cliff.

My heart caves into my chest as dread sets in. "I have to go to the hospital. I need to get Gloria."

"Chloe ..." His voice deepens as he erases the gap between us.

I push his chest and hold my finger up in front of him. "Don't." I walk away from him, and my voice trembles. "Don't you dare fucking say it!"

He grabs my shoulders, turns me around, and drags me into his chest. "Gloria was in the car with her."

"Don't you say it," I whisper, stifling a scream. "Don't you dare fucking say it!"

His hold on me tightens, and his lips brush against my hair. "I'm so sorry, Chloe."

"No! No!" I yell, flares of anger shooting through me as he grasps me. I struggle to break free. "Let me leave, Kyle!" My arms fly in every direction, and I'm certain they've made contact with him a few times, but he doesn't flinch, just keeps a secure hold on me.

"You're not driving in this condition," he says.

My body shakes. "I need to go to her!"

He pulls in a thick breath. "There's nowhere to go for her."

Kyle doesn't have to tell me. I already know.

"Whoa, whoa," Trey interrupts while stepping into the room, yawning. "What's going on in here?" He shoots Kyle a hard glare before puffing out his chest.

Kyle loosens his hold on me and makes sure I'm not a runner before releasing me completely. "Hey, buddy. Why don't you go to your room for a minute?" he tells Trey.

I rub my face, my eyes, my arms. My hands need to be busy or else I'll throw something across the room.

"I'm not going anywhere," Trey replies with a clenched jaw when he notices the condition I'm in. "Why are you here?"

I gulp and press my hand into Kyle's stomach, stopping him from telling Trey. I need to do it. I have to do it. Kyle only nods, and I make my way to Trey.

"There was an accident with your mom and Gloria," I whisper. "A car accident."

Trey tenses but stays quiet.

"Gloria ..."

Concern flickers across his face. He helped raise Gloria and was more of a father to her than her own. He was the one who made sure she went to school, had every meal, and did her homework.

"What happened to her?" Trey grits out with knotted fists.

"I'm sorry, honey, but Gloria ..." I glance over at Kyle for confirmation, just in case I'm wrong, and he gives me a solemn nod. I shake my head before giving him a look of desperation. I need him to say it, to make the final call, because those words can't leave my mouth. I'm too weak.

Kyle gives me another nod and steps to my side. "Gloria passed away tonight, Trey." His tone isn't one of a policeman breaking the news to an unsuspecting family. He's heartbroken. He feels for Trey. For *us. For Gloria.*

Trey's face twists in pain as he registers Kyle's statement, and his hands start shaking. "What? How? No, this can't be true. I saw her earlier today. She was fine. We went on a walk, and she told me about the new book she checked out from the library! She was fine!" His eyes change from a hardened state to a fearful one. "You're wrong, man. You're wrong!" Trey says with tears streaming down his face.

I rush forward to hug him. He shrugs away and pulls his phone from his pocket but is unable to hold it with his shaking hands. It falls to the floor, the thud ringing out through the grave silence, and he reaches down and picks it up in haste.

"I'm calling Mom," he explains, punching his fingers against the screen. "She'll tell you everything is okay. They're probably eating ice cream while Gloria talks about her dolls."

"Trey," Kyle says softly.

"No!" he screams. "I'm calling her! You've made a mistake!"

He holds the phone to his ear as tears slide down his face. "Pick up, Mom. Please. Just pick up the phone." His shouts grow louder. "Pick up!"

I know it goes to voice mail when he blurts out, "Goddamn it."

He starts to dial again, but Kyle takes the phone from him.

Surprisingly, Trey doesn't fight him for it back. Instead, he sinks down on the couch, his face stricken with tears. I rush over, wrapping my arms around him, capturing his loud sobs in my shoulder.

"I'm so sorry," I say over and over again while brushing my hand over his hair. "I'm so sorry, Trey."

His face is red when he pulls away. "Mom?"

"She's in the hospital right now. I'm not sure what's going on, but she's alive," I answer.

"I want to kill her," Trey blurts out. "I don't care what anyone says! She deserves to die for taking my sister away from me!" It's sad that Trey knows his mother well enough to know she played a part in Gloria's death—a destructive part.

I stroke Trey's back while he attempts to contain his hurt. When he starts to calm down, I inhale a deep breath and look at Kyle. I forgot he was there while I consoled Trey.

I calm my voice, and it turns flat. "I need you to drive me to the hospital, please. I need someone to scream at, and that somebody is Claudia."

Tears threaten his eyes as he stares at me. "I can't do that, Chloe. Even if I could, you wouldn't be able to see her since it's an ongoing investigation," he says, his voice almost cracking mid-sentence.

I ask, "When did it happen?" at the same time Trey asks, "How?"

He comes closer. "We're not entirely sure yet. Claudia was driving. Gloria was in the backseat, unbuckled, and there was no car seat either. The details are limited, and normally, we aren't supposed to notify anyone until all the details are confirmed, but I couldn't do that to you."

I nod—a silent thank-you. He nods back—a silent you're welcome.

"This is all my fault," Trey mutters. "It's all my fault for refusing to go with Mom tonight for her visitation. If I had been there, I could've stopped it from happening. I could've protected my baby sister."

I wrap my arm around Trey's shoulder and drag him into me again. "Trey, listen to me. This is in no way your fault."

It's my fault.

I allowed her to go with Claudia against my better judgment. Claudia was doing better after I gave her the cash. She dumped Roger. She threw no tantrums, no asking for money and no threatening to take the kids. She was sober and excited to spend time with Gloria when I dropped her off at the trailer. She never mentioned them leaving.

Kyle kneels down in front of Trey. He's fighting back his own pain. He didn't know Gloria for long, but the expression on his face shows he cared for her.

"We don't know if it's anyone's fault yet," he replies in a soothing voice. "It could've been weather or vehicle-related."

It was Claudia.

It's always fucking Claudia.

Even if the accident wasn't her fault, losing Gloria was. Claudia didn't have her in a car seat. She didn't protect her.

"Was she drunk? High?" I question.

"We won't know anything until the toxicology reports come back," Kyle answers.

"Don't bullshit me," I snap.

He sighs, terrified to tell me. "There was an opened alcohol bottle and drug paraphernalia in the vehicle." His voice softens. "I know there's nothing I can say or do for you" —his attention moves to Trey—"but I'm here. If you need *anything,* I'm right here."

No. He's not hitting me with this nightmare and then ending the conversation like this. I will not be given the *I'm sorry for your loss; I'm here* bullshit. I want my goddamn niece back in her goddamn bed with her goddamn dolls. I want goddamn answers.

I jump up from my seat. "Watch Trey." I sprint across the room and snag my keys. "I'm going to the hospital."

I make it outside, nearly to my car, when Kyle stops me. I fight him again, soaking wet this time, as he drags me back inside, slides my keys into his pocket, and locks the door.

"Chloe, you can't do that right now. As soon as the doctors give us the go-ahead, we can question her. Until then, it's better for us to sit here and wait."

"Sit here and wait?" I scream. "Claudia is not getting out of this, Kyle. She does not get to heal or rest. She doesn't even deserve another ounce of breath for what she did! You know who deserves that?" I seethe. "*The little girl she neglected!* That *I* neglected. That's who deserves it. Not you." I push him back again. "Not me." My finger shoves into my chest. "She was only four fucking years old!"

Kyle lets me take my anger out on him and waits until I'm finished before speaking. "As soon as I can, I'll take you to her. I swear it. I'll let you say whatever you need to without anyone stopping you, okay?"

"Where do we go from here?" I whisper.

"You grieve and let me handle the rest." He tilts his head toward Trey. "You two take care of each other."

He moves from me to Trey and pulls him into a hug. "I'll be home all night. Come over. Call. Anything you need, I'm here."

"Will you ... will you hang out here longer?" Trey asks, peering up at him.

"Of course," Kyle answers. He says it with no question, no hesitation, no asking for permission.

The rest of the night, I'm numb. Angry. Like I'm not even present or alive. I walk through my house, emotionless, consoling Trey. I take phone calls, give police information, and answer as many questions as I can, but mentally, I'm checked out, not with it. I feel nothing, and along with feeling nothing, I can't process my loss.

I go to bed with tears in my eyes.

When Kyle comes into my bedroom later, I don't stop him.

When he holds me as I fight myself to sleep, I don't stop him.

When I do fall asleep and wake up in the middle of the night, jerking from a nightmare, and he tightens his hold on me, I don't stop him.

He does it again and again.

His arms never leave my body. His voice in my ear is soothing.

And that confirms more than I already know.

This man I love has a heart of gold and deserves someone less messed up, less deceitful than me.

CHAPTER TWENTY-SEVEN

Chloe

THE WARMTH of Kyle's chest brushes against my back when I wake up, and his arm is draped along my waist—a security blanket. My heart sinks, the tears simmering, when my memory is refreshed from last night's nightmare. It wasn't a nightmare. It was my reality.

I wince and inhale a sharp breath, feeling too numb to move.

Grief. Hurt. Regret.

They sucker-punch me. It seems surreal, and I'm nearly tempted to roll out of bed, pad down the hallway, and go to her room in hopes that I'll find her sleeping. But it'd break me more. She's gone. I failed her.

His arm tightens around me when he realizes I'm awake.

"Hi," he simply says in a subdued voice.

I swallow. Even though his nearness provides comfort, it won't erase what he said and did the last time he was here. That's not important to bring up right now though. I'm too exhausted to fight, to nearly speak.

The sheets fall down my body, and his arms leave me when I sit up. My head spins, and seconds later, I'm close to falling back down. His arm curls around my stomach just in time, and a glass of water is offered my way.

"Here, drink this," he whispers as I turn to face him.

"Thank you." I gulp it down, realizing how dry my mouth was.

"What do you need me to do for you?" he asks, his tone gentle and kind, as if he's prepared to pull the weight of my pain off me.

"I need to see Claudia," is all I answer.

She got last night—more time than she deserved—and there's no way I can make it through the day without confronting her.

He nods. "Do you want me to stay with Trey?"

"Please."

"Of course. Anything you need, I'm here, Chloe."

"Thank you."

"Always."

———

I WAIT for Trey to wake up before leaving for the hospital. He walks into the kitchen with droopy shoulders, red eyes, and a puffy face, wearing the same clothes from last night. Even now, he looks to be on the verge of tears.

An hour after Kyle arrived and told us about the accident, Trey left for his bedroom with a bowed spine, and this is the first time I've seen him since.

I checked on him before going to bed, asking if he was all right through his closed door, and received a simple, "I'm fine."

He opens the fridge, snags a bottle of water, and leans back against the door after shutting it. "Are you going to see her today?"

I nod while sitting at the kitchen table. "I am."

I eventually pulled myself together, showered while having

practice conversations in my head of what I wanted to say when confronting Claudia, and then dressed before walking into the kitchen. Kyle was waiting with a coffee cup in his hand, and worry lined his features.

"Tell her I hate her fucking guts," Trey says in a flat, monotone voice, not seeming apologetic or concerned for his language.

I don't scold him because I don't blame him. Those words have been on the tip of my tongue since last night.

"I want you to say it," he goes on. "Word for word. Tell her I'm no longer her son and to forget about me." Tears lace his eyes again. "Tell her I'll never forgive her for taking my baby sister away from me. If there's anything you can do for me right now, Aunt Chloe, it's to relay that message to her. If you don't, I'll call an Uber and do it myself."

I gulp and stumble for the right words before speaking. "Do you want to go to the hospital with me?" *Say no.*

Even though I don't want him to, he deserves the choice. It's his mother. It was his sister she killed. He deserves it just as much as I do.

He shakes his head while tightly gripping the water bottle in his hand. "I never want to see her again. She should've died instead of Gloria. She's the one who deserved it."

Kyle finally steps into the conversation, clearly uncomfortable with Trey's choice of words. "I know you're angry."

Trey interrupts him. "No, dude, don't even. There's no talking me down from my hate toward her. I've thought about it all night. I couldn't sleep because all I could think about was, it's her fault I'll never see my sister again. She's not my mother. She's nothing to me." His sadness turns into anger. "I need to shower."

I stand up when Trey starts to leave the kitchen. "Trey."

He holds his palm out. "Just leave me alone for a while, okay?"

Kyle pulls out the chair next to mine when Trey leaves. "Are you sure you're ready to do this?"

"I was ready for it last night." I tilt my chin up to stare at him. "You need to swear to me, she won't get off the hook for this."

He takes my hand in his. "I promise I'll do everything I can for her to get what she deserves."

———

I'M FILLED with fury when I slam the door shut behind me, and I don't care who can hear when I scream my words out, "I fucking hate you!"

Claudia is in front of me, relaxing in a hospital bed, with IVs in her arm. One of her hands is cuffed to the bed rail. I don't know her condition or diagnosis, and I don't know if she'll even tell me. Right now, I don't even care.

A large bandage is stretched along her forehead, a dark bruise is around her eye, and there are scratches and cuts along her neck. Her blonde hair is matted along her hairline, and her eyes are slanted. I hate that she's here, hate that she was saved and given treatment even though she killed Gloria.

She looks down, playing with her hands, and shrugs. "What's new, Chloe?" The regret is clear on her face. She knows what she did, the part she played in Gloria's death. "You think I don't feel bad?" she yells. "You think I don't have to live with this guilt every day?"

I swallow. "Good. I hope it haunts you until you take your last breath." I step closer to her bed, and she tenses up. "Not only were you driving under the influence, but you were also too lazy and stupid to put her in a car seat. What were you thinking? I told you I'd pick her up after you were finished visiting!" I curl my hands into fists and stop myself from punching her in the face, my anger getting the best of me.

She rubs her head. "I wanted to take her out for a drive. I

wanted to be a normal mom for once and drive my daughter around."

"Stop with the fucking lies! They found your phone. You were meeting a drug dealer." I grip my hands around the bed rails and tilt my head forward until I'm in her face, not even bothered that she might be the one to punch me. "She's gone because you needed to get high."

"Fuck you!" Spit flies out with her words. "She was my child!"

I draw back, and my lips curl. "A child you never bothered to take care of. A child you failed."

"I want you to leave."

"I don't care what you want. You're going to lie there and listen to every single word I say because this will be the last visit I'll ever give you. If they give you a trial, which I'll fight for, I'll be there, but this will be our last conversation. Do you hear me?" I point my finger at her. "So, sit back, shut up, and listen to me tell you how much I fucking hate you. Listen to me tell you I will fight until the death of me to make sure you get in trouble for this."

She scratches her head. "Say whatever you want, Chloe. Make me feel like a piece of shit, like you've done since you were a kid."

I pace in front of her bed, holding my tongue the best that I can.

"I want to see Trey," she says, her voice scratchy. "I want to tell him I'm sorry and see him one more time."

That catches my attention, and I shift to face her. "Tough shit. He doesn't want to see you."

"Don't lie to me," she bites out.

"If he decides he wants to see you at any time, I'll give him that." I pause while briefly debating on whether to relay the message he gave me. "He said he hates your guts and you're dead to him." I'll give that to Trey. Right or wrong, he deserves to have his voice.

Her face and tone turn spiteful. "He might hate me, but as a minor, he has no say in what happens in his life. He can't stop me from demanding he live with his father instead of you."

I stumble back a step, her words catching me off guard. I pull in a sharp breath and straighten my back, appearing to brush off the threat lined between her words. "Not only is there no physical proof that Michael is Trey's father, I doubt he'll step up. Nice try though."

She shakes her head. "That's where you're wrong. Michael's name is on the birth certificate."

I gulp. "You're lying."

The corners of her mouth tilt up in a cold smirk. "He made me take a DNA test to prove Trey was his before supporting us. They already paid me a visit. They want to take him now that I'll be in jail."

"Bullshit. Michael never wanted Trey."

"True, but Michael is eating crow to regain his wife's trust, *and* how bad will it look if he turns his back on his son? They'll give him a stable home environment."

My snorting interrupts her. *Stable my ass.*

"I'll do everything in my power to make that happen."

"Don't. You know I've been there for Trey since day one."

"And, now, it's time for someone better to do it."

My heart races as fear sets in. "Fuck you, Claudia."

I charge out of the hospital with tears in my eyes.

More tears fall, and I scream to the emptiness of my car when I catch sight of a couple I recognize walking into the hospital.

CHAPTER TWENTY-EIGHT

Kyle

I GRAB my phone from the coffee table when it buzzes with a text.

Gage: We're en route to Chloe's with food.

He called earlier to check on me, asked about Chloe, and said him and Lauren would be over with enough baked goods to last a month—all prepared by Lauren's mother. I asked them to make a pit stop at the diner and pick up a takeout order for Trey and me.

I haven't heard from Chloe since she left for the hospital. She needs time and space to process everything.

Eventually, Trey wandered into the living room with a blank stare on his face. I handed him the remote when he sat down on the other end of the couch. He chose the movie, and we sat in silence while watching it. Just like with Chloe, I'm giving him time.

We haven't discussed us being brothers, but I'll approach the conversation when the time is right. The day after losing his sister isn't. I've been a good brother to my siblings, and I don't mind being the same for Trey.

My fallout with Chloe won't stop me from comforting her while she endures her loss. Have I forgotten about the chaos her family has caused mine? No. Right now, that issue isn't at the top of my priority list.

I didn't know Gloria long, but I cared for her. This morning, when Chloe asked me to shut Gloria's bedroom door, tears threatened my eyes when I noticed the sparkly red shoes in the corner and the stuffed Toto on the bed. My throat choked up as I took in the dolls, the coloring books, all the memories and toys of a sweet girl taken away too early.

Fuck. I want to kill Claudia myself.

Lauren wraps me in a hug as soon as I answer the door. She was on shift when Claudia was brought into the ER and assigned her nurse until she was transferred to another floor. Lauren said her tongue hurt from biting it all night while caring for her.

Claudia's toxicology report came back, confirming alcohol and heroin flowed through her bloodstream at the time of the accident. She'd fallen asleep at the wheel and suffered minor injuries—a concussion and internal bleeding. She'll be taken straight to the county jail upon her release.

Lauren and Gage don't stay long, and Trey devours his cheeseburger before moving on to the cupcakes. An hour later, he's asleep on the couch, and it's time for me to leave for work. Both my lieutenant and Gage offered to give me the evening off, but I declined. No one could cover my shift, and I wasn't going to leave Gage to work alone.

I text Chloe before leaving, telling her, if she needs anything, don't hesitate to call, but receive nothing back.

It's the same when my shift ends at midnight.

————

CHLOE'S CAR is in the driveway when Gage drops me off, and I dig out the house key she gave me earlier today after asking if I'd come over later. I was reluctant to come so late since she still hadn't returned my text, but my house key is here, so I have no choice.

The house is quiet when I walk in, and a light shines from the kitchen. I tiptoe down the hall to find Chloe sitting at the table, staring blankly at the papers and documents scattered along it. It appears to be work files, paperwork she was given last night regarding Claudia, Gloria, the accident, and bills. I stop mid-step when I notice what's in her hand—a packet regarding funeral arrangements.

She chokes out a cry, unaware I'm here, and slams her hand over her mouth, as if it were a crime for her to break down. I hesitate before moving closer, and she takes in my presence in discomfort.

"Chloe, talk to me," I beg.

She stiffens in her chair and avoids eye contact. "You don't have to be here." The words leave her mouth calmly but chillingly.

Where is this coming from?

Before she left for the hospital, she thanked me for being there for her and Trey. All of a sudden, in a ten-hour span, everything has changed.

Something happened.

I draw in closer and stop in front of the table. "I know, but I want to be here."

She stands, almost robotically. She grabs a bottle of water from the refrigerator and rests with her back against the cabinet. "Don't feel sorry for me. I don't need you to feel sorry for me."

"Feel sorry for you?" I throw back. "I'm hurting that you're hurting. Your heart is broken, and all I want to do is help! To make you feel better!"

She throws the bottle across the room before thrusting her finger in my direction. "Fuck you! You wanted nothing to do with me before Gloria's death. You came into my bedroom, fucked me, and then told me to *get fucked*! Don't think you can step in here and act like you're some hero. I can do it on my own! I can save myself. Now, I'm kindly asking you to leave."

It takes me what feels like a minute to speak. "Chloe."

She vacantly stares at me. "Leave."

My eyes lock with hers. "I'm sorry." Regret lodges in my throat. "I'm sorry," I repeat, not moving any closer to her. "I'm fucking sorry for not allowing you to explain yourself. It was my mistake, and I'm willing to listen when you're ready, but right now, right fucking now, that's the last of my concern. Does that mean I'll forget what went down? No, but you need a friend, and I'm here."

That vacant stare turns into one of defeat. "No, Kyle, I don't want to be *your friend*. I don't want anything to do with you or your family!"

I throw my arms up in the air. "Here we fucking go again with your fucking obsession with my family! The truth is out! It's over now!"

She lets out a cold laugh. "No, it's not over! You want to know why?" She advances my way. "Because, now that your father's secret is out, your parents want custody of Trey. They can provide a *better environment* for him."

Whoa. What?

"Who told you this?"

"Claudia."

I scowl. "You're believing *her* out of all people?" I rub at my brow. "Chloe, if my mother even *considered* taking custody of Trey, she would've told me. Claudia said that to hurt you."

"Really?" She raises her voice. "Did she tell you she visited Claudia in the hospital?"

I slam my mouth shut. "No."

"I saw them, Kyle! Your mom and dad were there!"

"Maybe for another reason. There's more than one patient in that hospital," I stupidly reply. "My mom does charity work there."

Annoyance floods her face.

I scrub my hands over my face. "Chloe … we … this." I'm at a loss for words. "Let me talk to my mother." I can't deny it because it sounds like my mother—always wanting to fix the problem and create a better life for someone. She sees Trey as a charity case.

She gestures between us. "This has to be done. Too much terrible shit has happened for us to ever have a healthy relationship. From what happened in high school to the secret about your father and now this. Too much damage has been done. We need to stop kidding ourselves that we'd ever work out."

My heart rages in my chest. *Is she fucking kidding me?* "Or maybe it's time to stop kidding ourselves and realize this can work between us. How about that, huh?"

She frantically shakes her head. "No. It'll never work. I'm asking you to leave."

"Chloe," I beg, another attempt for her to understand what she's doing.

"Leave!" she screams.

Anger crushes through me like a bullet. "Fine, keep pushing people away. Don't be upset when you're alone and nursing a broken heart for the rest of your life because you're so goddamn stubborn."

My words seem to add more power to her anger. "No, I'm being smart to stop my heartache. It's time I stop letting people in. All I get is pain and hurt."

"What have I done to hurt you? *What the flying fuck have I done?* I did something shitty in high school that I *thought* we'd moved on from. I said some stupid shit to you. Now, let's take a step back and talk about what you've done to hurt me. You've done nothing but lie to me—about my father, about me having a brother I never knew about, about my father fucking your sister behind my mother's back! I'm the one taking the risk with you, not the other way around."

"And I didn't know your mother would take custody of Trey!"

"Whoa, whoa. Who's taking custody of me?"

I whip around and spot Trey standing feet away from me with a dumbfounded look on his face.

He whips his arm out to me. "Your mom is trying to take me away from Aunt Chloe?"

I hold my palm out and shake my head. "It's a big misunderstanding."

"It's not," Chloe counters. "I called the social worker. They've talked to her, and with your parents' influence, cheating scandal or not, they have more power."

Horror flashes through Trey's eyes. "I'll never live with anyone else. Fuck that."

"Trey, watch your mouth," Chloe warns.

He shrugs. "Ground me. Do whatever. I've already lost enough anyway."

Chloe looks at me. "Kyle, please leave. It's over. We're over. Thank you for all you've done, but please, go home."

"Chloe." I draw out her name while fighting for the right words.

"Please," she begs.

It's too late. Even if I find the words, it's done.

I nod. "Thank you for clarifying all I needed to know. I'm glad this meant nothing to you."

With that, I grab my shit and leave.

CHAPTER TWENTY-NINE

Chloe

SMILES.

Funerals are full of them.

An entire range of smiles is what I've received today.

I never want to smile and thank someone for coming again.

The church is filled with people smiling while paying their respects. It should make me feel good for the support, but instead, it angers me. Most of these people didn't care about her kind until tragedy hit. Parents are here, who denied their children playdates with her because of where she came from. Even Mrs. Garfield shoots me an apologetic smile, a hint of shame in her eyes, when it's her turn to give her condolences.

Gloria's casket is small, and the bright pink flowers Trey picked out lie atop it. She's wearing her Dorothy costume, and her stuffed Toto is nestled at her side. I came early before the showing, sat in front of her casket, and apologized. I should've never trusted Claudia with her. *Never.* That's on me. Our little Dorothy will be buried today because of my stupid judgment.

When I look at her, it's a deeper cut into my heart, but I won't quit torturing myself. Every heart-shattering glance is worth it because, after today, I'll never be able to do it again. All I'll have is photos.

Adjusting to life without Gloria is a mixture of emotions— denial, disbelief, anger, regret, and sadness. As she was the youngest, Trey and I made Gloria the priority of our lives, and now, she's gone even though all the evidence of the space she filled in our hearts is everywhere.

Claudia put in a request to attend the funeral, but it was denied. Denied by *Mayor Lane.* She's facing a long list of charges for Gloria's death, including vehicular manslaughter. I haven't visited her again and don't plan to. Trey's attitude hasn't changed in the matter either.

I take a seat in the front row and look over to the corner where Kyle has stood since he came in. He's kept his distance, but even that is comforting. I never doubted he'd show.

I catch a glimpse of his family a few rows back—including his father. Sierra reached out to Trey a few days ago, inviting him over to her house for dinner. I'm not dumb. They want to warm themselves up to him. He declined, but he was nice about it. It's his sister, and he's having trouble coming to terms with that. He lost a sister, and now, a new one is coming around.

I've felt guilt over my wanting custody of him. He'll have more money, growing up as a Lane, but I can't lose him. I've already lost Gloria, and I won't survive another loss. I'm also not too selfish; if the time comes and Trey does want to live with them, I'd let him go.

I'd let him go because, unlike everyone else, it's his happiness that matters to me.

I look over when Kyle sits down next to me. There's been an empty chair there since I sat down. It's almost as if no one dared to take it.

"Hi," he says.

Him being at my side eases me.

"Hi," I reply.

When the service starts and the tears hit, he grabs my hand. I squeeze it tight. Trey gives the eulogy, keeping his sobs together to say his words. I'm mentally and physically depleted when it ends.

"Thank you for coming," I whisper as people clear out of the church.

"Always," he says.

The three of us stand, and Kyle looks from me to Trey. "I'm right next door and not going anywhere. If you need anything—sugar, a friend, a hug—you guys come knocking, okay?"

Trey and I nod.

His offer makes me smile for a brief moment—something I haven't done in what seems like weeks.

———

THE LOSS of Gloria hits Trey the hardest when we arrive home.

He plucks a picture of her from the fridge, sets it down on the table next to the pizza we picked up, and stares at it, tears resurfacing. "I wouldn't even dress up as a stupid scarecrow for her!" he says through sobs. "That's all she wanted—for her big brother to go trick-or-treating with her—and I let her down because I was being a stupid hard-ass." He ducks his head down in humiliation … anger … sadness. "God, what I'd do to have her back. I'd dress up as a scarecrow every day of my life. I'd do anything—*anything*—for her to be next to me right now."

I get up from my chair, stand behind him, and wrap my arms around his shoulders.

I don't know how long we cry and stare at her.

When Trey goes to bed, the pizza untouched, I tread into my bedroom.

Reality sinks through, drowning me like an anchor, and I

don't know if I'll ever be able to reach the surface again. I slide down the wall, raise my knees, and slack forward. I want to break down in tears but scream out in anger. Every emotion for every shitty thing in my life is finally pouring out of me like an overflowing stream.

A knock on the door breaks me away from my thoughts, and I sniffle, wiping my nose with my arm. The door opens, and I hear someone walk in. I shut my eyes and release a breath at his scent.

"Trey let me in," Kyle whispers into the darkness of my bedroom. I vaguely see his hand held out to me. "Come here."

I shake my head. "I need to get this out."

He nods, but instead of leaving, he slides down the wall and sits next to me. "Then, get it out."

He doesn't talk or touch me again. He sits there, assuring me I'm not alone, until I fall asleep.

When I wake up, he's gone.

CHAPTER THIRTY

Chloe

GLORIA'S FUNERAL was two days ago.

I've kept to myself, and Trey has done the same—playing video games and Netflix-bingeing. My phone keeps alerting me with reminders to call the social worker regarding Trey, but when I pick up the phone to do it, I can't. I'm scared. The fear of what she'll tell me knocks back my energy into making the call. I'm biding my time until they come knocking on the door, and I'll ready to fight like hell when they do.

My shoulders tense when I hear the doorbell ring, and my legs feel weak when I walk to the door. I question myself on answering when I look through the peephole, and worry seeps through me when I answer.

Nancy Lane is standing in front of me.

My breath catches in my throat while I wait for her to speak. I'm at a loss for words.

"Hi, Chloe," she bursts out in a sweet tone. "Can we talk?"

I blink, and it takes me a moment to reply. "Sure."

This is it.

This is where she tells Trey to pack his bags and leave me.

I lead her into my living room, and neither one of us is relaxed when we sit on the couch.

She cuts straight to the point. "I'm aware Claudia informed you that Michael and I felt it was in Trey's best interest if we raised him."

I grimace and ball my knuckles. "She did, and I respectively disagree." I'm biting back the angry words I want to scream at her.

"It seems you're not the only one."

Her response surprises me.

"I'm sorry ... what?"

Her eyes are glossy, and she places a finger underneath her nose as she tilts her head down. "I want to apologize." She blinks away tears. "I'm sorry if I'm being too emotional. Kyle came to talk to me. He explained that you've been the sole caretaker for Trey, that, since he was a baby, it's always been you. He asked me how I'd feel if someone tried to take my children away from me, and his words made me understand. My heart hurts if I caused you any pain. I only wanted to help Trey, but I understand now that helping him is having you. Trey can stay with you. Michael and I will not be pursuing any type of custody battle, and we have no issue with helping if need be—whether it be money, school assistance, anything like that. We're here." She sucks in a breath. "And, when you two feel comfortable, I'd love to get to know him. So would his brother and sisters."

Tears fill my eyes. "Thank you," I blurt out, my voice thick with emotions, so many damn emotions. "Thank you so much." I pull in a breath and wipe away my tears before clearing my throat. "And I'm sorry ... for keeping everything from you ... and, uh ... taking money away from your family."

She shakes her head. "Honey, you did that for those kids. Michael told me he had the checks made out to you because he knew you'd do the right thing and that you stopped accepting them when you had enough money to help them yourself. You doing that, even against your better judgment, only further proves how much you care for them." She grabs my hand and squeezes it. "And I am so, *so very sorry* about your loss."

We're both crying as we stand, and she wraps her arms around me before leaving. "My door is always open." She hands me a piece of paper when we separate. "Here's my number. If you need anything, Chloe, please let me know."

I sniffle. "Thank you again."

She gives me one last look before leaving. "Now, I understand why my son loves you so much." She sighs. "With four children, I try to steer clear of their love lives, but Kyle cares for you deeply. He's not perfect, and sometimes, he doesn't think before he speaks. But he's ready to take on every broken piece of you, and hopefully, you're willing to do the same with him."

CHAPTER THIRTY-ONE

Kyle

I'VE TOLD Chloe good morning for the past week.

I'm not greeted with curse words or finger signals.

I get a small glimmer of a smile and a bowed head.

That's it.

I should appreciate her lack of telling me to fuck off but don't. It further proves every light inside her has dimmed.

My family's disdain toward Chloe has lowered. We sat down after the funeral and all came to the understanding that she's not the bad person; he is.

I haven't forgiven my father, but I am giving him credit for stepping up. When he realized my mother was finally going to walk away, it sucker-punched him. My mom ignored his infidelities before because they were hidden, but when they were released in the open, that did her in. Not to mention, he produced a child with his mistress *years ago*. My siblings and I had begged her to leave him, but she didn't want to lose her family. I didn't agree with her decision, but I accepted it because I love her. She asked us to work on not hating our father, so for her, I've tried to keep a straight face and not punch him when he's around. But no matter what, I'll never have respect for him.

I slam the door shut after getting into the car with Gage. He's my best friend, but lately, he's proven to be more than that. He was there for Gloria's funeral, and that was a big step for him. Gage isn't one who frequents funerals, especially children's funerals, after what he experienced in Chicago. He came for me. He kicked away those fears for me.

He jerks his head toward Chloe's house. "Have you gone over and talked to her yet?"

He asks this every day.

I give him the same reply every day.

I shake my head and rub at my eyes. If you don't count my good mornings, then no. "I'm not sure what to say."

"She hasn't mentioned your mom's visit to her?"

"No."

"Use it as a conversation starter. Knock on her door and deliver the news as if you didn't know your mom had paid her a visit. You wanted to make sure she knew."

I blow out a breath. "I'm giving her time to grieve."

"You are one patient man."

———

"HEY THERE. NEW JOB?"

Trey is squatted down and sliding cans on a lower shelf in a grocery aisle at Garfield's. The last time I saw him here was for shoplifting, and now, they've given him a job.

Good for him.

Trey looks up at me with a nod before standing up. "Yeah. I need something to help pass my time before my mind goes crazy." His voice lowers. "I don't have a little sister to look after anymore, so it's all I think about in my downtime."

I've debated on reaching out to Trey after the funeral. I told them my door is open, so when they're ready, I'm ready.

I give him a hopeful look. "I'm sorry, buddy. My door is always open if you want to talk or hang out," I offer again.

He smiles and plays with the collar of his red work shirt. "I'm sorry for what I said when I eavesdropped on the conversation about your parents wanting custody of me. I was pissed. It was nothing against you."

I smile. "Don't worry about it."

He kicks his feet against the ground. "But I'm down for whatever. I got a new number."

He fishes his phone from his pocket. I grab mine, and we recite our numbers to each other.

"You know," he starts with hesitation, "I've always wanted a big brother."

I wink. "You have one now."

He grins wider before pointing to my cart. "That's a lot of food."

"My parents are having a dinner on Christmas. You're more than welcome to come with me if you'd like."

"Maybe. Aunt Chloe is making dinner on Christmas."

"That's scary," I joke.

He laughs. "I know, right? She wants us to have a traditional Christmas dinner." He pauses, and all friendliness on his face has disappeared and is replaced with sadness. "I'm worried about her. Gloria and I always spent the day with her, and now …"

I nod in response. "You be there for her, okay?"

"I'm trying my hardest to."

———

TREY TEXTS me the next day.

He asked Chloe if it was okay for him to hang out with me, and she approved.

We go out for pizza, and I take him to the arcade. We have a blast. He says Melanie has been hanging out at the house to keep Chloe's spirits up. He's still worried about her, and he knows she's hiding her sadness.

We brainstorm, coming up with ideas to help her through her pain.

CHAPTER THIRTY-TWO

Chloe

CHRISTMAS HAS NEVER BEEN exciting for me.

The holidays were never bright and cheery, growing up. When I was younger, I didn't know how I always managed to be on the naughty list. No matter how good I acted, Santa never visited our house. I never received coal either, so it was a confusing time for me. I promised myself that Trey and Gloria would never doubt where they stood with Santa. I worked my ass off to give them a decent Christmas every year.

This year, I've made an entire Christmas dinner with more food than Trey and I could eat in a month.

"I wish she were here with us," Trey mutters when I hand him his first gift. He frowns at the box, as if it's wrong for him to open it.

My brows scrunch together when he drops the box and grabs his phone after it beeps with a text message.

"Oh, yeah," he says. "I forgot to tell you that Mr. Garfield said they had extra pies at the market that are close to expiring, so they're dropping them off."

Trey brought up getting a job to me three days after Gloria's funeral. He needed a hobby to take his mind off his mother going to prison and his sister's death. I agreed and was surprised when he told me he'd been hired at Garfield's Grocery.

I'm doing the same. I work as often as I can and considered looking into a second job—not for financial reasons, but to keep my mind off my problems as well. Melanie has made it her mission to be my sidekick at all times, and even though I act like it's driving me crazy, I appreciate her company.

Then, there's Kyle. I feel terrible for not thanking him for talking to his mother. It's a bitch move on my part, but I'm terrified. He hasn't reached out since the night he consoled me and then disappeared, which I don't blame him for.

I sigh. Tomorrow, I'm going to his house and apologizing for my outburst, for kicking him out of my house, for not telling him everything about his father, and for not giving him a hug for saving me from the heartache of losing Trey.

I uncross my legs and stand up from the floor. "Aw, that's nice of them."

He pulls on his boots. "Can you give me a hand? They're old and it's snowing, so we should probably help them."

"Of course."

I put my shoes on and throw on a coat. "Are they not here yet?" I ask, shivering when we walk outside.

Trey is typing on his phone. "Hold on. They're texting me now."

I raise a brow in confusion. "The Garfields know how to text?"

He doesn't answer me, and seconds later, the abrupt sound of his voice cuts through the morning air. The deep voice brims with an overflow of emotions.

"Merry Christmas to the girl I love!"

My attention sweeps over to Kyle's porch to find him standing there, shirtless, wearing only his gray sweatpants, looking the same as he did every day before we started our relationship. A Santa hat is on his head, and I can't hold back my burst of laughter—my first loud, belly-aching laughter I've had in months.

"You're going to get hypothermia!" I yell back in exchange for, *Fuck off*.

He hops down the stairs, and Trey is beaming from the sidelines. Their setup is playing out smoothly.

"If I get hypothermia," he says when he reaches me, "I'm blaming you, babe."

I press my hand against my chest. "On me? It's not my fault you enjoy flaunting your naked self around in the freezing cold."

I can see his breath releasing into the cold. "Please be honest with me, Chloe. That's all I want for Christmas, and your honesty will provide me the energy to make my way back inside. Otherwise, I'll probably freeze outside and die."

I shake my head, still laughing. "I can't believe I'm even entertaining this."

He grabs me by my waist, and his chest is freezing. "Tell me how you feel about me, Chloe. No bullshit. Look at me and tell me you don't care about me the way I care about you."

I gulp, and my heart races so hard that I'm waiting for it to fall out of my chest. "I … I don't care about you, Kyle."

His face falls.

"I mean … I do … but I *more* than care about you."

A smile takes over his face. "Say it."

I cover my face with my hands. "Oh my God. I can't believe I'm about to declare my love to a half-naked man sporting a Santa hat, who looks like he should be featured in an X-rated Christmas calendar."

He takes my hand and kisses the top. "I'm more than happy to get you a calendar with my pictures in them."

A tear falls down my cheek, and his finger is cold when he wipes it away.

"I love you," I say with no hesitation, regret, or unease.

He stares down at me, his white teeth showing as he grins wildly. "And, damn, do I love you."

He tilts his head down and kisses me. He pulls away and inspects me, and then his lips hit mine again.

I glance back at Trey while smiling. "I take it, there are no pies?"

Trey shrugs. "They must have forgotten to stop on their way home."

"Did you say pie?" Kyle chimes in. "Weird, I have *plenty* of them in my house." He snags my hand in his and leads me toward his porch while calling out for Trey to come on.

"Did your mom make the pies?" I ask when we make it inside.

Kyle grins. "Would you think any different? I told you, I want to always impress you, not give you food poisoning."

————

"I GOT YOU SOMETHING," Kyle says.

After we devoured the sweets Kyle had brought home from his family Christmas dinner, we went to the living room to watch Christmas movies.

He hops off the couch and walks barefoot to his bedroom while Trey snores in the background.

"You ... you didn't have to do that," I say when he hands me a small box.

"I know I didn't. I *wanted* to."

I stare at it, moving the box around and inspecting it, before undoing the bow. I gulp, unsure of why I'm so nervous about opening a present. It's a jewelry box. My heart races when I pop it open.

Nestled inside is a necklace.

I pull it out, playing with the thin string, and inspect it. I cover my mouth to conceal my whimper, and tears flood my cheeks. On the necklace hangs a heart pendent that says *Mother* and inscribed are Trey's and Gloria's names.

"It's beautiful. Thank you," I whisper.

Kyle's face is filled with pride, and he nods toward Trey. "He helped me pick it out. He said he's always seen you as his mother, not anyone else, and we knew nothing better would suit you."

I frown, and he uses his thumb to gently rid me of my tears. "I didn't buy you a gift."

He tips his head down to kiss my lips. "Don't worry," he says against them in a low tone. "You can give me mine later."

The thought of him touching me, of being in his bed, of us together again, sparks happiness inside me. If Trey wasn't sleeping on the other side of the sectional, I'd be straddling Kyle right now.

I blush. "You can't joke around about that even if he is asleep."

He draws back with a grin. "Huh? I want a night full of you repeating you love me *over and over* again. That's what I want as my gift."

I chuckle. "This conversation is mirroring one of those Hallmark movies we just watched."

"I'll take it because Hallmark movies always end up with a happily ever after."

CHAPTER THIRTY-THREE

Chloe

Two Months Later

EVEN THOUGH TODAY is Trey's birthday, you'd think, with the excitement beaming from me, it was mine.

"It's official," Trey says. "You're my mother."

Tears fall from my eyes.

When we finally opened gifts on Christmas, Trey slipped me a letter, asking me to adopt him. Kyle talked to his parents, and Michael agreed to sign over custody to me. Trey still wants to get to know his family, but he wanted to make sure he was always *my son*. I'd been reluctant on adopting him for years in hopes that Claudia would change, but Trey deserves a good mother who loves and appreciates him.

I shut my eyes as a tear slips down my face. I wish I could've done the same for Gloria, wish I'd done it years ago. It's bittersweet, celebrating being Trey's parent while also wishing you could've done the same with his sister.

Kyle wraps his arm around my shoulders and walks with us. "You know, since we're in the county building, we can go upstairs and get married."

I throw my head back and laugh. "You always make jokes."

He squeezes my side. "No joking. You say the word, and I'm throwing you over my shoulder and making you my wife. Absolutely no fucking joke about that."

———

"I'M NERVOUS," Trey says from the backseat of Kyle's Jeep. "I'm meeting a brother and sisters I never knew I had."

"Hey, you met me before," Kyle says in an attempt to lighten his nervousness.

"Yes, but you were super cool when we first met."

Kyle elbows me from the driver's side while I'm in the passenger seat. "Listen to that. He knows I'm super cool."

I shake my head. "He's calling you *super cool* because you got him out of a shoplifting charge."

Kyle's grin drops. "Ah, man, and here I thought, we were best friends."

Trey smacks his shoulder. "Trust me, dude; we are best friends. Any other cop would've arrested me with no questions asked. You never made me feel like anything but a normal kid."

Happiness radiates through my chest—the opposite of how I thought it'd be when we got here. I'm going inside, facing Nancy and Michael while we share a dinner. Michael and Nancy reached out, and before we threw Trey into the mix, we had a meeting at Kyle's house. Michael apologized. I accepted but will never forgive him for the pain he'd caused my family. Trey needs a father, and he's working on accepting Michael not being there for him before.

We're taking chances in our lives.

Losing Gloria convinced me to take a step back and realize what I wanted in life—to stop being scared and be happy.

We count to three before getting out of the Jeep, and Trey looks around in awe at the home.

We see Sierra first when we walk in. She's skipping down the stairs with her boyfriend trailing behind her.

"I don't understand why you keep hanging out with Maliki," he mutters behind her. "You close the bar with him every night, and it's not even your job."

"He's my friend. Get over it," she snaps.

Her boyfriend snorts. "I bet you wouldn't be okay with me having a friend who was a girl."

Their conversation ends when they notice us.

"What's up, big and little brother?" she greets.

I cover my face to stop the joyful tears. She's treating Trey as if he's one of them and not creating any awkwardness.

"I'm Sierra, the best sister in the world," she adds.

"Hell yes!" Rex comes roaring through next. "I'm your big bro, Rex. If you think Kyle is cool, prepared to be shocked by the increased coolness factor of me!"

I glance at Trey, expecting him to be nervous, but he's smiling from ear to ear.

Dinner goes by smoothly. I don't share words with Michael, but he acknowledges Trey and isn't acting like an asshole, like the first time I had dinner here. Kyle said he's changed since news of his affair broke out. Nancy was done, her children supporting her when she called a divorce lawyer, and it opened Michael's eyes.

By the time we're loading back into the Jeep, Trey and Rex have plans to go to the arcade tomorrow.

———

KYLE SLIDES into bed next to me after we finish brushing our teeth. We're shoulder-to-shoulder as we lean back against the headboard.

He stares ahead when he speaks. "I know you just adopted

Trey, but you told me you wanted another child as well. *Children*, if I'm certain."

My attention shoots straight to him, and my eyes meet his green ones. I clutch my stomach and swallow without saying a word.

He doesn't stop for my reply. "I did some research and got in touch with organizations I know through the force." He turns, opens the nightstand on his side, and eases a folder from inside it. "Here's a list of babies in need of adoption. There are other options, Chloe, *so many* other options, and I will be by your side on any path you go on."

I cover my mouth, my hands shaking as I open the green folder, and tears glisten in my eyes. "You did all this ... for me?"

"Yes, because I love you more than I've loved anyone in my life. You own every part of me, and I'd love nothing more than to create a family with you, a life with you, with us turning old and gray together. I want us to live together, so I can always say my good mornings from *our* bed."

The tears fall, landing on the paperwork on the folder, and I set it aside to curl into his arms. "Thank you, Kyle. You are everything to me. I never believed in love, never thought I'd have it, until you barreled through my insecurities."

He kisses the top of my head, my nose, before tilting my chin up to kiss me on the lips. "Also, let me know when you're ready to be my wife." He winks. "They say it makes it *much* easier to adopt when you're married."

I grin and shuffle through the folder. "Get me a folder with a marriage license to sign, and I'm game."

KEEP UP WITH THE BLUE BEECH SERIES

All books can be read as standalones

Just A Fling
(Hudson and Stella's story)
Just One Night
(Dallas and Willow's story)
Just Exes
(Gage and Lauren's story)
Just Neighbors
(Kyle and Chloe's story)
Just Roommates
(Maliki and Sierra's story)
Just Friends
(Rex and Carolina's story)

OTHER BOOKS BY CHARITY

RISKY DUET

Risky

Worth The Risk

ACKNOWLEDGMENTS

My Other Half: Without your support and everything you do, I wouldn't be able to write as much as I do. So, thank you for everything—accepting that home cook meals are a rare occurrence in our lives, when I tell you we're stuck in the house because I'm meeting deadlines, and telling more people about my books than I do.

To the Readers, Bloggers, and Book Community: You're the real MVP. Thank you times infinity. Everything you do seriously means the world to me. You take so much time helping authors, promoting them, reading, and reviewing.

Jill: I can get a little … okay, a lot of anxiety not only when I'm writing but with the behind the scenes business. You've helped me with Just Neighbors *so much* with everything from plotting, beta reading, dealing with my doubts, and going out of your way to help me. I'm so glad Dallas brought us together and now you're stuck with me forever.

Jovana: Best. Editor. Ever. You do so much magic on my books, and I'm grateful that even when I ask last minute or am running behind, you work with me.

Virginia: Thank you for taking me in last minute with the proofreading.

Paris and Zoe: Forever my BFFs.

Ivy: For setting goals with me that are rarely met.

Much love,

Charity

Made in the USA
Monee, IL
24 August 2021